Put a rocket under your revision with CGP!

GCSE Physics isn't the easiest subject on Earth, and that's putting it mildly.
Luckily, we've squeezed all the facts, theory and practical skills you'll need into this CGP book —
plus exam practice questions to put your new-found Physics knowledge to the test.

How to access your free Online Edition

This book includes a free Online Edition to read on your PC, Mac or tablet.
To access it, just go to **cgpbooks.co.uk/extras** and enter this code...

1589 8572 2396 1676

By the way, this code only works for one person. If somebody else has used
this book before you, they might have already claimed the Online Edition.

CGP — still the best! ☺

Our sole aim here at CGP is to produce the highest quality books —
carefully written, immaculately presented and dangerously close to being funny.

Then we work our socks off to get them out to you
— at the cheapest possible prices.

Contents

Published by CGP.

From original material by Richard Parsons.

Editors: Robin Flello, Emily Garrett, Sharon Keeley-Holden, Duncan Lindsay, Frances Rooney, Sarah Oxley, Charlotte Whiteley, Sarah Williams.

Contributors: Paddy Gannon

Graph to show trend in atmospheric CO_2 concentration and global temperature on page 10 based on data by EPICA community members 2004 and Siegenthaler et al 2005.

Stopping distance data on page 63 from the Highway Code. Contains public sector information licensed under the Open Government Licence v3.0. http://www.nationalarchives.gov.uk/doc/open-government-licence/version/3/

ISBN: 978 1 78294 563 5

With thanks to Matthew Benyohai for the proofreading.

With thanks to Ana Pungartnik for the copyright research.

Printed by Elanders Ltd, Newcastle upon Tyne.
Clipart from Corel®

Waves

Waves transfer <u>energy</u> from one place to another without transferring any <u>matter</u> (stuff). Clever so and so's.

Waves Transfer Energy in the Direction they are Travelling

A <u>wave</u> is a <u>regular disturbance</u> (i.e. a uniform pattern of <u>movement</u>) that <u>transfers energy</u>. For waves travelling through a medium, the <u>particles</u> (see p.78) of the medium <u>vibrate</u> and <u>transfer energy</u> between each other. BUT overall, the particles stay in the <u>same place</u> — <u>only energy</u> is transferred.

> For example, if you drop a twig into a calm pool of water, <u>ripples</u> form on the surface. The ripples <u>don't</u> carry the <u>water</u> (or the twig) away with them though.
>
> Similarly, if you strum a <u>guitar string</u> and create a <u>sound wave</u>, the sound wave travels to your <u>ear</u> but it doesn't carry the <u>air</u> away from the guitar — if it did, it would create a <u>vacuum</u>.

1) The <u>amplitude</u> of a wave is the <u>displacement</u> from the <u>rest position</u> to a <u>crest</u> or <u>trough</u>.

2) The <u>wavelength</u> is the distance between the same points on <u>two adjacent</u> (neighbouring) <u>disturbances</u> (e.g. from <u>crest to crest</u> or from <u>compression</u> to <u>compression</u>, see below), i.e. one <u>full cycle</u> of the wave.

3) <u>Frequency</u> is the <u>number of complete waves</u> made by the source, <u>or the cycles</u> passing a certain point <u>per second</u>. Frequency is measured in <u>hertz (Hz)</u>. 1 Hz is <u>1 wave per second</u>.

4) The <u>period</u> of a wave is the <u>number of seconds</u> it takes for <u>one full cycle</u> to pass a certain point. <u>Period = 1 ÷ frequency</u>.

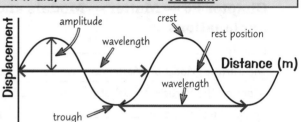

> Waves (or the wave model) can be used to describe and predict how one object affects another object that is some distance away from it by transferring energy to it by waves.

Transverse Waves Have Perpendicular Disturbances

1) For <u>transverse waves</u> the disturbance of the medium is <u>perpendicular</u> (at 90°) to the <u>direction</u> the wave travels.

2) <u>Most waves</u> are transverse, including <u>electromagnetic waves</u> (p.5), <u>S-waves</u> (see p.18) waves in <u>water</u> (see p.2) and waves on a <u>rope</u>.

A rope wiggled <u>up and down</u> gives a <u>transverse</u> wave.

Wave travels this way.

Disturbances go up and down.

Longitudinal Waves Have Parallel Disturbances

1) For <u>longitudinal waves</u>, the disturbance of the medium is <u>parallel</u> to the <u>direction</u> the wave travels.

2) Examples are <u>sound waves</u> in air (p.16) and <u>P-waves</u> (p.18).

3) Longitudinal waves <u>squash up</u> and <u>stretch out</u> the arrangement of particles in the medium they pass through, making <u>compressions</u> (<u>high pressure</u>, lots of particles) and <u>rarefactions</u> (<u>low pressure</u>, fewer particles).

If you <u>push</u> and <u>pull</u> the end of a spring, you send a wave of <u>compression pulses</u> down the spring — a <u>longitudinal</u> wave.

Disturbances in the same direction as the wave travels.

compressions

rarefactions

> A wavelength is still one complete cycle, e.g. from one compression to another.

Learn the Wave Speed Equation

It can be used for <u>all types</u> of wave, including <u>water</u>, <u>sound</u> and <u>EM waves</u>.

> **wave speed (m/s) = frequency (Hz) × wavelength (m)**

Wave frequencies are often given in <u>kHz</u> (kilohertz) or <u>MHz</u> (megahertz). Change them to Hz to use them in the equation (see p.97). <u>1 kHz = 1000 Hz</u> and <u>1 MHz = 1 000 000 Hz</u>.

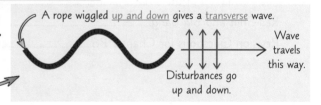

What about Mexican waves...

You won't get far unless you understand these wave basics. Try a question to test your knowledge.

Q1   A wave has a speed of 0.15 m/s and a wavelength of 7.5 cm. Calculate its frequency.   [3 marks]

Wave Experiments

Time to <u>experiment</u>. Microphones and ripple tanks — sounds like fun, just don't mix them together...

Use an Oscilloscope to Measure the Speed of Sound

By attaching a <u>signal generator</u> to a speaker you can generate sounds with a specific <u>frequency</u>.
You can use <u>two microphones</u> and an <u>oscilloscope</u> to find the <u>wavelength</u> of the sound waves generated.

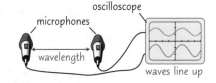

speaker attached to signal generator
microphones
oscilloscope
wavelength
waves line up

1) Set up the oscilloscope so the <u>detected waves</u> at each microphone are shown as <u>separate waves</u>.

2) Start with <u>both microphones</u> next to the speaker, then slowly <u>move one away</u> until the two waves are <u>aligned</u> on the display, but have moved <u>exactly one wavelength apart</u>.

3) Measure the <u>distance between the microphones</u> to find one <u>wavelength</u> (λ).

4) You can then use the formula <u>$v = f\lambda$</u> to find the <u>speed</u> (*v*) of the <u>sound waves</u> passing through the <u>air</u> — the <u>frequency</u> (*f*) is whatever you set the <u>signal generator</u> to in the first place.

Measure Speed, Frequency and Wavelength with a Ripple Tank

PRACTICAL

You can generate <u>waves</u> in a <u>ripple tank</u> using a <u>variable power supply</u> attached to a <u>dipper</u>.
The dipper moves up and down to create water waves at a fixed frequency. Or you can use
a <u>signal generator</u> which generates waves with a <u>known</u> fixed <u>frequency</u>.

The frequency is the number of waves made by the dipper (the source) per second.

To measure the <u>frequency</u>, you'll need a <u>cork</u> and a <u>stopwatch</u>:

1) <u>Float</u> the cork in the ripple tank. It should <u>bob up and down</u> as the waves pass it.

2) When the cork is at the <u>top</u> of a 'bob', <u>start the stopwatch</u>. <u>Time</u> how long the cork takes to complete <u>10 bobs</u>.

3) <u>Divide</u> this <u>time</u> by 10 to get the time for <u>one bob</u> — the <u>period</u>.

4) Calculate the <u>frequency</u> using the formula <u>frequency = 1 ÷ period</u>.

dipper attached to variable power supply

cork bobs up and down

(If you used a signal generator, your result should match its frequency.)

To measure the <u>wavelength</u>, use a <u>strobe light</u>:

1) Place a card covered with <u>centimetre-squared paper</u> behind the ripple tank.

2) Turn on the <u>strobe light</u> and <u>adjust its frequency</u> until the waves appear to '<u>freeze</u>'.

3) Using the squared paper, measure the <u>distance</u> that, e.g. <u>five</u> waves cover. Divide this distance by the number of waves to get an <u>average wavelength</u>.

strobe light
five waves
card

Measure the <u>wave speed</u> using a <u>pencil</u> and a <u>stopwatch</u>:

You need <u>two</u> people for this.

As $v = f\lambda$, you could measure two of these quantities and calculate the third.

1) Place a <u>large piece of paper</u> next to the tank.

2) As the <u>waves move</u> across the tank, one of you should <u>track the path</u> of one of the crests on the paper using the <u>pencil</u>. Using a ruler will help make sure your line is <u>parallel</u> to the direction the wave travels.

3) The other should <u>time</u> how long it takes the first to draw a line of a <u>certain length</u>, e.g. 20 cm.

4) <u>Calculate wave speed</u> by plugging the <u>length of the line</u> (the distance) and the <u>time taken</u> to draw it into the formula <u>speed = distance ÷ time</u>.

pencil tracks this wave crest

line drawn along the paper as the crest moves

As always, for <u>each</u> of these experiments make sure you do at least three <u>repeats</u> and take an <u>average</u>.
Also, make sure it's a <u>fair test</u> — keep the <u>equipment</u> the <u>same</u> and the <u>variables</u> you <u>aren't testing</u> the <u>same</u> every time, e.g. the <u>position</u> of the dipper, the <u>voltage</u> of the power supply, the <u>depth</u> of the water...

Disco time in the physics lab...

Sound waves always travel at the same speed in air — about 330 m/s. So your value should be in that ball park.

Q1   Describe an experiment in which a water wave is produced and its frequency measured.   [4 marks]

Reflection and Refraction

All waves <u>reflect</u> and <u>refract</u>. 'What does that mean?' you ask. Read on...

Waves Are Absorbed, Transmitted and Reflected at Boundaries

When a <u>wave</u> meets a <u>boundary</u> between two materials (a <u>material interface</u>), <u>three</u> things can happen:

1) The wave is <u>ABSORBED</u> by the second material — its energy is <u>transferred</u> to the material, often causing <u>heating</u>.

2) The wave is <u>TRANSMITTED</u> through the second material — the wave <u>carries on travelling</u> through the new material. This often leads to <u>refraction</u> (see below).

3) The wave is <u>REFLECTED</u> — this is where the incoming ray is neither <u>absorbed</u> nor <u>transmitted</u>, but instead is '<u>sent back</u>' away from the second material (see p.11).

What actually happens depends on the wavelength of the wave and the properties of the materials involved.

This is true for <u>all types of wave</u>, including EM waves (see p.5), sound waves (see p.16) and water waves.

Refraction — Waves Changing Direction at a Boundary

1) Waves travel at <u>different speeds</u> in different materials. So when a wave crosses a <u>boundary</u> between materials it <u>changes speed</u>.

2) The <u>frequency</u> of a wave <u>stays the same</u> (it can't change) as it crosses a boundary from one medium (material) to another. As $v = f\lambda$, this means if the speed of the wave changes, the <u>wavelength</u> must also change. The wavelength <u>decreases</u> if the wave <u>slows down</u>, and <u>increases</u> if it <u>speeds up</u>.

3) If the wave hits the boundary at an <u>angle</u> to the normal, this change of <u>speed</u> causes a <u>change in direction</u> — this is <u>refraction</u>. If the wave is travelling <u>along the normal</u> it will <u>change speed</u>, but it's <u>NOT refracted</u>.

A normal is an imaginary line at right angles to the surface at the point the wave hits it.

4) The <u>wavefront diagrams</u> below show a wave slowing down as it crosses a boundary.

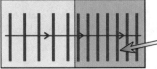

The wavefronts are closer together, showing a decrease in wavelength (and so a decrease in velocity).

The wave hits a different medium at an angle, so the wave changes direction.

A wavefront is a line used to represent a crest (or trough) of a wave.

5) The <u>greater</u> the <u>change</u> in speed, the <u>more</u> a wave <u>bends</u> (changes direction).

6) The wave bends <u>towards the normal</u> if it <u>slows down</u>, and <u>away</u> from the normal if it <u>speeds up</u>.

Light and Sound Waves can be Modelled by Water Waves

<u>Water waves</u> show some of the behaviours of <u>light</u> and <u>sound</u> waves — and the best thing is, you can actually <u>see</u> the <u>wavefronts</u>. A <u>ripple tank</u> can be used to demonstrate reflection and refraction.

REFLECTION:

When water waves hit an object, they are <u>reflected</u> by it. The <u>angles</u> the incident and reflected waves make with the normal always <u>match</u> each other (just like with sound and light waves — see p.11).

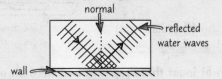

REFRACTION:

When water waves pass into <u>shallower</u> water, they <u>slow down</u>. If they're at an angle to the normal, they'll <u>refract</u>.

The boundary in this diagram is where the depth of water suddenly changes.

deep water

shallow water

I'll give you some time to reflect on this page...

So the angle at which a wave hits a boundary determines whether it refracts or not. How fantabulous.

Q1   Explain what happens to the wavelength of a wave when it passes into a different medium and slows down.   [3 marks]

Reflection and Refraction Experiments

Experiments are what science is all about. And here are some beauties involving refraction and reflection.

You can Investigate Reflection Using a Ray Box and a Mirror

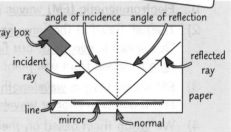

1) Take a piece of paper and draw a solid line across it using a ruler. Then draw a dotted line at 90° to the solid line (your normal).
2) Place a plane (flat) mirror so it lines up with the solid line.
3) Using a ray box, shine a thin beam of white light at the mirror, so the light hits the mirror where the normal meets the mirror.
4) Trace the incident and reflected light rays.

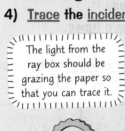

The light from the ray box should be grazing the paper so that you can trace it.

5) Measure the angle between the incident ray and the normal (the angle of incidence) and the angle between the reflected ray and the normal (the angle of reflection) using a protractor.
6) Repeat these steps, varying the angle of incidence. You should find that no matter its value, the angle of incidence ALWAYS equals the angle of reflection.

Do this experiment in a dark room. Keep the light levels the same throughout your experiment.

7) As always, keep your test fair by keeping other variables the same, e.g. same mirror, same width and brightness of beam.
8) You should see that the reflected ray is as thin and bright as the incident ray — a plane mirror gives a clear reflection and none of the light is absorbed.

You can Investigate the Refraction of Light using a Prism

You'll need a light source, such as a laser (lasers produce only a single wavelength of light), and a triangular glass prism on a piece of paper:

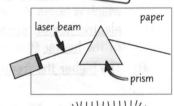

1) Draw a solid line around the prism on to the paper.
2) Then shine the laser beam into the prism at an angle to its surface. (Some light will be reflected.)
3) Trace the incident and emerging rays onto the paper and remove the prism.
4) Draw the refracted ray by joining the ends of the other two rays with a straight line.
5) You can then measure the angles of incidence and refraction:

See p.12 for definitions of these angles.

- Draw normals at the points where the ray enters and leaves the prism. Do this by drawing dotted lines at 90° to the sides of the prism at the entry and exit points.
- You then have two sets of angles of incidence and refraction to mark and measure. There's the set where the ray enters the prism and the set where it leaves.

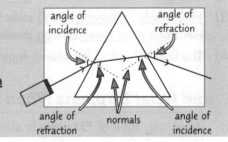

6) Electromagnetic (EM) waves (see p.5) like light usually travel more slowly in denser materials.
7) So, when entering glass from the air, they bend towards the normal (if they refract that is). So at the point of entry, the angle of incidence will be greater than the angle of refraction.
8) The opposite happens when they leave the prism — they speed up, bending away from the normal.
9) If you repeated the investigation using a prism made out of a different material, you'd get different angles of refraction as the wave would change speed by a different amount.

Lights, camera, refraction...

Make sure you know how to conduct these experiments and what you would expect to see from the results.

Q1   Describe an investigation you could do to compare the refraction of light waves through a sapphire prism and a glass prism.   [5 marks]

The Electromagnetic Spectrum

So you know that light is a wave, but did you know that light's just one small part of the EM spectrum...

There's a Continuous Spectrum of EM Waves

> Electromagnetic waves are vibrations of electric and magnetic fields (rather than vibrations of particles). This means they can travel through a vacuum.

1) Electromagnetic (EM) waves are transverse waves (p.1).

2) They all travel at the same speed through space (a vacuum). This speed is very fast, but finite (so it always takes EM waves some time to travel from one point to another). However, they travel at different speeds in different materials.

3) EM waves vary in wavelength from around 10^{-15} m to more than 10^4 m, and those with shorter wavelengths have higher frequencies (from $v = f\lambda$ on page 1).

4) We group them based on their wavelength and frequency — there are seven basic types, but the different groups merge to form a continuous spectrum.

5) Our eyes can only detect a small part of this spectrum — visible light. Different colours of light have different wavelengths. From longest to shortest — red, orange, yellow, green, blue, indigo, violet.

RADIO WAVES	MICRO WAVES	INFRA RED	VISIBLE LIGHT	ULTRA VIOLET	X-RAYS	GAMMA RAYS
1 m – 10^4 m	10^{-2} m	10^{-5} m	10^{-7} m	10^{-8} m	10^{-10} m	10^{-15} m

wavelength

Long wavelength, low frequency and low energy.

Short wavelength, high frequency and high energy.

6) What we see as white light is actually a mixture of all of the colours across the visible spectrum.

7) EM waves spread out from a source and transfer energy to an absorber, which is some distance away. For example, when you warm yourself by an electric heater, infrared waves transfer energy from the thermal energy store of the heater (the source) to your thermal energy store (the absorber).

> You might see this explanation of how energy is transferred by radiation called a radiation model.

8) The higher the frequency of the EM wave, the more energy it transfers.

> EM waves are sometimes called EM radiation.

You Need to Know how Some EM Waves are Emitted...

1) A wide range of EM radiation can be released when changes occur in nuclei, atoms or molecules.

2) Changes in nuclei can cause gamma rays to be emitted — this is radioactive decay.

3) Visible light, ultraviolet (UV) radiation and X-rays are emitted when electrons drop down energy levels (shown on p.6).

4) The bonds holding the atoms together in molecules vibrate — this generates infrared radiation.

... and What Happens When EM Waves are Absorbed

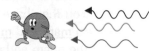

1) When any type of EM wave is absorbed, it ceases to exist as radiation and causes heating. However, high-energy UV, X-rays and gamma rays have so much energy that they don't just cause heating, but can cause ionisation when they're absorbed by atoms (p.6).

2) Infrared radiation is absorbed by molecules (as well as being emitted by them, see above).

3) UV radiation from the Sun is absorbed by oxygen molecules (O_2) in the upper atmosphere, forming ozone (O_3). This ozone then absorbs large amounts of ionising UV radiation from the Sun, protecting living things (especially animals) from its damaging effects.

Learn about the EM spectrum and wave goodbye to exam woe...

Here's a handy mnemonic for the order of EM waves: 'Rock Music Is Very Useful for eXperiments with Goats'.

Q1   Put the following in order of increasing wavelength: microwaves, X-rays, visible light.   [1 mark]

Q2   Give one way in which gamma rays can be produced.   [1 mark]

Energy Levels and Ionisation

Some electromagnetic radiation can have <u>dangerous</u> effects on humans. Don't worry though, it's not all bad.

Electrons Can be Excited to Higher Energy Levels

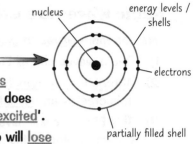

nucleus · energy levels / shells

electrons

partially filled shell

1) <u>Electrons</u> in an atom (or molecule) sit in <u>different energy levels</u> or shells (see p.69). Each <u>energy level</u> is a different distance from the <u>nucleus</u>. ⟶

2) An electron can <u>move up</u> one or more energy levels in one go if it <u>absorbs</u> <u>electromagnetic (EM) radiation</u> with the right amount of <u>energy</u>. When it does move up, it moves to a <u>partially filled</u> (or <u>empty</u>) <u>shell</u> and is said to be 'excited'.

3) The electron will then <u>fall back</u> to its <u>original energy level</u>, and in doing so will <u>lose</u> the <u>same amount</u> of <u>energy</u> it <u>absorbed</u>. The energy is <u>carried away</u> by <u>EM radiation</u>.

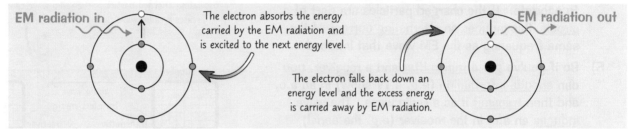

EM radiation in

The electron absorbs the energy carried by the EM radiation and is excited to the next energy level.

EM radiation out

The electron falls back down an energy level and the excess energy is carried away by EM radiation.

4) <u>Visible light</u>, <u>ultraviolet light</u> and <u>X-rays</u> are all created when atoms <u>lose energy</u> by an electron dropping <u>down</u> an energy level and emitting energy in the form of <u>EM radiation</u>.

5) The part of the <u>EM spectrum</u> the radiation is from depends on its <u>energy</u> (which depends on <u>the energy levels</u> the electron moves between). A <u>higher energy</u> means a <u>higher frequency</u> of EM radiation — which is more <u>dangerous</u> for humans.

An Atom is Ionised if it Loses an Electron

1) If an <u>outer electron</u> absorbs radiation with <u>enough energy</u>, it can move <u>so far</u> that it <u>leaves the atom</u> (or <u>molecule</u>). It is now a <u>free electron</u> and the atom is said to have been <u>ionised</u>.

2) The atom is now a <u>positive ion</u>. It's <u>positive</u> because it now consists of <u>more protons</u> than <u>electrons</u>. The positive ion can go on to take part in <u>other chemical reactions</u>.

3) Atoms can lose <u>more than one electron</u>. The <u>more</u> electrons it loses, the <u>greater</u> its positive charge.

Ionising Radiation Harms Living Cells

1) <u>Gamma rays</u>, <u>high-energy ultraviolet</u> and <u>X-rays</u> are types of <u>ionising radiation</u> — they carry enough energy to <u>knock electrons off some atoms and molecules</u>.

2) <u>High amounts</u> of <u>exposure</u> to ionising radiation is <u>dangerous</u> as ionised atoms or molecules can go on to <u>react further</u> causing <u>cell damage</u> and possible <u>cell destruction</u>. <u>Lower amounts</u> of <u>exposure</u> can <u>change</u> cells making them more likely to grow in an <u>uncontrolled way</u>, possibly <u>leading to cancer</u>.

- <u>Ultraviolet</u> (<u>UV</u>) is <u>absorbed</u> by the skin, where it can cause <u>damage</u> to <u>cells</u>, possibly leading to <u>skin cancer</u>. It can also damage your <u>eyes</u> and possibly even cause <u>blindness</u>.

- <u>X-rays</u> and <u>gamma rays</u> can cause mutations and damage cells too (which can lead to cancer). They can be very dangerous as they transfer <u>a lot of energy</u> and are <u>penetrating</u> — they pass through the skin and are absorbed by <u>deeper tissues</u>.

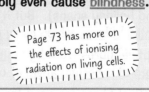

Page 73 has more on the effects of ionising radiation on living cells.

3) <u>Low energy</u> waves like <u>radio waves</u> are transmitted through the body <u>without</u> being <u>absorbed</u>.

What's an atom's favourite chore? Ioning...

So some types of EM radiation are really scary. However, other types are totally safe. It depends on their energy.

Q1 Describe how the absorption of radiation can affect the arrangement of electrons in an atom. **[1 mark]**

Q2 Explain why exposure to gamma radiation can lead to cancer. **[2 marks]**

Chapter P1 — Radiation and Waves

Uses of EM Radiation

How EM waves <u>behave</u> in materials varies, which means we use <u>different types</u> of EM waves in <u>different ways</u>...

Radio Waves are used for Communications

We use <u>radio waves</u> to <u>transmit information</u> like <u>television</u> and <u>radio shows</u> from one place to another:

1) Radio waves and all EM waves are just <u>oscillating electric</u> (p.28) <u>and magnetic fields</u> (p.37).

2) <u>Alternating currents</u> (a.c.) in electrical circuits cause <u>charges to oscillate</u>. This creates an <u>oscillating electric and magnetic field</u> — an EM wave.

There's more on a.c. on p.26.

3) This EM wave will have the <u>same frequency</u> as the current that created it. So a current with a frequency corresponding to the <u>radio wave</u> part of the spectrum is used so that <u>radio waves</u> are produced.

4) EM waves also <u>cause</u> charged particles in a conductor to oscillate. If the charged particles are part of a <u>circuit</u>, this <u>induces</u> an <u>alternating current</u> of the same frequency as the EM wave that induced it.

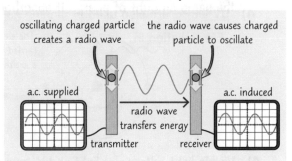

oscillating charged particle creates a radio wave — the radio wave causes charged particle to oscillate

a.c. supplied — radio wave transfers energy — a.c. induced

transmitter — receiver

5) So if you've got a <u>transmitter</u> and a <u>receiver</u>, you can <u>encode information</u> (e.g. a TV show) in an a.c. and then <u>transmit</u> it as a radio wave. The wave <u>induces</u> an a.c. in the receiver (e.g. the aerial) and bam, you've got your information.

Microwaves are Used for Communications and Cooking

1) Communication to and from <u>satellites</u> (including <u>satellite TV</u> signals and <u>mobile phones</u>) uses <u>microwaves</u> with a wavelength that can <u>pass easily</u> through the Earth's <u>watery atmosphere</u>.

2) We also use microwaves to <u>cook food</u>. These microwaves penetrate up to a few centimetres into the food before being <u>absorbed</u> and <u>transferring</u> energy to <u>water molecules</u> in the food, causing the water to <u>heat up</u>. The water molecules then <u>transfer</u> this energy to the rest of the molecules in the food <u>by heating</u> — which <u>quickly cooks</u> the food.

Infrared Radiation Can be Used to Increase or Monitor Temperature

1) <u>Infrared</u> (IR) radiation is <u>given off</u> by all <u>objects</u>. The <u>hotter</u> the object, the <u>more</u> it gives off (see p.9).

2) <u>Infrared cameras</u> can detect IR radiation and <u>monitor temperature</u>. They <u>detect</u> the IR and turn it into an <u>electrical signal</u>, which is <u>displayed on a screen</u> as a picture. The <u>hotter</u> an object is, the <u>brighter</u> it appears. E.g. IR is used in <u>night-vision</u> cameras.

night-vision camera

hot man hiding in the bushes

3) <u>Absorbing</u> IR radiation also causes objects to get <u>hotter</u>. <u>Food</u> can be <u>cooked</u> using IR radiation — the <u>temperature</u> of the food increases when it <u>absorbs</u> IR radiation, e.g. from a toaster's heating element.

Light Signals Can Travel Through Optical Fibres

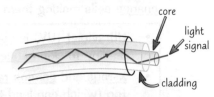

core

light signal

cladding

1) <u>Light</u> is used to <u>look at things</u> (and to take endless selfies and holiday snaps). But it's also used for <u>communication</u> using <u>optical fibres</u>, which carry <u>data</u> over long distances as <u>pulses</u> of <u>light</u>.

2) Optical fibres work by <u>bouncing light</u> off the sides of a very narrow <u>core</u>. The pulse of light <u>enters the core</u> at a <u>certain angle</u> at one end and is reflected <u>again and again</u> until it emerges at the other end.

3) Optical fibres are used for <u>telephone</u> and <u>internet cables</u>. They're also used for <u>medical</u> purposes to <u>see inside</u> the body — only a <u>small hole</u> is needed for the optical fibre (and any instruments) to enter the body, which is better than having <u>more major surgery</u>.

IR can be used in optical fibres too.

Or you could just stream the radio over the Internet...

EM waves are ace — it's the difference in how they behave at boundaries that means they're suited to varied uses.

Q1 Explain how an alternating current in a transmitter produces a radio wave. [2 marks]

More Uses of EM Radiation

If you enjoyed the last page, you're in for a real treat. If not, well, you've just got to suck it up.

Ultraviolet is Used in Fluorescent Lamps

1) Fluorescence is a property of certain chemicals, where ultraviolet (UV) radiation is absorbed and then visible light is emitted. That's why fluorescent colours look so bright — they actually emit light.

2) Fluorescent lights use UV radiation to emit visible light. They're energy-efficient (p.22) so they're good to use when light is needed for long periods (like in your classroom).

3) Security pens can be used to mark property (e.g. laptops). UV light causes the ink to fluoresce (emit visible light), but the ink remains invisible in visible light.

4) UV lamps are also used in tanning salons to give people an artificial suntan.

Skin produces a brown pigment melanin in response to UV radiation — melanin absorbs UV radiation and protects the cells from damage.

X-rays Let Us See Inside Things

1) X-rays can be used to view the internal structure of objects and materials, including our bodies.

2) Radiographers in hospitals take X-ray images to help doctors diagnose broken bones — X-rays are transmitted by flesh but are absorbed by denser material like bones or metal.

3) To produce an X-ray image, X-ray radiation is directed through the object or body onto a detector plate. The brighter bits of the image are where fewer X-rays get through, producing a negative image (the plate starts off all white).

4) Exposure to X-rays can cause cell damage (p.73), so radiographers and patients are protected as much as possible, e.g. by lead aprons and shields, and exposure to the radiation is kept to a minimum.

Gamma Rays are Used for Sterilising Things

1) Gamma rays are used to sterilise medical instruments. If they're absorbed by microbes (e.g. bacteria), they kill them. They also pass through the instruments to reach any microbes hiding in crevices.

2) This is better than trying to boil plastic instruments, which might be damaged by high temperatures.

3) Food can be sterilised in the same way — again killing microbes. This keeps the food fresh for longer, without having to freeze it, cook it or preserve it some other way, and it's perfectly safe to eat.

4) Gamma radiation is also used in cancer treatments (p.74) — radiation is targeted at cancer cells to kill them. Doctors have to be careful to minimise the damage to healthy cells when treating cancer like this.

5) We also use gamma radiation in medical imaging (see p.74).

The Risks and Benefits of Technology Must be Evaluated

1) Technology has been (and continues to be) developed to make use of every part of the electromagnetic spectrum. However useful EM waves might be, they can also be dangerous — the risks involved with using them need to be considered.

> For example, X-rays were used in some airport body scanners that were intended to improve airport security. They were initially considered safe as the radiation dose from them should be very low. However, some scientists have claimed that they do increase the risk of cancer. This has contributed to that type of scanner being banned in many countries.

2) People often have different opinions about the use of new technologies. However, decisions about whether or not to use new technology need to be justified with data and scientific explanation, rather than opinion.

Phones, lights, sterilisation — what can't EM radiation do?

You've probably got the idea now that we use EM waves an awful lot — much more than the examples on the last couple of pages even. If you get asked about an example you haven't come across before in the exam, don't panic — just apply what you do know about the electromagnetic spectrum and you'll be fine.

Q1   Give two uses of gamma rays.   [2 marks]

Absorbing and Emitting Radiation

<u>All</u> objects, including yourself, <u>emit</u> and <u>absorb</u> radiation constantly. No wonder I'm so tired all the time...

All Objects Emit Radiation

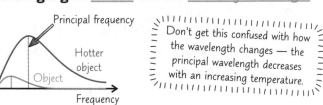

1) <u>All objects</u> emit <u>electromagnetic (EM) radiation</u> over a continuous <u>range</u> of <u>wavelengths</u> (and so over a range of <u>frequencies</u>).

2) The intensity (<u>power per unit area</u>) and wavelength (or frequency) distribution of radiation emitted depends on the object's <u>temperature</u>. The wavelength of radiation the object emits most of (i.e. has the <u>highest intensity</u>) is called the <u>principal (or peak) wavelength</u>.

3) The <u>y-axis</u> of the graph on the right shows how much <u>energy</u> each wavelength of the emitted radiation <u>transfers</u> to a given <u>area</u> in a <u>certain amount of time</u>.

4) As the <u>temperature</u> of an object <u>increases</u>, the <u>intensity</u> of <u>every emitted wavelength</u> increases.

5) However, the intensity increases <u>more</u> for <u>shorter wavelengths</u> than longer wavelengths (because shorter wavelengths of EM radiation <u>transfer more energy</u>, p.5). This causes the <u>principal wavelength</u> to <u>decrease</u>. So as objects get <u>hotter</u>, the <u>principal</u> wavelength gets <u>shorter</u> and the <u>intensity-wavelength distribution</u> becomes <u>less symmetrical</u>.

6) The <u>principal frequency</u> is the frequency of radiation that an object emits the most of. The principal frequency <u>increases</u> as the <u>temperature</u> of an object <u>increases</u>.

Don't get this confused with how the wavelength changes — the principal wavelength decreases with an increasing temperature.

Every Object Absorbs Radiation Too

As you saw above, all objects are continually <u>emitting radiation</u>, but they're also continually <u>absorbing radiation</u> too. The <u>balance</u> between absorbed and emitted radiation affects an object's <u>temperature</u>:

1) An object that's <u>hotter</u> than its surroundings <u>emits more radiation</u> than it <u>absorbs</u>. So over time, it <u>cools</u> down (like a cup of tea left on your desk).

2) An object that's <u>cooler</u> than its surroundings <u>absorbs more radiation</u> than it <u>emits</u>. Over time, the cool object warms up (e.g. ice cream on a hot day).

Hot objects give out more IR radiation than they absorb, so they cool down.

3) When an object emits the <u>same amount</u> of radiation as it absorbs, its temperature will <u>stay the same</u>.

Not all of the radiation hitting an object (<u>incoming radiation</u>) is absorbed — some is <u>reflected away</u>.

Radiation Affects the Earth's Temperature

1) The overall temperature of the Earth depends on the amount of radiation it <u>reflects</u>, <u>absorbs</u> and <u>emits</u>.

2) <u>During the day</u>, <u>lots</u> of EM radiation is transferred to the Earth from the Sun. The <u>atmosphere</u> allows some of it to pass through to be <u>absorbed</u> by the <u>Earth's surface</u>. This <u>warms</u> it and causes an <u>increase</u> in <u>local</u> temperature.

3) At <u>night</u>, less EM radiation is being <u>absorbed</u> than is being <u>emitted</u>, causing a <u>decrease</u> in the <u>local</u> temperature.

4) <u>Overall</u>, the <u>temperature</u> of the Earth stays <u>fairly constant</u>. This diagram shows the flow of EM <u>radiation</u> for the Earth.

5) <u>Changes</u> to the atmosphere can cause a change to the Earth's <u>overall temperature</u> — for example, global warming (see p.10).

Some radiation is reflected by the atmosphere, clouds and the Earth's surface.

The absorbed radiation is later emitted, some of which is absorbed by the atmosphere.

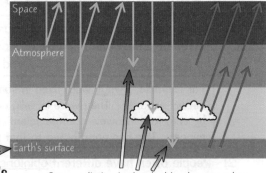

Space

Atmosphere

Earth's surface

Some radiation is absorbed by the atmosphere, clouds and the Earth's surface.

Don't let this get you hot under the collar...

The principal wavelength of radiation you emit is about 9.4×10^{-6} Hz — and you thought this page was dull...

Q1 The principal frequency of light from Star A is about 6×10^{14} Hz. The principal frequency of light from Star B is at about 3.5×10^{14} Hz. Which star is hotter? Explain your answer. [2 marks]

The Greenhouse Effect

Greenhouse gases are useful but can also cause problems — it's all about keeping a delicate balance.

Carbon Dioxide is one of the Main Greenhouse Gases

Greenhouse gases like carbon dioxide (CO_2), methane and water vapour trap radiation in the Earth's atmosphere — this, amongst other factors, allows the Earth to be warm enough to support life. Although CO_2 and methane are only present in small amounts, they have a large effect on the temperature of Earth:

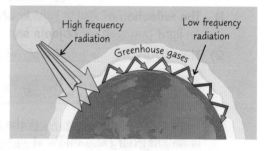

High frequency radiation

Low frequency radiation

Greenhouse gases

1) The Earth is cooler than the Sun, so the principal frequency of the radiation it emits is lower than that emitted by the Sun (see previous page).

2) All particles absorb certain frequencies of radiation. Greenhouse gases (e.g. CO_2 and methane) absorb lower frequency radiation, so they absorb a large amount of the radiation emitted by the Earth (they absorb less of the radiation emitted by the Sun as its frequency tends to be too high). The greenhouse gases then re-emit the radiation in all directions — including back towards the Earth.

3) The more greenhouse gases there are in the atmosphere, the more this happens. This is known as the greenhouse effect — it results in the Earth being warmer than it would otherwise be.

4) Some forms of human activity affect the amount of greenhouse gases in the atmosphere. E.g:

- Deforestation: This is where humans cut down and burn forests to clear land, e.g. for farming. Fewer trees means less CO_2 is removed from the atmosphere.
- Burning fossil fuels for energy (see p.23): carbon that was 'locked up' in these fuels is released as CO_2.
- Agriculture: more farm animals produce more methane through their digestive processes.
- Creating waste: more landfill sites and more waste from agriculture means more CO_2 and methane released as waste decays.

Increasing Carbon Dioxide is Linked to Climate Change

1) Over the last 200 years, the percentage of carbon dioxide in the atmosphere has increased — this is mainly due to an increased burning of fossil fuels as an energy source and deforestation by people.

2) The Earth's temperature varies naturally, but recently the average temperature of the Earth's surface has been increasing. Most scientists agree that the extra carbon dioxide from human activity is causing this increase — which is known as global warming.

3) Although most scientists also agree that global warming will lead to climate change, it's hard to fully understand the Earth's climate. This is because it's so complex, and there are so many variables, that it's very hard to make a model that isn't oversimplified.

4) However, the computer models that have been developed do show that human activity is causing global warming.

5) As more and more data is gathered using a large range of technologies, the models can be refined (made more accurate) and we can use them to make better predictions.

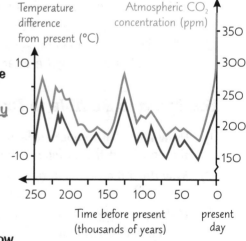

Temperature difference from present (°C)

Atmospheric CO_2 concentration (ppm)

Time before present (thousands of years)

present day

Eee, problems, problems — there's always summat goin' wrong...

Everyone's talking about climate change these days — and it might come up in the exam, so make sure you get it.

Q1   Give the names of three greenhouse gases present in the Earth's atmosphere.   [3 marks]

Q2   Describe how human activities result in global warming.   [4 marks]

Reflection and Ray Diagrams

Light <u>reflects</u> off lots of stuff. Which is pretty useful, or you wouldn't be able to read this book.

Reflection — *Light Bouncing off a Surface*

1) The reflection of <u>visible light</u> is what lets us see things — light <u>bounces off</u> objects and into our eyes.

2) There's <u>one simple rule</u> for <u>all reflected</u> waves:

> Angle of Incidence = Angle of Reflection

3) Each angle is <u>measured from</u> the <u>normal</u> — remember, this is an imaginary line that's at <u>right angles</u> to the surface at the point the light hits it (drawn with a <u>dotted</u> line).

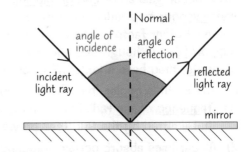

- <u>White light</u> is a <u>mixture</u> of all the <u>different colours</u> of light, which all have a different <u>wavelength</u>.
- <u>All the colours</u> of light in white light are reflected at the <u>same angle</u> — white light <u>doesn't split</u> into the different colours when it reflects, as all the wavelengths <u>follow the rule</u> above.
- So if a <u>beam of light</u> hits a mirror with an <u>angle of incidence</u> of <u>35°</u>, a <u>beam of light</u> will be reflected off the mirror with an angle of reflection of <u>35°</u>.

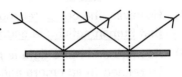

Reflection can be *Specular or Scattered*

1) Waves are <u>reflected</u> by <u>different boundaries</u> in <u>different ways</u>.

2) <u>Specular reflection</u> is when parallel incident waves are reflected in a <u>single direction</u> by a <u>smooth surface</u>.

3) This means you get a <u>clear reflection</u>, e.g. when <u>light</u> is reflected by a <u>mirror</u>.

4) <u>Scattering</u> occurs when parallel incident waves are reflected by an <u>uneven surface</u> (e.g. paper) and the waves are <u>reflected</u> in <u>all directions</u>.

5) This happens because the <u>normal</u> is <u>different</u> for each incident ray, so each ray has a different <u>angle of incidence</u>. The rule <u>angle of incidence = angle of reflection</u> still applies.

6) When light is reflected by <u>something rough</u>, the surface looks <u>matt</u>, and you <u>don't</u> get a clear reflection.

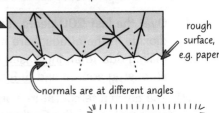

smooth surface, e.g. mirror

normals are all parallel

rough surface, e.g. paper

normals are at different angles

You Need to Be Able to Draw Ray Diagrams for Reflection

1) Draw a <u>normal</u> to your surface and a <u>light ray</u> that meets the normal at the surface — this is your <u>incident ray</u>.

2) Now draw the <u>reflected ray</u>, remembering that the <u>angle of incidence</u> must always <u>equal</u> the <u>angle of reflection</u>.

3) If there are <u>multiple</u> rays which are <u>parallel</u> (e.g. the light source is distant) and they're reflecting off a <u>smooth surface</u>, then the <u>reflected rays</u> will also all be <u>parallel</u> to each other.

4) Remember to use a <u>ruler</u> (and <u>protractor</u> if required) and <u>always</u> put <u>arrows</u> on your rays.

A ray diagram shows the path of a wave.

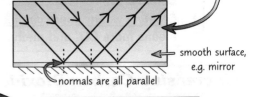

angles should be equal

incident ray

reflected ray

normal

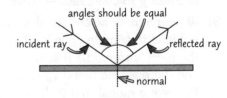

Ray Diagrams — *top bloke...*

More on reflection, will it ever end? Only time, tea and more revision will tell. It's all rather important though and those ray diagrams can be life savers in exams. Best sharpen your pencil and practise.

Q1   Sketch a ray diagram showing parallel rays of red and violet light reflecting off a mirror at 45° to the normal.

[3 marks]

Refraction, Ray Diagrams and Prisms

Remember refraction from page 3? Well, here's some more stuff you need to know about it.

Refraction can be Shown on a Ray Diagram

Refraction happens when a wave crosses a boundary between substances at an angle. The wave's change in speed results in a change in direction — see page 3.

Here's how to draw a ray diagram to show refraction:

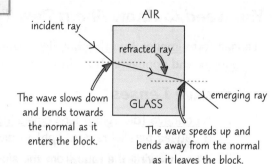

AIR
incident ray
refracted ray
GLASS
emerging ray

The wave slows down and bends towards the normal as it enters the block.

The wave speeds up and bends away from the normal as it leaves the block.

1) Draw a normal where any ray meets a boundary.
    (A normal is a line at 90° to a boundary — use a dotted line for it.)

2) If the light ray slows down as it crosses a boundary, it will bend TOWARDS the normal.

3) If the light ray speeds up as it crosses a boundary, it will bend AWAY from the normal.

4) If a light ray is travelling through a rectangular block, the emerging ray and the incident ray will be parallel.

5) Remember to use a ruler and add arrows to your rays to show direction.

- The angle of incidence is between the incident ray and the normal.
- The angle of refraction is between the refracted ray and the normal.

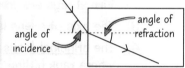

angle of incidence

angle of refraction

Different Colours of Light Travel at Different Speeds through Substances

Different wavelengths (colours) of light travel at the same speed in air, but at different speeds in different materials (e.g. glass, water or perspex®). This means they refract by different amounts.

Remember, in order of decreasing wavelength, the colours of light are: red, orange, yellow, green, blue, indigo, violet.

The shorter the wavelength, the slower the light travels in a material. For example, violet light travels more slowly in glass than red light does, meaning violet light refracts more than red.

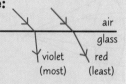

air
glass
violet (most)   red (least)

White light is a mixture of all the colours of light (p.5).

The Wave Model Explains Why Prisms Disperse White Light

The speed differences between colours explains why a beam of white light disperses (spreads out) when it passes through a triangular prism and you see the colours of the spectrum (a rainbow):

You need to be able to draw a ray diagram to show this:

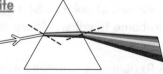

Because of the prism's shape, the wavelengths spread out even more when leaving the prism.

1) Draw a triangular prism and a single ray hitting one side of it at an angle. Draw a normal to the prism at the point where the light ray hits it.

2) Draw two rays refracting to represent two different wavelengths of light — each ray should bend towards the normal by a different amount as it enters the prism. Label each ray (the blue ray will have refracted more than the red).

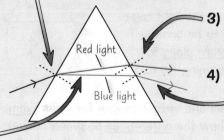

Red light

Blue light

3) At the points where each ray leaves the prism, draw a normal to the prism.

4) Draw each ray bending away from the normal as they leave the prism (and speed up). Again, the blue ray refracts more than the red.

Did you see the match? There was some great ref action...

Refraction is the reason that you see rainbows. However, the pot of gold at the end is due to leprechauns...

Q1 a) Draw a ray diagram to show the refraction of a beam of red light as it enters a glass block at an angle to the surface of the block, and slows down. Label the angles of incidence and refraction. [4 marks]

   b) Explain why you would expect the angle of refraction to be different for a beam of green light. [2 marks]

Lenses

Refraction is more than just a straw looking bent in your glass of fizzy pop.
It is how our eyes see (and how your glasses work if your eyes aren't quite getting it spot on).

You Need to Know About Two Types of Lens

Lenses form images by refracting light (p.3), which changes its direction. There are two main types of lens — convex and concave. They have different shapes and have opposite effects on light rays:

Concave Lenses

1) A concave (diverging) lens caves inwards. It causes parallel rays of light to diverge (spread out).

2) When viewing the rays from the side of the lens from which the rays emerge, it will look like the rays have come from somewhere else. We show this using a virtual ray — a ray that isn't actually there (see below). Virtual rays are drawn by tracing the emerging rays back.

3) The axis of a lens is a line through the middle of the lens.

4) The principal focus (focal point) of a concave lens is the point where rays hitting the lens parallel to the axis appear to come from. The virtual rays all meet up at this single point.

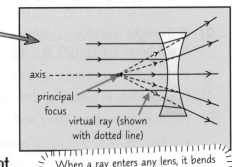

axis

principal focus

virtual ray (shown with dotted line)

When a ray enters any lens, it bends towards the normal. When it leaves, it bends away from the normal (p.12).

Convex Lenses

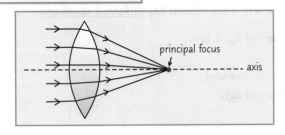

principal focus

axis

1) A convex (converging) lens bulges outwards. It causes parallel rays of light to converge (be brought together).

2) The principal focus of a convex lens is where rays hitting the lens parallel to the axis all meet.

3) For any lens, the distance from the centre of the lens to the principal focus is called the focal length. There's a principal focus on each side of any lens.

Images can be Real or Virtual

Images are formed at points where all the light rays from a certain point on an object come together or appear to come together. These are two types of images that can be formed by lenses:

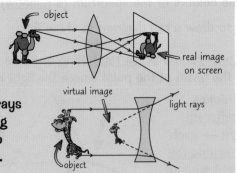

1) A REAL image is formed when the light rays actually come together to form the image.

object — real image on screen

2) A VIRTUAL image is when the light rays from the object appear to be coming from a completely different place to where they're actually coming from.

virtual image — light rays — object

You don't need to know about real and virtual images for your exam, but it'll help you be able to use ray diagrams to show the differences between convex and concave lenses, which you do need to know. More coming up on that on the next page.

Contact lenses — ring them up and say hello...

Make sure you know the differences between real and virtual images — they can be pretty tough.

Q1 Copy and complete this diagram to show the path taken by the light rays as they pass through the lens, and after they emerge from the other side. The principal focus is labelled p.

• p [3 marks]

Ray Diagrams of Lenses

Ray diagrams of lenses show the position, orientation and size of the image formed. Learn how to...

Draw a Ray Diagram for an Image Through a Convex Lens

1) Pick a point on the top of the object. Draw a ray going from the object to the lens parallel to the axis of the lens.

2) Draw another ray from the top of the object going right through the middle of the lens.

3) The incident ray that's parallel to the axis is refracted through the principal focus (F). Draw a refracted ray passing through F.

4) The ray passing through the middle of the lens doesn't bend.

5) Mark where the rays meet. That's the top of the image.

6) Repeat the process for a point on the bottom of the object. When the bottom of the object is on the axis, the bottom of the image is also on the axis.

In ray diagrams, this represents a convex lens.

The distance from the lens to the object affects the size and position of the image:

1) An object 2F (two focal lengths) from the lens produces a real, inverted (upside down) image the same size as the object and at 2F on the other side of the lens.

2) An object between F and 2F will make a real, inverted image bigger than the object and beyond 2F.

3) An object nearer than F will make a virtual image the right way up, bigger than the object and on the same side of the lens.

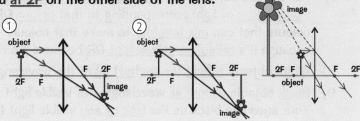

Draw a Ray Diagram for an Image Through a Concave Lens

1) Pick a point on the top of the object. Draw a ray going from the object to the lens parallel to the axis of the lens.

2) Draw another ray from the top of the object going right through the middle of the lens.

3) The incident ray that's parallel to the axis is refracted so it appears to have come from the principal focus (F). Draw a ray from the principal focus. Make it dotted before it reaches the lens (as it's virtual here).

4) The ray passing through the middle of the lens doesn't bend.

5) Mark where this ray meets the virtual ray. That's the top of the image.

6) Repeat the process for a point on the bottom of the object. When the bottom of the object is on the axis, the bottom of the image is also on the axis.

In ray diagrams, this represents a concave lens.

A concave lens always produces a virtual image. The image is the right way up, smaller than the object and on the same side of the lens as the object — no matter where the object is.

Convex and Concave Lenses have Similarities and Differences

1) You've just seen how concave lenses don't have much variety in their image type. Convex lenses have loads in comparison. They can produce both real and virtual images, upright and inverted, on either side of the lens, not to mention images of any size. It's a key difference between the lens types.

2) There are a few similarities too — convex and concave lenses both have a principal focus along the axis on each side. Also, rays passing through the centre of either lens are never refracted.

The lens said to the policeman, "I've been framed"...

Phew, that's the last page on ray diagrams, but probably the most complicated. You know what to do, practise.

Q1 Draw a ray diagram for an object at a distance between F and 2F in front of a convex lens. [3 marks]

Visible Light and Colour

Time for a bit more about the different <u>wavelengths of light</u>. Look at all the <u>pretty colours</u>...

Colour and Transparency Depend on Absorbed Wavelengths

1) The <u>colour</u> of an object depends on the differences in its <u>absorption</u>, <u>transmission</u> and <u>reflection</u> of <u>different wavelengths</u>.

2) <u>Each colour</u> has its own narrow <u>range</u> of <u>wavelengths</u>.

3) Colours can also <u>mix together</u> to make other colours.
The only colours you <u>can't</u> make by mixing are the <u>primary</u> colours: pure <u>red</u>, <u>green</u> and <u>blue</u>.
When <u>all</u> of these different colours are put together, it creates <u>white light</u> (p.5).

long wavelength   short wavelength

low frequency   high frequency

4) Different objects <u>absorb</u>, <u>transmit</u> and <u>reflect</u> different <u>wavelengths</u> of light <u>differently</u>.

5) <u>Opaque</u> objects are objects that <u>do not transmit light</u>.
When visible light waves hit them, they <u>absorb</u> some wavelengths of light and <u>reflect</u> others.

6) The <u>colour</u> of the object depends on <u>which wavelengths</u> of light are <u>reflected</u>. E.g. a <u>red</u> apple appears to be red because the wavelengths corresponding to the <u>red part</u> of the <u>visible spectrum</u> are reflected. The other <u>wavelengths</u> of light are <u>absorbed</u>.

7) For opaque objects that <u>aren't a primary colour</u>, they may be reflecting either the <u>wavelengths</u> of light corresponding to that <u>colour</u> OR the wavelengths of the <u>primary</u> colours that can <u>mix together</u> to make that colour. So a banana may look <u>yellow</u> because it's <u>reflecting yellow light</u> OR because it's reflecting <u>both red and green light</u>.

How I love my coat that reflects different wavelengths of li-ight!!!

8) <u>White</u> objects <u>reflect</u> (or <u>scatter</u>) <u>all</u> of the wavelengths of visible light <u>equally</u>.

9) <u>Black</u> objects <u>absorb all</u> wavelengths of visible light (and <u>scatters none</u>).
Your eyes see black as the <u>lack of</u> any visible light (i.e. the lack of any <u>colour</u>).

10) <u>Transparent</u> (see-through) and <u>translucent</u> (partially see-through) objects <u>transmit light</u>, i.e. not all light that hits the surface of the object is absorbed or reflected — some can <u>pass through</u> (<u>most</u> can for transparent objects).

Colour filters are translucent objects.

11) Some wavelengths of light may be <u>absorbed</u> or <u>reflected</u> by translucent objects (and to a lesser extent by transparent objects). These objects will appear to be the colour of light that corresponds to the wavelengths most <u>strongly transmitted</u> by the object.

Colour Filters Only Let Through Particular Wavelengths

1) Colour filters are used to <u>filter out</u> different <u>wavelengths</u> of light, so that only <u>certain wavelengths</u> are <u>transmitted</u>.

2) A <u>primary colour filter</u> only <u>transmits</u> that <u>colour</u>, e.g. if <u>white light</u> is shone at a <u>blue</u> colour filter, <u>only</u> blue light will be let through. The rest of the light will be <u>absorbed</u>.

3) If you look at a <u>blue object</u> through a blue <u>colour filter</u>, it would still look <u>blue</u>.
Blue light is <u>reflected</u> from the object's surface and is <u>transmitted</u> by the filter.

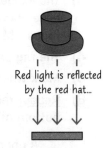

Red light is reflected by the red hat...

4) However, if the object was e.g. <u>red</u> (or any colour <u>not made from blue light</u>), the object would appear <u>black</u> when viewed through a blue filter.
<u>All</u> of the light <u>reflected</u> by the object will be <u>absorbed</u> by the filter.

...but it's not transmitted by the blue colour filter...

5) <u>Filters</u> that <u>aren't</u> for <u>primary</u> colours let through <u>both</u> the <u>wavelengths</u> of light for that <u>colour</u> AND the wavelengths of the <u>primary</u> colours that add together to make that colour.

...so the hat appears black.

Have you seen my white shirt? It's red and yellow and green and...

Hopefully you now know enough about absorption and reflection that you're feeling pretty confident. Once you've got them down, this page is pretty easy — red objects reflect red light and red filters let red light through. Simple.

Q1   a) Explain why a cucumber looks green.   [2 marks]
             b) State the colour a cucumber would look if you looked at it through a red filter.   [1 mark]

Sound Waves

We hear sounds when <u>vibrations</u> reach our <u>eardrums</u>. I'm picking up good vibrations about this page...

Sound Travels as a Wave

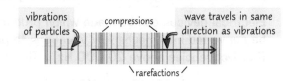

vibrations of particles   compressions   wave travels in same direction as vibrations

rarefactions

1) <u>Sound waves</u> are caused by <u>vibrating objects</u>.

2) These vibrations are passed through the surrounding medium as a series of <u>compressions</u> and <u>rarefactions</u>. They're a type of <u>longitudinal wave</u> (see page 1).

3) When a sound wave travels <u>through a solid</u> it does so by causing <u>vibrations</u> of the <u>particles</u> in that solid.

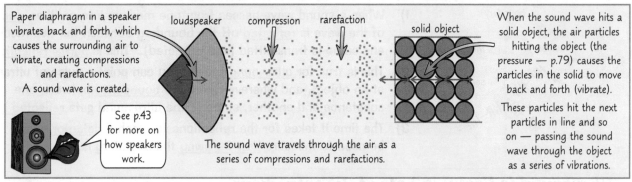

Paper diaphragm in a speaker vibrates back and forth, which causes the surrounding air to vibrate, creating compressions and rarefactions. A sound wave is created.

See p.43 for more on how speakers work.

loudspeaker   compression   rarefaction

The sound wave travels through the air as a series of compressions and rarefactions.

solid object

When the sound wave hits a solid object, the air particles hitting the object (the pressure — p.79) causes the particles in the solid to move back and forth (vibrate).

These particles hit the next particles in line and so on — passing the sound wave through the object as a series of vibrations.

4) Sound travels at <u>different speeds</u> in <u>different media</u> — it generally travels <u>faster in solids</u> than in <u>liquids</u>, and <u>faster in liquids</u> than in <u>gases</u>. The speed of sound is <u>much slower</u> than the speed of light.

5) The <u>frequency</u> of sound <u>doesn't change</u> when it passes from one medium into another. But because $v = f\lambda$ (p.1) the <u>wavelength</u> does — it gets <u>longer</u> when it <u>speeds up</u>, and <u>shorter</u> when it <u>slows down</u>.

6) So sound waves can <u>refract</u> as they enter <u>different media</u> (see p.3). (However, since sound waves are always spreading out so much, the change in direction is <u>hard to spot</u> under normal circumstances.)

7) <u>Sound waves</u> will be <u>reflected</u> by <u>hard flat surfaces</u>. <u>Echoes</u> are just reflected sound waves.

8) Sound can't travel in <u>space</u> because it's mostly a <u>vacuum</u> (there are no particles to move or vibrate).

You Hear Sound When Your Eardrum Vibrates

1) Sound waves that reach your <u>eardrum</u> cause it to <u>vibrate</u>.

2) These <u>vibrations</u> are passed on to <u>tiny bones</u> in your ear called <u>ossicles</u>, through the <u>semi-circular canal</u> and to the <u>cochlea</u>.

3) The <u>cochlea</u> turns these vibrations into <u>electrical signals</u> which get sent to your <u>brain</u>.

4) The brain <u>interprets</u> the signals as sounds of different <u>pitches</u> and <u>volumes</u>, depending on their <u>frequency</u> and <u>intensity</u>. A <u>higher frequency</u> sound wave has a <u>higher pitch</u>.

5) <u>Human hearing</u> (<u>audition</u>) is limited by the <u>size</u> and <u>shape</u> of our <u>eardrum</u>, and the <u>structure</u> of all the parts within the ear that <u>vibrate</u> to transmit the sound wave.

6) The bones in the middle ear (ossicles) only work over a <u>limited frequency range</u>, which means humans can't hear <u>very low-pitched</u> or <u>very high-pitched</u> sounds. The bones transmit frequencies in the range 1 kHz to 3 kHz <u>most efficiently</u>, but <u>young people</u> can hear frequencies ranging from about <u>20 Hz</u> (low pitch) up to <u>20 000 Hz</u> (high pitch). As you get <u>older</u>, the <u>upper limit decreases</u>, and sounds may need to be <u>louder</u> for you to hear them. This is mainly due to <u>wear and tear</u> of the <u>cochlea</u> or <u>auditory nerve</u>.

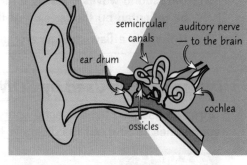

outer ear   middle ear   inner ear

semicircular canals   auditory nerve — to the brain

ear drum

ossicles

cochlea

Sorry, listening to the radio doesn't count as revision...

It's amazing how our ears and brains make sense of pulsating air molecules. Anyway, no time for awe — try this.

Q1   Explain why you wouldn't hear an explosion in space.   [2 marks]

Q2   Explain how your ears allow you to hear sounds.   [3 marks]

Ultrasound and SONAR

Can you hear <u>that</u>? If not, '<u>that</u>' could be <u>ultrasound</u> — a handy wave used for <u>seeing hidden objects</u>.

Ultrasound is Sound with Frequencies Higher Than 20 000 Hz

Electrical devices can be made which produce <u>electrical oscillations</u> of <u>any frequency</u>. These can easily be converted into <u>mechanical vibrations</u> to produce <u>sound</u> waves <u>beyond the range of human hearing</u> (i.e. frequencies above 20 000 Hz). This is called <u>ultrasound</u> and it pops up all over the place.

Sound Waves Get Partially Reflected at Boundaries

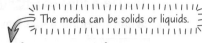
The media can be solids or liquids.

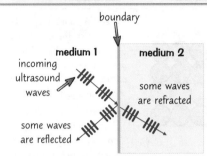
boundary
medium 1   medium 2
incoming ultrasound waves
some waves are refracted
some waves are reflected

1) When a sound wave passes from one medium into another, <u>some</u> of the wave is <u>reflected</u> off the boundary between the two media, and some is transmitted (and refracted). This is <u>partial reflection</u>.

2) This is true for <u>ultrasound</u> too — you can point a pulse of ultrasound at an object, and wherever there are <u>boundaries</u> between one substance and another, some of the ultrasound gets <u>reflected back</u>.

3) The time it takes for the reflections to reach a <u>detector</u> can be used to measure <u>how far away</u> the boundary is.

Ultrasound is Useful in Lots of Different Ways

<u>Medical imaging, e.g. pre-natal scanning of a foetus</u>

1) <u>Ultrasound waves</u> can pass through the body, but whenever they reach a boundary between <u>two different media</u> (like fluid in the womb and the skin of the foetus) some of the wave is <u>reflected back</u> and <u>detected</u>.

2) The exact <u>timing and distribution</u> of these <u>echoes</u> are processed by a computer to produce a <u>video image</u> of the foetus.

3) As far as we know, ultrasound imaging like this is <u>perfectly safe</u>.

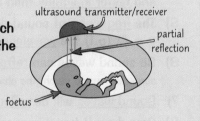
ultrasound transmitter/receiver
partial reflection
foetus

<u>Industrial imaging, e.g. finding flaws in materials</u>

1) Ultrasound can also be used to find <u>flaws</u> in objects such as <u>pipes</u> or <u>materials</u> such as wood or metal.

2) Ultrasound waves entering a material will usually be <u>reflected</u> by the <u>far side</u> of the material.

3) If there is a flaw such as a <u>crack</u> inside the object, the wave will be <u>reflected sooner</u>.

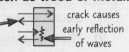
ultrasound waves reflected by far side of material
crack causes early reflection of waves

Ultrasound is Used by SONAR Underwater

Ultrasound is also used in <u>echo sounding</u>, which is a type of <u>SONAR</u> used by boats and submarines to find out the <u>distance to the seabed</u> or to <u>locate</u> objects in <u>deep water</u>.

EXAMPLE:

A pulse of ultrasound takes 4.5 seconds to travel from a submarine to the seabed and back again. If the speed of sound in seawater is 1520 m/s, how far away is the submarine from the seabed?

1) The 4.5 s is for there <u>and</u> back, so <u>halve</u> the time.

2) Use <u>distance = average speed × time</u> (p.49).

$4.5 \div 2 = 2.25$ s

distance $= 1520 \times 2.25$
$= 3420$ m

pulse sent
pulse back

Partially reflected — completely revised...

Ultrasound waves are really useful, so make sure you can describe how looking at the time taken for them to be reflected can let you see the structure of things you would otherwise be unable to — like the inside of a metal.

Q1   Describe how ultrasound waves can be used to scan a foetus.   [3 marks]

Seismic Waves

<u>Ultrasound</u> waves can be used to <u>explore structures</u> that we can't <u>see</u>, but they're <u>not</u> the <u>only</u> ones...

Waves Can Be Used to Detect and Explore

1) Waves have <u>different properties</u> (e.g. speed) depending on the <u>material</u> they're travelling through.

2) When a wave arrives at a <u>boundary</u> between materials, a number of things can happen.

3) It can be <u>completely reflected</u> or <u>partially reflected</u> (like in <u>ultrasound</u> imaging, see page 17). The wave may continue travelling in the same direction but at a <u>different speed</u>, or it may be <u>refracted</u> (p.3) or <u>absorbed</u> (like <u>S-waves</u> below).

4) Studying the properties and paths of <u>waves</u> through structures can give you clues to some of the properties of the structure that you can't <u>see</u> by eye. You can do this with lots of <u>different waves</u> — ultrasound (see previous page) and seismic waves are two good, well-known <u>examples</u>.

Earthquakes and Explosions Cause Seismic Waves

> Seismic waves also sometimes called 'earthquake waves'.

1) When there's an <u>earthquake</u> somewhere, it produces <u>seismic waves</u> which travel out through the Earth. We <u>detect</u> these waves all over the surface of the planet using <u>seismometers</u>.

2) <u>Seismologists</u> work out the <u>time</u> it takes for the shock waves to reach each seismometer. They also note which parts of the Earth <u>don't receive the shock waves</u> at all.

3) When <u>seismic waves</u> reach a <u>boundary</u> between different layers of <u>material</u> (which all have different <u>properties</u>, like density) inside the Earth, some waves will be <u>absorbed</u> and some will be <u>refracted</u>.

4) Most of the time, if the waves are <u>refracted</u> they change speed <u>gradually</u>, resulting in a <u>curved path</u>. But when the properties change <u>suddenly</u>, the wave speed changes abruptly, and the path has a <u>kink</u>.

P-waves can Travel through the Earth's Core, S-Waves Can't

1) There are <u>three different types</u> of seismic waves you need to learn — P-waves and S-waves (see below), and L-waves which travel on the <u>surface</u> of the Earth moving the ground <u>up and down</u>.

2) By observing how seismic waves are <u>absorbed</u> and <u>refracted</u>, scientists have been able to work out <u>where</u> the properties of the Earth change <u>dramatically</u>. Our current understanding of the <u>internal structure</u> of the Earth and the <u>size</u> of the <u>Earth's core</u> is based on these <u>observations</u>.

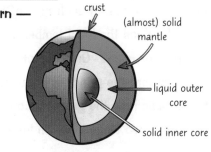

P-waves inside the Earth

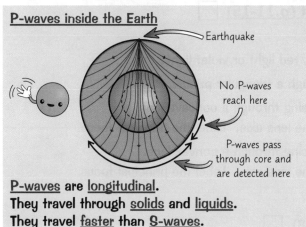

<u>P-waves</u> are <u>longitudinal</u>.
They travel through <u>solids</u> and <u>liquids</u>.
They travel <u>faster</u> than <u>S-waves</u>.

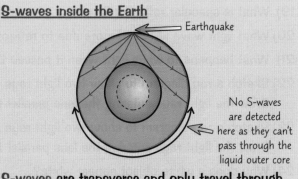

<u>S-waves</u> are transverse and only travel through <u>solids</u>. They're <u>slower</u> than <u>P-waves</u>.

I'll take an Earth with metal filling and a crispy crust to go...

Wow, who knew earthquakes could be so educational as well as destructive...

Q1   S-waves produced at the Earth's North Pole would not be detected at the South Pole. Suggest one conclusion you can make about the Earth's core from the observation. Explain your answer.   [2 marks]

Revision Questions for Chapter P1

Well, that wraps up <u>Chapter P1</u> — hopefully that got you warmed up. First chapter down, seven to go.
- Try these questions and <u>tick off each one</u> when you <u>get it right</u>.
- When you've done <u>all the questions</u> for a topic and are <u>completely happy</u> with it, tick off the topic.

<u>Wave Basics (p.1-2)</u> ☑

1) What is the amplitude, wavelength, frequency and period of a wave? ☑

2) What is the difference between a transverse wave and a longitudinal wave?
Give one example of each type of wave. ☑

3) State the wave speed equation. ☑

4) Describe an experiment to measure the speed of sound in air. ☑

5) Describe an experiment to measure the wavelength of a water wave. ☑

<u>Reflection and Refraction Basics (p.3-4)</u> ☑

6) What three things can happen to a wave when it hits a boundary between two different materials? ☑

7) Out of velocity, frequency and wavelength, which change when a wave refracts? ☑

8) Describe an experiment for investigating the reflection of light. ☑

<u>Uses and Dangers of Electromagnetic Waves (p.5-10)</u> ☑

9) Are EM waves transverse or longitudinal? ☑

10) List the waves in the EM spectrum, in order of increasing wavelength. ☑

11) What happens when an electron drops down an energy level? ☑

12) What is meant by ionising radiation? ☑

13) Give one use of each type of EM wave. ☑

14) Why does the local temperature of the Earth increase during the day but decrease at night? ☑

15) True or false? Only objects warmer than their surroundings emit infrared radiation. ☑

16) Compare the principal frequency of the radiation emitted by the Earth with that emitted by the Sun. ☑

17) Explain how the greenhouse effect keeps the Earth warm. ☑

18) State two ways in which human activity is leading to an increase in carbon dioxide in the atmosphere. ☑

<u>Ray diagrams, Lenses and Visible Light (p.11-15)</u> ☑

19) What is specular reflection? ☑

20) What light wave will bend more due to refraction, red light or violet light? ☑

21) What happens to white light when it passes through a triangular prism? ☑

22) Sketch a ray diagram to show two light rays passing through a concave lens.
Draw the light rays entering the lens parallel to the lens axis. Label the principal focus. ☑

23) Sketch a ray diagram to show two light rays passing through a convex lens.
Draw the light rays entering the lens parallel to the lens axis. Label the principal focus. ☑

24) Why does a white object appear white? ☑

<u>Sound and Exploring Structures (p.16-18)</u> ☑

25) How does the wavelength of a sound wave change as it passes from one medium
to another and speeds up? ☑

26) What is SONAR used for? ☑

27) Name three kinds of wave produced by an earthquake. What are the main differences between them? ☑

Energy Stores and Transfers

Energy is <u>never used up</u>. Instead it's just <u>transferred</u> between different <u>energy stores</u> and different objects...

Energy is Transferred Between Stores

Energy can be held in a limited number of different <u>stores</u>. Here are the stores you need to learn:

1) <u>Thermal</u> energy stores
2) <u>Kinetic</u> energy stores — p.66
3) <u>Gravitational potential</u> energy stores — p.66
4) <u>Elastic</u> energy stores — p.85
5) <u>Chemical</u> energy stores
6) <u>Nuclear</u> energy stores

7) <u>Electromagnetic</u> energy stores
— two objects will have energy in this store if they exert a magnetic force on each other.
8) <u>Electrostatic</u> energy stores
— two objects will have energy in this store if they exert an electrostatic force on each other (see p.28).

<u>Energy is transferred</u> whenever a <u>system changes</u>. A <u>system</u> is just a fancy word for a <u>single</u> object (e.g. the air in a piston) or a <u>group</u> of <u>objects</u> (e.g. two colliding vehicles) that you're interested in. A system can be <u>changed</u> by <u>heating</u> or by <u>working</u>.

Energy can be Transferred by Heating...

Energy transfer <u>by heating</u> is where energy is transferred from a <u>hotter</u> region to a <u>colder</u> region. Energy can be transferred by heating in different ways:

• <u>Conduction</u> is where the <u>vibrating particles</u> of a substance transfer energy to <u>neighbouring particles</u>.
• <u>Convection</u> is where the energetic particles of a substance <u>move away</u> from <u>hotter to cooler</u> regions.

Energy can also be transferred by <u>radiation</u>, e.g. electromagnetic/sound <u>waves</u>. The energy is often transferred directly to <u>thermal energy stores</u>.

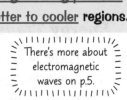
There's more about electromagnetic waves on p.5.

...or by Working

1) <u>Work done</u> is just another way of saying <u>energy transferred</u> — they're the <u>same thing</u>.
2) <u>Work</u> can be done <u>mechanically</u> (an object moving due to a <u>force</u> doing work on it, e.g. pushing, pulling or stretching) or <u>electrically</u> (a charge doing <u>electrical work</u> against resistance, e.g. charges moving round a circuit). For example:

> <u>A battery-operated heater</u> — energy is transferred <u>electrically</u> from the <u>chemical</u> energy store of the <u>battery</u> to the <u>thermal</u> energy store of the <u>electric heater</u>. This energy is then transferred to the <u>surroundings</u> by <u>heating</u>.

> A <u>motor</u> connected to the <u>mains</u> — in a <u>power station</u>, energy is transferred from the <u>chemical</u> energy store of the <u>fuel</u> to the <u>thermal</u> energy store of <u>water</u> in the boiler. This is then transferred to the <u>kinetic</u> energy stores of <u>turbines</u> and <u>generators</u> which produce electricity. Energy is transferred by the <u>electric current</u> (electrically) to the <u>kinetic</u> energy store of the <u>motor</u>.

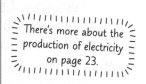
There's more about the production of electricity on page 23.

3) For both battery- and mains-operated devices (where the mains electricity has come from burning fossil fuels in a power station, see p.23), the <u>electric current</u> transfers energy from the <u>chemical energy store</u> of the fuel and <u>does work</u> on the device.

4) Transferring energy by <u>electricity</u> from a power station to consumers is <u>convenient</u> as it can travel over <u>long distances</u>. Electricity can be <u>used</u> in many ways, e.g. <u>driving motors</u> (which are used to lift or move objects) or <u>heating</u>.

All this work, I can feel my energy stores being drained...

Energy stores pop up everywhere in physics, the pesky scoundrels — make sure you've got to grips with them.

Q1   Describe the energy transfers that occur in a battery-operated motor.   [3 marks]

Conservation of Energy and Power

Repeat after me: <u>energy</u> is <u>NEVER</u> destroyed. Make sure you learn that fact, it's really important.

You Need to Know the Conservation of Energy Principle

1) The <u>conservation of energy principle</u> says that energy is <u>always</u> conserved:

   > Energy can be <u>transferred</u> usefully, stored or dissipated, but can <u>never</u> be <u>created</u> or <u>destroyed</u>.

2) When energy is <u>transferred</u> between stores, not <u>all</u> of the energy is transferred <u>usefully</u> to the store you want. Some of the energy is <u>dissipated</u> (usually to the thermal energy stores of the <u>surroundings</u>).

3) Dissipated energy is sometimes called '<u>wasted energy</u>' because the energy is being <u>stored</u> in a way that is <u>not useful</u> and that you <u>can't access</u>. <u>Eventually</u>, wasted energy ends up in <u>thermal</u> energy stores.

   > A mobile phone is a <u>system</u>. When you charge the phone, energy is <u>usefully</u> transferred <u>into</u> the system to the <u>chemical</u> energy store of the phone's <u>battery</u>. But some of the energy is <u>wasted</u> to the <u>thermal</u> energy store of the <u>phone</u> (you may have noticed your phone feels warm if it's been charging).

4) You need to be able to describe energy transfers for <u>closed systems</u> (systems where neither <u>matter</u> nor energy can enter or leave). The <u>net change</u> in the <u>total energy</u> of a <u>closed system</u> is <u>always zero</u>.

   > A <u>cold spoon</u> is dropped into an insulated flask of <u>hot soup</u>, which is then sealed. You can assume that the flask is a <u>perfect thermal insulator</u> so the <u>spoon</u> and the <u>soup</u> form a <u>closed system</u>. Energy is transferred from the <u>thermal</u> energy store of the <u>soup</u> to the <u>useless</u> thermal energy store of the <u>spoon</u> (causing the soup to cool down slightly). Energy transfers have occurred <u>within</u> the system, but no energy has <u>left</u> the system — so the net change in energy is <u>zero</u>.

Energy Transferred Depends on the Power

1) <u>Power</u> is the <u>rate of energy transfer</u>, i.e. how much energy is transferred between stores <u>per second</u>.

2) <u>Domestic electrical appliances</u> usually have <u>power ratings</u>. These are their <u>maximum operating powers</u>.

3) Devices with <u>higher</u> power ratings transfer <u>more</u> energy <u>per second</u> — e.g. a 1200 W heater will transfer <u>twice</u> as much energy per second than a 600 W heater. There's more on power on p.67.

4) The <u>total</u> energy transferred (work done) by an <u>electrical appliance</u> depends on its <u>power rating</u> and <u>how long</u> the appliance is on for.

Phenomenal cosmic power...

5) The amount of <u>energy transferred electrically</u> is given by:

   > energy transferred (J) = power (W) × time (s) $E = P \times t$

6) <u>Energy</u> is usually given in <u>joules</u>, but for <u>electrical devices</u> you may also see it given in <u>kilowatt-hours</u>.

7) A kilowatt-hour (kWh) is the amount of energy a device with a <u>power of 1 kW</u> (1000 W) <u>transfers</u> in <u>1 hour</u> of operation. It's <u>much bigger</u> than a joule, so it's useful for when you're dealing with <u>large amounts</u> of energy — 1 kWh is equal to <u>3 600 000 J</u>.

8) To calculate the energy transferred in kWh, you need <u>power</u> in <u>kilowatts</u>, <u>kW</u>, and the <u>time</u> in <u>hours</u>, <u>h</u>.

9) <u>Electricity bills</u> are based on the number of <u>kWh</u> used by a household. You need to be able to <u>calculate the cost</u> of using an <u>electrical device</u> for a given amount of time:

   1) Find the <u>amount of energy transferred</u> to the device in a <u>certain amount of time</u> in <u>kWh</u>.

   2) The cost is usually given in <u>pence per kilowatt-hour</u> (p per kWh). So just <u>multiply</u> the <u>cost per kWh</u> by the <u>number of kilowatt-hours used</u> to find the <u>total cost</u> of running the device.

Energy can't be created or destroyed — only talked about a lot...

Make sure you get your head around kWh, they can be a bit tough until you've practised using them.

Q1 A motor transfers 4.8 kJ of energy in 2 minutes. Calculate its power in watts. [3 marks]

Q2 A clothes dryer has a power rating of 4.0 kW. It takes 45 minutes to dry one load of clothes. The cost of electricity is 14p per kWh. Calculate the cost of drying one load of clothes. [4 marks]

Efficiency and Sankey Diagrams

More! More! Tell me more about energy transfers please! Oh go on then, since you insist...

Most Energy Transfers Involve Some Energy Being Wasted

1) No device is 100% efficient — whenever work is done, some of the energy transferred is always wasted.

2) The less energy that is 'wasted', the more efficient the device is said to be.

3) The efficiency for any energy transfer can be worked out using this equation:

$$\text{efficiency} = \frac{\text{useful energy transferred}}{\text{total energy transferred}}$$

You can give efficiency as a decimal or you can multiply your answer by 100 to get a percentage, i.e. 0.75 or 75%.

EXAMPLE: A food blender is 70% efficient. 6000 J of energy is transferred to it. Calculate the useful energy transferred by the blender.

1) Change the efficiency from a percentage to a decimal. efficiency = 70% = 0.7
2) Rearrange the equation for useful energy transferred. useful energy transferred
3) Stick in the numbers you're given. = efficiency × total energy transferred
= 0.7 × 6000 = 4200 J

4) The efficiency of any energy transfer can be increased by reducing unwanted energy transfers.

5) You can increase the efficiency of a device (e.g. a motor) by lubricating it. You can also improve efficiency of a device by making them more streamlined. Both of these methods reduce unwanted energy transfers caused by work done against frictional forces.

Reducing energy losses in buildings

• Unwanted energy losses by heating can be reduced by using thermal insulation. E.g. loft insulation, thick curtains and cavity walls with insulation reduce conduction and convection. Double glazed windows and hot water tank jackets reduce conduction and draught excluders reduce convection.

• The thickness and thermal conductivity of (solid) walls also affects how quickly energy is transferred out of a building. The thicker the walls, the lower the rate of energy transfer. The lower the thermal conductivity of the material the walls are made from, the lower the rate of energy transfer. So thick walls with a low thermal conductivity increase the time taken for a building to cool down.

You can Use Sankey Diagrams to Show Efficiency

You can use a Sankey diagram like the one below. to show all the energy transfers made by a device. From it you can work out the efficiency of the device.

You can also sketch Sankey diagrams — where the width still represents the amount of energy transferred, but the diagram isn't to scale.

Diagram for an electric motor with 80% efficiency:

In this diagram, the width of one square on the grid represents 20 J. The thickness of the arrows represents how much energy is being transferred. The length has nothing to do with it.

The total energy transferred by the motor equals the sum of the energy transferred to useful and wasted stores because energy is always conserved (p.21).

Total energy transferred by motor = 100 J

ENERGY TRANSFER

Useful energy transferred to kinetic energy stores = 80 J

Here, the wasted energy splits off.

Energy wasted to thermal energy stores (dissipated to the surroundings) = 20 J

Don't waste your energy — turn the TV off while you revise...

Unwanted energy transfers can cost you a lot in energy bills — that's why so many people invest in home insulation.

Q1 A motor in a remote-controlled car transfers 300 J of energy to the car's energy stores. 225 J is transferred to the car's kinetic energy stores. The rest is transferred to its thermal energy store. Calculate the efficiency of the motor. Give your answer as a percentage. [3 marks]

Energy Resources

We use <u>A LOT</u> of electricity (just look around you) — the energy to power it all has to come from <u>somewhere</u>.

Energy Resources Can Either be Renewable or Non-Renewable

1) We get <u>some</u> of our energy from <u>non-renewable</u> resources — resources that will <u>run out</u> one day.

2) The main non-renewable energy resources on Earth are the three <u>fossil fuels</u> (<u>coal</u>, <u>oil</u> and <u>gas</u>) and <u>nuclear fuels</u> (<u>uranium</u> and <u>plutonium</u>).

Peat (a biofuel made of decayed plants) is sometimes called a non-renewable resource too, because it can't be quickly replaced.

3) One of the <u>advantages</u> of using these energy resources is that <u>they're reliable</u>. There's enough <u>fossil</u> and <u>nuclear fuels</u> to meet <u>current demand</u>, and they are extracted from the Earth at a <u>fast enough rate</u> that power stations always have fuel in stock. This means non-renewable power stations can respond <u>quickly</u> to <u>changes in demand</u>.

4) One of the <u>disadvantages</u> of fossil fuels is they <u>damage the environment</u> when they're being used:

• Coal, oil and gas release CO_2 into the atmosphere when they're <u>burned</u>. All this CO_2 adds to the <u>greenhouse effect</u>, and contributes to <u>global warming</u> (p.10).

Some environmental problems are unpredictable, e.g. oil spillages affect mammals and birds.

• Burning coal and oil also releases <u>sulfur dioxide</u>, which causes <u>acid rain</u>.

5) One of the main <u>issues</u> with using <u>nuclear fuel</u> is that <u>nuclear waste</u> is <u>dangerous</u> and difficult to <u>dispose of</u>. Take a look at p.75 for more on this.

1) A <u>renewable energy resource</u> is one that will <u>never run out</u>.

2) Most of them do <u>some damage to the environment</u>, but in <u>less nasty</u> ways than non-renewables.

3) They <u>don't</u> provide as much energy as <u>non-renewables</u> and the <u>weather-dependent</u> ones can be <u>unreliable</u>.

4) The main renewable resources are <u>biofuels</u>, <u>wind</u>, the <u>Sun</u>, <u>hydroelectricity</u> and the <u>tides</u>.

Most Power Stations Use Steam to Drive a Turbine

They said turbine, Dave.

The <u>set-up costs</u> for fossil fuel power stations is <u>high</u>, but the <u>running costs</u> are <u>low</u>.
We currently generate some of our electricity using <u>steam-driven turbines</u> like this:

1) As the fossil fuel <u>burns</u> the <u>water</u> is heated.

2) The water <u>boils</u> to form <u>steam</u>, which moves and <u>turns</u> a <u>turbine</u>.

Boiler · steam · Turbine · Generator · Fuel · water · Grid

3) The turbine is connected to an <u>electrical generator</u>, which generates a <u>potential difference</u> across (and so a <u>current</u> through) a wire by spinning a <u>magnet</u> near to the <u>wire</u>, p.41.

4) The current produced by the generator flows through the <u>national grid</u> (p.26).

The only type of power generation that doesn't use a turbine and generator system is solar power.

A similar set-up is used for most <u>other types</u> of electricity generation as well.
In <u>nuclear</u> power stations, energy from <u>nuclear fission</u> (p.75) is used to heat the water. In <u>hydroelectric</u>, <u>tidal</u> and <u>wind</u> power, the turbine is turned <u>directly</u> without needing to heat water to form steam first.

Wind Power — Lots of Little Wind Turbines

1) Each wind turbine has a <u>generator</u> inside it. The rotating <u>blades</u> turn the generator and produce <u>electricity</u>.

2) They have quite a <u>high set-up cost</u> but <u>no fuel costs</u>.

3) There's <u>no pollution</u> (except for a little bit when they're manufactured).

4) But some people think they <u>spoil the view</u> and they can be <u>very noisy</u>, which can be annoying for people living nearby. However, they can be placed <u>offshore</u> which actually generates <u>more</u> energy.

5) They <u>only</u> work when it's <u>windy</u>, so you can't always <u>supply</u> electricity, or respond to <u>high demand</u>.

It all boils down to steam...

Power stations can be made into combined heat and power stations. As they create steam, some of the energy is wasted to surrounding thermal stores. This wasted energy can be used to heat a small number of nearby homes.

Q1   State two renewable energy resources.   [2 marks]

Renewable Energy Resources

Renewable energy resources see (p.23) are generally <u>better for the environment</u>, but they all have <u>drawbacks</u>...

Solar Cells — Expensive but No Environmental Damage

Time to recharge.

1) <u>Solar power</u> is often used in <u>remote places</u> where there's not much choice (e.g. the Australian outback) and to power electric <u>road signs</u> and <u>satellites</u>.
2) <u>Initial costs</u> are <u>high</u> but after that the energy is <u>free</u> and <u>running costs almost nil</u>.
3) There's <u>no pollution</u> when they're being used. (Although they do use quite a lot of energy to make.)
4) Solar cells are mainly used to generate electricity on a relatively <u>small scale</u>, e.g. in <u>homes</u>.
5) Solar power is most suitable for <u>sunny countries</u>, but it can be used in <u>cloudy countries</u> like Britain.
6) And of course, you <u>can't</u> make solar power at <u>night</u> or <u>increase production</u> when there's extra demand.

Biofuels are Made from Plants and Waste

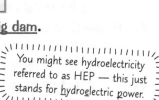

1) <u>Biofuels</u> can be made from many different things, from <u>farm waste</u>, <u>animal droppings</u> and <u>landfill rubbish</u> to <u>specially grown crops</u> (e.g. sugar cane, vegetable oils or trees).
2) They're renewable because we can just <u>grow more</u>.
3) They can be burnt to produce <u>electricity</u> or used to run <u>cars</u> in the same way as <u>fossil fuels</u>.
4) Burning them releases <u>CO_2</u>, but the plants you grow (either to burn or as animal feed) <u>remove CO_2</u> from the atmosphere (so there's <u>no net change</u> in the atmosphere). There's <u>debate</u> about whether there's no net change, as this only works if you keep growing plants at <u>at least the rate</u> that you're burning things.
5) Biofuels are fairly <u>reliable</u> as they can be generated fairly quickly and easily. But it's harder to respond to <u>immediate energy demands</u>, as crops <u>take time</u> to grow (you can <u>stockpile</u> biofuels to combat this).
6) The <u>cost</u> to make <u>biofuels</u> is <u>very high</u> and some worry that growing crops specifically for biofuels could lead to there not being enough <u>space</u> or <u>water</u> to grow enough crops for <u>food</u> for everyone.
7) In some places, large areas of <u>land</u> have been <u>cleared</u> to grow <u>biofuels</u>, resulting in species losing their <u>habitats</u>. The <u>decay</u> and <u>burning</u> of this vegetation also increases <u>CO_2</u> and <u>methane</u> emissions.

Hydroelectricity — Building Dams and Flooding Valleys

1) <u>Producing hydroelectricity</u> usually involves <u>flooding</u> a <u>valley</u> by building a <u>big dam</u>.
2) <u>Water</u> is stored and allowed out <u>through turbines</u>.
3) There is a <u>big impact</u> on the <u>environment</u> due to the flooding of the valley and possible <u>loss of habitat</u> for some species.

> You might see hydroelectricity referred to as HEP — this just stands for <u>hydro</u>electric power.

4) A <u>big advantage</u> is <u>immediate response</u> to increased electricity demand — <u>more</u> water can be let out through the turbines to generate more electricity.
5) <u>Initial costs are often high</u> but there are <u>minimal running costs</u> and it's a <u>reliable</u> energy source.

Tidal Barrages — Using the Sun and Moon's Gravity

1) <u>Tidal barrages</u> are <u>big dams</u> built across <u>river estuaries</u> with <u>turbines</u> in them.
2) As the <u>tide comes in</u> it fills up the estuary. The water is then let out <u>through turbines</u> at a set speed.
3) There is <u>no pollution</u> but they <u>affect boat access</u>, can <u>spoil the view</u> and they <u>alter the habitat</u> for wildlife, e.g. wading birds.
4) Tides are pretty <u>reliable</u> (they always happen twice a day). But the <u>height</u> is <u>variable</u> and tidal barrages don't work when the water <u>level</u> is the <u>same either side</u>.
5) Even though it can only be used in <u>some estuaries</u>, tidal barrages have <u>great potential</u> as an alternative to non-renewable energy sources.

Burning poo... lovely...

Make sure you can describe the energy resources above and the effect on the environment when using them.

Q1   Give one advantage and one disadvantage of generating electricity using solar power. [2 marks]

Trends in Energy Use

Over time, the types of energy resources we use change. There are many reasons for this...

There are Disadvantages and Benefits for Each Energy Resource

1) The risks, drawbacks and benefits need to be weighed up when deciding the best energy resource to use.

2) Which resources are easily available, their cost and how reliably they can produce the energy we need must be considered, along with their environmental impact and any opportunities (e.g. jobs) they create.

3) Of course, everyone has different priorities and opinions. This means that there's often no 'right' answer — so decisions about which resources to use vary depending on the circumstances.

- For example, a government may think hydroelectric power (p.24) is a great, reliable and (relatively) environmentally-friendly way to generate electricity. But, if there's nowhere suitable to build a hydroelectric power station then they can't use it as an energy resource. Similarly, the high cost of building the power station may put them off — even if some people think it's worth the money.

- They may decide nuclear fuel is a good, clean and reliable energy resource to use. Setting up and shutting down a nuclear power station provides many jobs but is difficult and costly. Nuclear power also always carries the small risk of a major catastrophe, which can cause lots of debate — some say the benefits outweigh the risk, whilst others say the potential damage isn't worth it (p.75).

Our Energy Demands are Changing

1) The world demand for energy is continually increasing. This is down to the population increasing, technological advances (e.g. most homes and workplaces now have computers and electronic devices) and our lifestyles.

2) The growing demand raises questions over how we will be able to keep up with it — what the future availability of energy resources will be, and how sustainable the energy resources and the methods we use to generate electricity today are.

> Sustainable energy resources are those that we can keep on using in the long term. Renewable resrouces tend to be sustainable as they won't run out and aren't usually too damaging to the environment.

3) Concerns about sustainability have led people to make changes in their everyday lives and to put pressure on their governments in order to cause national changes. This has led to countries creating targets for using renewable resources, which in turn puts pressure on other countries to do the same.

4) Research is being done to find new energy resources, as well as looking at improving the ways we use our current ones. The research into, and development of, new energy resources provides jobs, as does the building of any new power stations.

5) These factors have all led to an increase in the use of renewable energy resources.

> In the UK we generate some electricity from fossil fuels. They're also used for heating and transport, as they're relatively cheap, efficient and reliable. But we can't keep using them long-term — they're not sustainable. So slowly, the UK is trying to increase its use of more sustainable energy resources.

6) However, it's not something that will change overnight. Research and development takes time and money. Governments need to balance this investment against spending on other areas of national interest.

7) And just like many of our current energy resources, new energy resources may also bring with them new technological and environmental challenges as well as benefits.

> For example, nuclear energy was first used to generate electricity in the 1950s. It took a long time to develop the technology to release energy from nuclear fuels using a nuclear reaction. It took even longer to develop the technology to house and control the nuclear reaction to make it safe enough to generate electricity. Even though nuclear fuel is now a relatively safe and reliable energy resource, it generates radioactive waste which is highly toxic for a very long time. This could greatly damage the environment if not treated and stored correctly — an unforseen challenge when nuclear fuel was first proposed.

Going green is on-trend this season...

So energy demands are increasing, and the energy sources we're using are changing. Just not particularly quickly.

Q1   Suggest two reasons why a government may choose to invest in nuclear power.   [2 marks]

The National Grid

Once <u>electricity</u> has been produced using <u>energy resources</u> (p.23), it has to be transported to <u>consumers</u> (you).

Electricity is Distributed via the National Grid

1) The <u>national grid</u> is a giant web of <u>wires</u> and <u>transformers</u> (p.43) that covers the UK and connects <u>power stations</u> to <u>consumers</u> (anyone who is using electricity).

2) The <u>national grid</u> transfers energy electrically from <u>power stations</u> anywhere on the grid (the <u>supply</u>) to anywhere else on the grid where it's needed (the <u>demand</u>) — e.g. <u>homes</u> and <u>industry</u>.

3) <u>Transformers</u> (p.43) are used to increase the generated electricity to a very <u>high potential difference</u> (p.d.) before it is transmitted through the <u>network</u> of the national grid. <u>Transferring electrical power</u> at a very high p.d. helps to <u>reduce energy losses</u> (see p.44). The p.d. is then <u>reduced</u> by another transformer to a level that is safe for use before being supplied to <u>homes</u> and <u>businesses</u>.

Mains Supply is a.c., Battery Supply is d.c.

Take a look at page 42 for how a.c. and d.c. are generated.

1) There are two types of electric current — <u>alternating current</u> (a.c.) and <u>direct current</u> (d.c.).

2) In <u>a.c. supplies</u> the current is <u>constantly</u> changing direction. <u>Alternating currents</u> are produced by <u>alternating voltages</u> in which the <u>positive</u> and <u>negative</u> ends of the potential difference keep <u>alternating</u>.

3) The <u>UK domestic</u> (<u>mains</u>) <u>supply</u> (the electricity in your home) is an a.c. supply at around <u>230 V</u>.

4) The frequency of the a.c. mains supply is <u>50 cycles per second</u> or <u>50 Hz</u>.

5) By contrast, cells and batteries supply <u>direct current</u> (d.c.).

6) <u>Direct current</u> is a current that is always flowing in the <u>same direction</u>. It's created by a <u>direct voltage</u> (remember — voltage is the <u>same</u> as p.d., p.29). This voltage is usually smoothed out to provide a straight line on a graph of <u>p.d.</u> (voltage) against <u>time</u>.

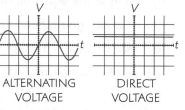

ALTERNATING VOLTAGE   DIRECT VOLTAGE

Most Plugs Contain Three Wires

Mains appliances usually have a <u>3-core cable</u>, which contains <u>three wires</u>.

1) <u>LIVE WIRE</u> — <u>brown</u>. The live wire carries the voltage (potential difference, p.d.). It alternates between a <u>high positive and negative voltage</u> of about <u>230 V</u>.

2) <u>NEUTRAL WIRE</u> — <u>blue</u>. The neutral wire <u>completes</u> the circuit — when the appliance is operating normally, current flows through the <u>live</u> and <u>neutral</u> wires. It is around <u>0 V</u>.

3) <u>EARTH WIRE</u> — <u>green</u> and <u>yellow</u>. The earth wire is for <u>safety</u>. It carries the current away if something goes wrong. It's <u>also</u> at 0 V.

1) The <u>p.d.</u> between the <u>live wire</u> and the <u>neutral wire</u> equals the <u>supply p.d.</u> (<u>230 V</u> for the mains).

2) The <u>p.d.</u> between the <u>live wire</u> and the <u>earth wire</u> is also <u>230 V</u> for a mains-connected appliance.

3) There is <u>no p.d.</u> between the <u>neutral wire</u> and the <u>earth wire</u> — they're both at 0 V.

4) Your <u>body</u> is an example of an earthed conductor, and is also at <u>0 V</u>. This means if you touched the <u>live wire</u>, there'd be a <u>large p.d.</u> across your body and a <u>current</u> would flow through you. This large <u>electric shock</u> could injure or even kill you.

5) Even if a plug socket is <u>off</u> (i.e. the switch is <u>open</u>) there is still a <u>danger</u> you could get an electric shock. A current <u>isn't flowing</u>, but there is still a <u>p.d.</u> in the live part of the socket, so your body could provide a <u>link</u> between the supply and the earth if you made <u>contact</u> with it.

Why are earth wires green and yellow — when mud is brown..?

Make sure you can explain why touching a live wire is dangerous. It's all to do with our old pal, potential difference.

Q1   Explain the difference between alternating current and direct current.   [2 marks]

Q2   State the potential difference of the live, neutral and earth wires in an appliance.   [3 marks]

Revision Questions for Chapter P2

Hope you've still got some energy left to have a go at these revision questions to see what you've learnt.

- Try these questions and tick off each one when you get it right.
- When you've done all the questions for a topic and are completely happy with it, tick off the topic.

Energy Stores, Energy Transfers and Efficiency (p.20-22) ☑

1) Name the eight energy stores.
2) How can energy be transferred between stores?
3) Why is transferring energy by electricity convenient?
4) State the conservation of energy principle.
5) What does 'dissipated energy' mean?
6) True or false? The net change in the total energy of a closed system is always zero.
7) What does the power rating of an electrical appliance describe?
8) Write down the equation that links energy transferred, power and time.
9) What is a kilowatt-hour (kWh)?
10) In which energy store does wasted energy eventually end up?
11) What is the equation for calculating the efficiency of an energy transfer?
12) How can you reduce unwanted energy transfers in a motor?
13) True or false? Thicker walls make a house cool down quicker.
14) What does the thickness of an arrow in a Sankey diagram represent?

Energy Sources and Trends in their Use (p.23-25) ☑

15) Name four renewable energy resources and four non-renewable energy resources.
16) What is the difference between renewable and non-renewable energy resources?
17) Give three disadvantages of using fossil fuels. Suggest a way to reduce their negative impact.
18) Give one advantage and one disadvantage of using nuclear power.
19) Explain how a power station uses fossil fuels to produce electricity.
20) Give two advantages and two disadvantages of solar power and wind power.
21) Describe the benefits and drawbacks of using biofuels.
22) True or false? Tidal barrages are useful for storing energy to be used during times of high demand.
23) Compare the reliability of hydroelectricity and tidal barrages.
24) Describe how the energy usage in the UK has changed over recent years.
25) Suggest one reason why this change has occurred.
26) Explain why the UK plans to use more renewable energy resources in the future.

The National Grid (p.26) ☑

27) What is the national grid?
28) State the frequency and potential difference of the UK mains supply.
29) True or false? The UK mains supply is a direct current.
30) What type of current do batteries supply?
31) What is meant by a direct current?
32) State the colours of the live, neutral and earth wires in a plug.
33) Why is it dangerous to provide a link between the live wire and the ground?

Static Electricity

Static electricity builds up when electrons are transferred between surfaces that rub together.

Build-up of Static is Caused by Transferring Electrons

All matter contains charges — atoms contain positive protons and negative electrons (p.69).
Neutral matter contains an equal number of positive and negative charges,
so their effects cancel each other out (the matter has zero net charge).
But in some situations charge can build up on objects — this is static electricity.

1) When certain insulating materials are rubbed together, negatively charged electrons will be scraped off one and dumped on the other.

2) This will leave the materials electrically charged, with a positive static charge on one and an equal negative static charge on the other.

3) Which way the electrons are transferred depends on the two materials involved.

4) If enough charge builds up, it can suddenly move, causing sparks or shocks (see below).

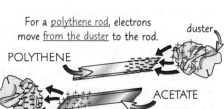

For a polythene rod, electrons move from the duster to the rod.

For an acetate rod, electrons move from the rod to the duster.

Similar Charges Repel, Opposite Charges Attract

1) Electrically charged objects exert a force on one another.

2) Things with opposite electric charges attract each other, things with similar (or like) electric charges repel each other.

3) The force between two charged objects is known as electrostatic attraction (if they attract each other), or electrostatic repulsion (if they repel).

4) It's a non-contact force — the objects don't need to touch.

5) If you hang a charged rod from a string and put an object with the same charge near the rod, they will move away from each other. An oppositely-charged object will attract the rod towards it.

All Electric Charges Have an Electric Field

1) An electric field is the space surrounding any electric charge, where its effects can be felt.

2) So when a charge is placed in the electric field of another charge, a force is exerted on both charges. This force is caused by the electric fields of the two charges interacting.

3) The size of the force between two charges depends on the strength of their electric fields.

4) The strength of a charge's electric field depends on the size of the charge and how far away from the charge you are — the field gets stronger the closer to the charge you are.

5) Sparking can also be explained using electric fields.

6) If the surfaces of two objects have been rubbed together to transfer electrons from one to the other, and then placed near each other, there will be a force between them.

7) If the forces acting on the charged objects due to their electric fields are big enough, then electrons will 'jump' from the negatively charged object to the positively charged object. This is a spark.

Come on, think positive...

Remember — no matter whether it's a positive or negative static charge, electrons always move to create it.

Q1   Explain what is meant by an electric field.   [1 mark]

Circuits — The Basics

It's pretty bad news if the word <u>current</u> makes you think of delicious cakes instead of physics. Learn what it means, as well as some handy <u>symbols</u> to show items like <u>batteries</u> and <u>switches</u> in a circuit.

Current can Only Flow Round a Closed Circuit

1) <u>Electric current</u> is the rate of flow of <u>electrical charge</u>. Electrical charge will <u>only flow</u> if a circuit is closed (a complete loop) and if there's a source of potential difference, e.g. a battery. The unit of current is the <u>ampere</u>, A.

2) In a <u>single</u>, closed <u>loop</u> (like the one on the right) the current has the same value <u>everywhere</u> in the circuit (see p.34).

3) <u>Potential difference</u> (or voltage) is the <u>driving force</u> that <u>pushes</u> the charge round. Its unit is the <u>volt</u>, V.

4) <u>Resistance</u> is anything that <u>resists</u> the <u>flow of charge</u>. <u>All</u> circuit components have a <u>resistance</u>, but you can usually <u>ignore</u> the resistance from <u>wires</u> connecting components as it's so small. Unit: <u>ohm</u>, Ω.

5) Resistance, current and potential difference are all <u>related</u> — if one of them <u>changes</u>, at least one of the others must <u>change too</u> (in fact there's an equation that links them, see the next page).

6) If the <u>potential difference</u> (p.d.) of a circuit is <u>increased</u> whilst the <u>resistance</u> of the circuit <u>stays the same</u>, then the <u>current will increase</u>. If the <u>resistance</u> of a circuit is <u>increased</u> whilst the <u>potential difference stays the same</u>, the <u>current</u> will <u>decrease</u>.

> You can think of an <u>electric circuit</u> as being like a set of <u>pipes</u>. The <u>current</u> is the <u>rate of flow of water</u> around the pipes and the <u>p.d.</u> is the <u>water pump</u> pushing the water around. <u>Resistance</u> is any sort of <u>narrowing</u> of the pipes which the water pressure has to <u>work against</u>. If you turn up the <u>pump</u>, more <u>force</u> is provided and the flow is <u>increased</u>. If you add more <u>narrow sections</u>, the flow <u>decreases</u>.

7) Charges going round a circuit flow in a <u>continuous loop</u>. They are <u>not used up</u>, but transfer energy to components as they do <u>work</u> (p.33).

8) <u>Metal conductors</u> (e.g. components and wires) have <u>lots of charges</u> that are free to move. A <u>battery</u> (or other p.d. source) in a circuit is what <u>causes</u> these charges to flow.

Total Charge Through a Circuit Depends on Current and Time

1) You can find the amount of <u>charge</u> that has flowed through a component in a <u>given time</u> using:

> charge (coloumbs, C) = current (A) × time (s)

2) So <u>more charge</u> passes around a circuit every second when a <u>larger current</u> flows.

Circuit Symbols You Should Know

There's more about a.c. and d.c. on p.26.

cell	battery	open switch	closed switch	filament lamp	fuse	LED	power supply

resistor	variable resistor	ammeter	voltmeter	diode	LDR	thermistor	motor

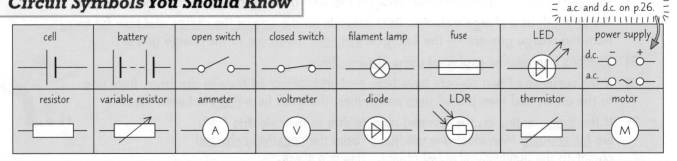

I think it's about time you took charge...

You've no doubt seen some of those circuit symbols before, but take a good look at all of them and practise drawing them. It's no good if you get asked to draw a circuit diagram and you can't tell a resistor from a thermistor.

Q1   A laptop charger passes a current of 8.0 A through a laptop battery. Calculate how long the charger needs to be connected to the battery for 28 800 C of charge to be transferred to the laptop.   [2 marks]

Resistance and $V = I \times R$

Ooh experiments, you've gotta love 'em. Here's a <u>simple experiment</u> for investigating resistance.

There's a Formula Linking Potential Difference and Current

<u>Current</u>, <u>potential difference</u> (p.d.) and <u>resistance</u> are all linked by this simple <u>formula</u>:

> potential difference (V)= current (A) × resistance (Ω)
>
> $V = IR$

You can use this equation for <u>whole circuits</u> or <u>individual components</u>.

You Can Investigate the Factors Affecting Resistance   PRACTICAL

The <u>resistance</u> of a component can depend on a number of factors. One thing you can easily investigate is how the <u>length of a wire</u> affects its resistance. You can do this using the set up shown on the right, which you need to be able to draw the <u>circuit diagram</u> for.

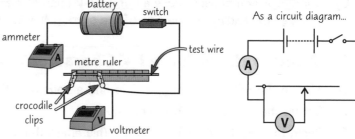

The circuit contains:

- <u>Ammeter</u> — this measures the <u>current</u> (in amps) flowing through the test wire. It can be put <u>anywhere</u> in the <u>main circuit</u> — but it must be placed <u>in series</u> (p.34) with the test wire, <u>never</u> in <u>parallel</u>.
- <u>Voltmeter</u> — this measures the <u>potential difference</u> across the test wire (in volts). It must be placed <u>in parallel</u> (p.35) with the <u>wire</u>, <u>NOT</u> any other bit of the circuit, e.g. the battery.

1) Attach a <u>crocodile clip</u> to the wire level with <u>0 cm</u> on the ruler.
2) Attach the <u>second crocodile clip</u> to the wire, e.g. 10 cm away from the first clip. Write down the <u>length</u> of the wire between the clips.
3) <u>Close the switch</u>, then record the <u>current</u> through the wire and the <u>p.d.</u> across it.
4) <u>Open the switch</u>, then move the second crocodile clip, e.g. another 10 cm, along the wire. Close the switch again, then record the <u>new length</u>, <u>current</u> and <u>p.d.</u>.
5) <u>Repeat</u> this for a number of <u>different</u> lengths of wire between the crocodile clips.
6) Use your measurements of current and p.d. to <u>calculate</u> the resistance for each length of wire, using $R = V \div I$ (from $V = IR$).
7) Plot a <u>graph</u> of <u>resistance</u> against <u>wire length</u> and draw a <u>line of best fit</u> (p.95).
8) You should find that the <u>longer the wire</u>, the <u>greater the resistance</u>.
9) Your graph should be a <u>straight line</u> through the <u>origin</u> — showing that resistance is <u>directly proportional</u> to length.
10) If your graph <u>doesn't</u> go through the origin, it could be because the <u>first clip</u> wasn't attached exactly at 0 cm, so all of your length readings are a <u>bit out</u>. This is a <u>systematic error</u> (p.94).

> A thin wire will give you the best results. Make sure it's as straight as possible so your length measurements are accurate.

> The wire may heat up during the experiment, which will affect its resistance. Leave the switch open for a bit between readings to let the circuit cool down.

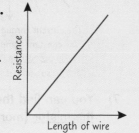

From your results you can also find the <u>resistance per unit length</u> of a wire. This is equal to the <u>gradient</u> of the graph shown above. You can use this to <u>estimate the resistance</u> of <u>any length</u> of the same wire (resistance = length × resistance per unit length).

Measure gymnastics — use a vaultmeter...

You could also investigate the effect of diameter or material on the resistance of a wire. What fun.

Q1   An appliance is connected to a 230 V source.
Calculate the resistance of the appliance if a current of 5.0 A is flowing through it.   [2 marks]

Resistance and *I-V* Characteristics

And we're not done with the experiments just yet. Time to draw some sweet *I-V characteristics*...

Components are Either Linear or Non-Linear

1) The term '*I-V characteristic*' refers to a graph which shows how the current (*I*) flowing through a component changes as the potential difference (*V*) across it is increased.

2) *I-V* characteristics show how the resistance of the component changes with current. Since *V = IR*, you can calculate the resistance at any point on an *I-V* characteristic by calculating *R = V/I*.

3) The resistance of some conductors remains constant (e.g. a fixed resistor at a fixed temperature), but the resistance of other components can vary (e.g. a heating element or a filament lamp).

4) Linear components have a constant resistance. Their *I-V* characteristic is a straight line.

5) Non-linear components have a curved *I-V* characteristic. Their resistance changes depending on the size of the current flowing through them.

You Need to Know Some I-V Characteristics

You can do the following experiment to find a component's *I-V characteristic*:

1) Set up the test circuit shown on the right.

2) Begin to vary the variable resistor. This alters the current flowing through the circuit and the potential difference across the component.

3) Take several pairs of readings from the ammeter and voltmeter to see how the potential difference across the component varies as the current changes. Repeat each reading twice more to get an average p.d. at each current.

4) Swap over the wires connected to the cell, so the direction of the current is reversed.

5) Repeat steps 2 and 3. Plot a graph of current against voltage for the component.

6) The *I-V* characteristics you get for resistors, a filament lamp and a diode should look like this:

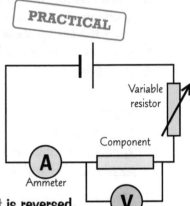

PRACTICAL

Variable resistor

Component

A — Ammeter

V — Voltmeter

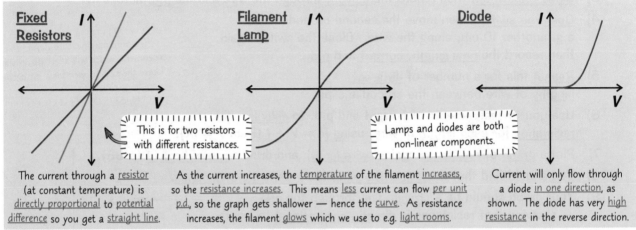

Fixed Resistors

This is for two resistors with different resistances.

The current through a resistor (at constant temperature) is directly proportional to potential difference so you get a straight line.

Filament Lamp

Lamps and diodes are both non-linear components.

As the current increases, the temperature of the filament increases, so the resistance increases. This means less current can flow per unit p.d., so the graph gets shallower — hence the curve. As resistance increases, the filament glows which we use to e.g. light rooms.

Diode

Current will only flow through a diode in one direction, as shown. The diode has very high resistance in the reverse direction.

7) You can find the *I-V* characteristics for an LDR and a thermistor (more about these on the next page).

8) In constant conditions (i.e. a constant room temperature or constant light levels) their *I-V* characteristics look like this:

The resistance of a thermistor is dependent on its temperature (see p.32) — as the current increases, the thermistor warms up, so the resistance decreases, which is why it has a curved *I-V* characteristic.

Thermistor

LDR

In the end you'll have to learn this — resistance is futile...

Draw out those graphs and make sure you can tell whether they're showing a linear or non-linear component.

Q1   Draw the *I-V* characteristic for: a) an LDR in constant conditions   b) a filament lamp.   [2 marks]

Circuit Devices

Now it's time to see what <u>diodes</u>, <u>LDRs</u> and <u>thermistors</u> can do, and why they're so useful.

Current Only Flows in One Direction through a Diode

1) A diode is a special device made from <u>semiconductor</u> material such as <u>silicon</u>.

2) It lets current flow freely through it in <u>one direction</u>, but <u>not</u> in the other (i.e. there's a very high resistance in the <u>reverse</u> direction). This is shown by the <u>I-V characteristic</u> (see previous page).

3) This turns out to be really useful in various <u>electronic circuits</u>, e.g. in <u>radio receivers</u>. Diodes can also be used to get <u>direct current</u> from an <u>alternating</u> supply (see p.26).

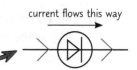

current flows this way

You can Use a d.c. Circuit to Test LDRs and Thermistors

Direct current (d.c.) means the current always flows in the same direction.

1) The <u>resistance</u> of some resistors is <u>dependent</u> on the <u>environment</u>.

2) If you set up the <u>circuit</u> shown on the right, you can <u>change the environment</u> the resistor is in to see the <u>effect</u> on its <u>resistance</u>.

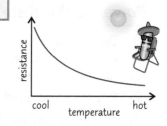

resistor being tested

LDR Stands for Light-Dependent Resistor

1) An LDR is a resistor that's <u>dependent</u> on the <u>intensity</u> of <u>light</u>. At a <u>constant light level</u>, its <u>resistance</u> is <u>constant</u> (p.31).

2) In <u>darkness</u>, the resistance is <u>highest</u>. As light levels <u>increase</u> the resistance <u>falls</u> so (for a given p.d.) the <u>current</u> through the LDR <u>increases</u>.

3) You can <u>test</u> this by gradually <u>covering up</u> the surface of the LDR with a piece of thick paper.

4) They have lots of applications including <u>automatic night lights</u>, <u>outdoor lighting</u> and <u>burglar detectors</u>.

A Thermistor is a Type of Temperature-Dependent Resistor

1) In <u>hot</u> conditions, the resistance of a thermistor <u>drops</u>. In <u>cool</u> conditions, the resistance goes <u>up</u>.

You can test this by placing the thermistor into a <u>beaker of hot water</u> and taking measurements as the water cools down and the <u>temperature</u> of the thermistor <u>decreases</u>.

2) They're used as <u>temperature detectors</u>, in e.g. <u>thermostats</u>, <u>irons</u> and <u>car engines</u>.

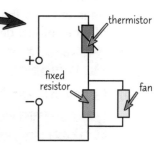

You Can Use LDRs and Thermistors in Sensing Circuits

1) <u>Sensing circuits</u> can be used to <u>turn on</u> or <u>increase the power</u> to components depending on the <u>conditions</u> that they are in.

2) The circuit on the right is a <u>sensing circuit</u> in a room.

3) As the room gets hotter, the resistance of the thermistor <u>decreases</u> and it takes a <u>smaller share</u> of the p.d. from the power supply (take a look at page 34 as to why this happens). So the p.d. across the fixed resistor and the fan <u>rises</u>, making the fan go faster.

4) You can use a <u>similar</u> setup for a sensing circuit containing an LDR. You just have to connect the <u>component</u> (most likely a <u>bulb</u>) <u>across</u> the LDR.

thermistor

fixed resistor

fan

Permistors — resistance decreases with curliness of hair...

Bonus fact — circuits like the ones above are called potential dividers (because they divide up p.d.).

Q1   Sketch a circuit that could be used to show how an LDR's resistance changes with light intensity. [2 marks]

Energy and Power in Circuits

All electrical devices <u>transfer energy</u> — their <u>power</u> is how <u>quickly</u> they do it.

Potential Difference is the Work Done Per Unit Charge

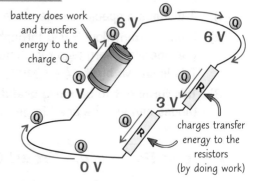

battery does work and transfers energy to the charge Q

charges transfer energy to the resistors (by doing work)

1) An electrical <u>current transfers energy</u> from a <u>power supply</u>, e.g. cells, batteries, generators (p.42) etc.

2) A <u>power supply</u> does <u>work</u> on a <u>charge</u> and so transfers <u>energy</u> to it.

3) <u>Charges transfer energy</u> to a <u>component</u> as they pass through it, by doing <u>work against</u> the <u>resistance</u> of the component.

> For example, in a handheld fan, energy is transferred <u>electrically</u> from the <u>battery's chemical energy store</u> to the <u>kinetic energy store</u> of the fan's <u>motor</u> — this is because a <u>current flows</u> and <u>does work</u> against the <u>resistance</u> of the <u>motor</u>.

4) The <u>potential difference</u> between two points is equal to the <u>work done per unit charge</u> flowing between those two points. A power supply with a <u>bigger p.d.</u> will do <u>more work</u> on each charge, so it will transfer <u>more energy</u> to the circuit for every <u>coulomb</u> (unit) of charge which flows round it.

5) There's a simple <u>formula</u> which relates the <u>potential difference</u> (V) between <u>two points</u>, the <u>work done</u> (J) either <u>on</u> or <u>by</u> a charge passing between the points and the total <u>charge</u> (C) that passes:

> **potential difference = work done (energy transferred) ÷ charge**

These two equations are just the same equation rearranged.

6) The <u>energy transferred</u> to a <u>component</u> in an <u>electric circuit</u> is dependent on the <u>total amount of charge</u> that passes through the component and the <u>potential difference</u> across the component. It can be calculated using the formula:

> **energy transferred (work done) = charge × potential difference.**

Power is the Rate of Energy Transfer

1) Devices have <u>power ratings</u> (see p.21) which tell you the <u>rate</u> that energy is transferred <u>to them</u> from a <u>power supply</u>. Some of this energy will be transferred to the <u>surroundings</u> (see p.22).

The power rating of a device is actually the maximum power at which the device can operate, but you can usually assume that devices are operating at their maximum powers.

2) Power is measured in <u>watts</u>, <u>W</u> — <u>1 W = 1 J/s</u> (see p.67).

3) You can calculate the <u>power transfer</u> in a circuit device from the <u>amount of energy transferred</u> to the <u>device</u> in the circuit in a given amount of <u>time</u> using the formula:

> **power (W) = energy (J) ÷ time (s)** $P = E \div t$

4) The <u>higher</u> the <u>potential difference</u> across a component is, the <u>more energy</u> each charge passing through will have and the <u>faster</u> they will move (i.e. a higher current). This means there will be <u>more energy</u> transferred to the component in a <u>given time</u>, so its <u>power</u> will be <u>higher</u>. You can calculate the <u>power</u> of an electrical device using the potential difference <u>across the device</u> and the current <u>through it</u>:

> **power (W) = potential difference (V) × current (A)** $P = VI$

5) <u>Or</u> you can use the current through the device and its <u>resistance</u>:

> **power (W) = current² (A²) × resistance (Ω)** $P = I^2R$

This equation has come from substituting V = IR (from p.30) into P = VI.

You have the power — now use your potential...

There are a lot of equations to get your head around — practise using them until you can remember them all.

Q1   A 1.5×10^3 W hairdryer is turned on for 11 minutes. Calculate the energy transferred.   [3 marks]

Series and Parallel Circuits

Ooh series and parallel circuits — my favourite. And soon to be yours too. Maybe.

Series and Parallel Circuits are Connected Differently

1) In series circuits, the different components are connected in a line, end to end, between the +ve and –ve terminals of the power supply.

2) Connecting several cells in series, all the same way (+ to –) gives a bigger total p.d. — because each charge in the circuit passes through each cell and gets a 'push' from each one. So two 1.5 V cells in series would supply 3 V in total.

3) In parallel circuits (p.35) each branch is separately connected to the +ve and –ve terminals of the supply.

4) Parallel circuits are usually the most sensible way to connect things, for example in cars and in household electrics, where you have to be able to switch everything on and off separately.

5) Connecting cells in parallel doesn't increase the total p.d. as each charge will only get a 'push' from one of the cells. So two 1.5 V cells in parallel would supply 1.5 V in total.

Series Circuits — Everything in a Line

Potential Difference is Shared

1) In series circuits, the total potential difference (p.d.) of the supply is shared between the various components. So the p.d.s across the components in a series circuit always add up to equal the p.d. across the power supply:

$$V = V_1 + V_2$$

2) This is because the work done by the battery on each unit of charge equals the total work done on the components by each unit of charge (p.33).

3) Work done and energy transferred are the same thing (see p.20), so the total energy transferred to the charges in the circuit by the power supply equals the total energy transferred from the charges to the components (p.33).

Remember, always connect ammeters in series and voltmeters in parallel.

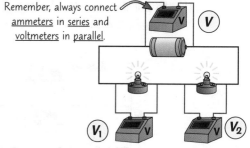

Current is the Same Everywhere

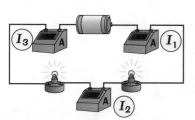

1) In a series circuit, each charge has to flow through all of the components to get round the circuit.

2) So the same current flows through all parts of the circuit:

$$I_1 = I_2 = I_3$$

3) The size of the current is determined by the total p.d. of the power supply and the net resistance of the circuit, i.e. $I = V/R$ (p.30).

Resistance Adds Up

1) The resistance of two (or more) resistors in series is bigger than the resistance of just one of the resistors on its own. That's because the battery has to push each charge through all of them.

2) So the net resistance (R) of a series circuit is just the sum of the individual resistances:

$$R = R_1 + R_2 + R_3$$

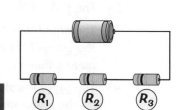

3) You might also see the net resistance called the equivalent resistance or the effective resistance.

I like series circuits so much I bought the box set...

If one of the bulbs in the diagrams above blew, it'd break the circuit, so they'd both go out. Sad times.

Q1   Calculate the net resistance of a series circuit containing three 2 Ω resistors.   [1 mark]

More on Series and Parallel Circuits

Move over series circuits, it's time for <u>parallel circuits</u> to have their say.

Parallel Circuits — Independence and Isolation

Potential Difference is the Same Across All Branches

1) In parallel circuits <u>all</u> branches have the <u>power supply p.d.</u> across them, so the p.d. is the <u>same</u> across all branches:

$$V_1 = V_2 = V_3$$

2) The <u>work done</u> (p.33) <u>per unit charge</u> in a branch is the <u>same for all branches</u> and is equal to the work done per unit charge <u>by the battery</u>.

3) This is because <u>each charge</u> can only pass down <u>one branch</u> of the circuit, so it must <u>transfer all the energy</u> supplied to it by the <u>source p.d.</u> to whatever's on that branch (see page 33).

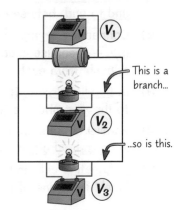

This is a branch...

...so is this.

Current is Shared Between Branches

1) In parallel circuits the <u>total current</u> flowing round the circuit equals the <u>total</u> of all the currents through the <u>separate branches</u>:

$$I = I_1 + I_2$$

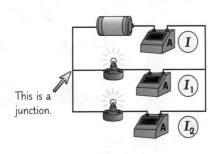

This is a junction.

2) In a parallel circuit, there are <u>junctions</u> where the current either <u>splits</u> or <u>rejoins</u>. The total current going <u>into</u> a junction has to equal the total current <u>leaving</u> it.

3) You can find the current in a branch using $\underline{I = V/R}$ (p.30), where *V* is the <u>p.d. across the branch</u> and *R* is the <u>net resistance</u> of the <u>branch</u>. All branches have the <u>same p.d.</u> as the battery across them — so the branch with the <u>lowest net resistance</u> will have the <u>largest current</u> flowing through it.

Resistance is Tricky

You <u>don't</u> need to be able to calculate the <u>net resistance</u> (see p.34) of a parallel circuit, just know that it <u>decreases</u> as you <u>add</u> resistors in parallel and why.

1) In the diagram opposite, when R_2 is added in <u>parallel</u> to R_1, the <u>charge flowing</u> round the circuit has <u>more than one</u> branch to take. This means <u>more</u> charge flows round the circuit in a <u>certain time</u> — i.e. there is a <u>higher total current</u>.

2) The p.d. of the circuit is the <u>same everywhere</u> (see above).

3) The equation $\underline{R = V \div I}$ (see page 30) shows that <u>increasing the current</u> through the circuit and keeping the <u>p.d. fixed</u> means that the <u>net resistance of the circuit</u> must <u>decrease</u>.

4) The <u>more</u> resistors added in parallel, the <u>higher</u> the current, so the <u>lower</u> the net resistance of the circuit.

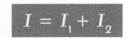

net $R < R_1$ and net $R < R_2$

The net resistance of the circuit will be lower than the resistors by themselves or having them connected in series.

After this page, your circuits knowledge will be unparalleled...

Remember, in parallel circuits, each branch has the same p.d., but the total current is shared between branches.

Q1   If 3 identical bulbs are connected in parallel to a 3.5 V battery, state the p.d. across each bulb.   [1 mark]

Investigating Series and Parallel Circuits

If you're not a fan of series and parallel circuits yet, this page is sure to <u>tickle your fancy</u>. **Maybe.**

Changing One Resistor Affects the Net Resistance of the Circuit

1) The <u>net resistance</u> of a circuit containing two or more components depends on the <u>resistance</u> of the components.

2) The resistance of some components <u>can change</u> (e.g. if it's a variable resistor, light-dependent resistor or thermistor). The <u>effect</u> this will have on the net resistance of the circuit depends on whether you're using a <u>series</u> or <u>parallel circuit</u>.

3) <u>Changing the resistance</u> of one component can also affect the <u>potential difference</u> and <u>current</u> within a circuit.

   <u>In series circuit</u>

   • For two components in series, the <u>bigger</u> the resistance of one of the components, the bigger its <u>share</u> of the <u>total p.d.</u> across it. This is because more <u>energy is transferred</u> from the charge when moving through a <u>large</u> resistance (see p.33).

   • So if the resistance of <u>one</u> component <u>changes</u>, the <u>potential difference</u> across all the components will <u>change</u>. The <u>net resistance</u> will also have changed, so the <u>current</u> through the components will <u>change too</u>.

   <u>In a parallel circuit</u>

   • For two components in a parallel circuit, if the resistance of <u>one</u> component <u>changes</u> then the current through <u>that branch</u> will <u>change</u>, but the current through the <u>other branches</u> and the <u>p.d.</u> across them will remain the <u>same</u>.

> Remember — the potential difference of the supply is shared out between the components in a series circuit (p.34) and is equal across parallel components in a parallel circuit.

You Can Investigate Series and Parallel Circuits using Bulbs

PRACTICAL

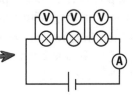

1) Set up a <u>circuit</u> consisting of a <u>power supply</u> and a <u>bulb</u>. Use a <u>voltmeter</u> to measure the <u>p.d.</u> across the bulb, and an <u>ammeter</u> to measure the <u>current</u> in the circuit.

2) One at a time, add <u>identical bulbs</u> in <u>series</u>. Each time, measure the current through the circuit and the p.d. across each bulb. The bulbs should look <u>dimmer</u> each time.

3) You'll find that each time you <u>add a bulb</u>, the <u>p.d.</u> across each bulb <u>falls</u> — this is because the p.d.s across the bulbs in the circuit need to <u>add up</u> to the <u>source p.d.</u>.

4) The <u>current</u> also <u>falls</u> each time you add a bulb, because you're increasing the <u>resistance</u> of the circuit.

5) <u>Less current</u> and <u>less p.d.</u> means the bulbs get <u>dimmer</u> (the power of each bulb is decreasing — p.33).

6) Repeat the experiment, this time adding each bulb in <u>parallel</u> on a <u>new branch</u>. You'll need to measure the <u>current</u> on <u>each branch</u> each time you add a bulb.

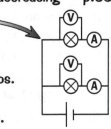

7) You should find that the bulbs <u>don't get dimmer</u> as you add more to the circuit.

8) The p.d. across <u>each bulb</u> is <u>equal</u> to the <u>source p.d.</u>, no matter the number of bulbs.

9) The <u>current</u> on each branch is <u>the same</u>, and <u>doesn't change</u> when you add more bulbs, because the resistance of and p.d. across each branch stays the same.

I can't resist a good practical...

Make sure you can explain the effects of changing a component's resistance, be it in a series or parallel circuit. This should include how it affects the net resistance of the circuit, the p.d. and the current.

Q1   Draw a diagram of a single circuit that could be used to investigate the effect of adding identical bulbs in parallel.

             [2 marks]

Permanent and Induced Magnets

I think magnetism is an <u>attractive</u> subject, but don't get <u>repelled</u> by the exams — <u>revise</u>.

Magnets Produce Magnetic Fields

1) All magnets have <u>two poles</u> — <u>north</u> (or N-pole) and <u>south</u> (or S-pole).

2) All magnets produce a <u>magnetic field</u> — a region where <u>other magnets</u> or <u>magnetic materials</u> (e.g. iron, steel, nickel and cobalt) experience a <u>force</u>. This is the <u>magnetic effect</u> — a <u>non-contact force</u> similar to the force on charges in an electric field, like you saw on page 28.

3) You can show a magnetic field by drawing <u>magnetic field lines</u>.

4) The lines always go from <u>north to south</u> and they show <u>which way</u> a force would act on a <u>north pole</u> of a small magnet if it was put at that point in the field.

5) The <u>closer together</u> the lines are, the <u>stronger</u> the magnetic field. The <u>further away</u> from a magnet you get, the <u>weaker</u> the field is.

6) The magnetic field is <u>strongest</u> at the <u>poles</u> of a magnet. This means that the <u>magnetic forces</u> are also <u>strongest</u> at the poles.

7) The force between a <u>magnet</u> and a <u>magnetic material</u> is <u>always attractive</u>, no matter the pole.

8) Between <u>two magnets</u> the force can be <u>attractive</u> or <u>repulsive</u>. Two poles that are the same (these are called <u>like poles</u>) will <u>repel</u> each other. Two <u>unlike</u> poles will <u>attract</u> each other.

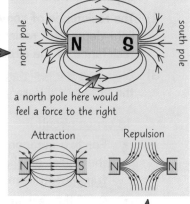

a north pole here would feel a force to the right

Attraction | Repulsion

Compasses Show the Directions of Magnetic Fields

1) Inside a compass is a tiny <u>bar magnet</u>. The <u>north</u> pole of this magnet is attracted to the south pole of any other magnet it is near. So the compass <u>points</u> in the direction of the magnetic field it is in.

2) You can move a compass around a magnet and <u>trace</u> its position on some paper to build up a picture of what the magnetic field <u>looks like</u>.

3) When they're not near a magnet, compasses always point <u>north</u>. This is because the <u>Earth</u> generates its own <u>magnetic field</u> (which looks a lot like the field of a <u>big bar magnet</u>). This is evidence that the <u>inside</u> (<u>core</u>) of the Earth must be <u>magnetic</u>.

The north pole of the magnet in the compass points along the field line towards the south pole of the bar magnet.

The <u>N-pole</u> of the compass is <u>attracted</u> towards the <u>Magnetic North Pole</u> — the <u>magnetic pole</u> near to the <u>geographic</u> North Pole. The Magnetic North Pole has a confusing name — it is actually a <u>magnetic south pole</u> but is called 'north' because it's close to <u>geographic north</u>. There's also a <u>magnetic north pole</u> near the <u>geographic South Pole</u>.

Magnets Can be Permanent or Induced

1) There are <u>two types</u> of magnet — <u>permanent</u> magnets and <u>induced</u> magnets.

2) <u>Permanent</u> magnets produce their <u>own</u> magnetic field.

3) <u>Induced</u> magnets are <u>magnetic materials</u> that <u>turn into</u> a magnet when they're put into a <u>magnetic field</u>.

4) When you <u>take away</u> the magnetic field, induced magnets quickly return to normal and <u>stop producing</u> a magnetic field (they <u>lose</u> their <u>magnetisation</u>).

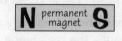

The magnetic material becomes magnetised when it is brought near the bar magnet. It has its own poles and magnetic field:

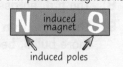

induced poles

Magnets are like farmers — surrounded by fields...

Magnetism can get quite tough quite quickly. Learn these basics — you'll need them for the rest of the chapter.

Q1 State where the magnetic field produced by a bar magnet is strongest. [1 mark]

Q2 Give two differences between permanent and induced magnets. [2 marks]

Electromagnetism

On this page you'll see that a <u>magnetic field</u> is also found around a <u>wire</u> that has a <u>current</u> passing through it.

A Moving Charge Creates a Magnetic Effect

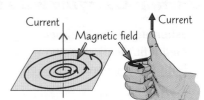

The Right-Hand Thumb Rule
Using your right hand, point your thumb in the direction of current and curl your fingers. The direction of your fingers is the direction of the field.

1) When a <u>current flows</u> through a <u>wire</u>, a <u>magnetic field</u> is created <u>around</u> the wire.

2) The field is made up of <u>concentric circles</u> perpendicular to the wire, with the wire in the centre.

3) You can see this by placing a <u>compass</u> near a <u>wire</u> that is carrying a <u>current</u>. As you move the compass, its needle will <u>trace</u> the direction of the magnetic field.

4) Changing the <u>direction</u> of the <u>current</u> changes the direction of the <u>magnetic field</u> — use the <u>right-hand thumb rule</u> to work out which way it goes.

5) The <u>strength</u> of the magnetic field produced <u>changes</u> with the <u>current</u> and the <u>distance</u> from the wire. The <u>larger</u> the current through the wire, or the <u>closer</u> to the wire you are, the <u>stronger</u> the field is.

A Solenoid is a Coil of Wire

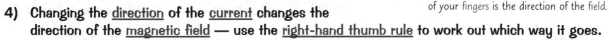

1) You can <u>increase</u> the <u>strength</u> of the magnetic field that a current-carrying wire produces by <u>wrapping</u> the wire into a <u>coil</u> called a <u>solenoid</u>.

2) The magnetic field strength <u>increases</u> because the fields around each <u>turn</u> (or loop) of wire <u>line up</u> with each other (and so 'add together').

3) The magnetic field <u>inside</u> a solenoid is <u>strong</u> and <u>uniform</u> (it has the <u>same strength</u> and <u>direction</u> at every point in that region).

4) <u>Outside</u> the coil, the magnetic field is just like the one round a <u>bar magnet</u>.

5) The <u>magnetic effect</u> (field strength) of a solenoid can be <u>increased</u> by: increasing the <u>current</u> through the coil, increasing the <u>number of turns</u> but keeping the <u>length</u> the <u>same</u>, and <u>decreasing</u> the <u>cross-sectional area</u> of the solenoid.

6) You can also add a block of <u>iron</u> in the <u>centre</u> of the coil. This <u>iron core</u> becomes an <u>induced</u> magnet whenever current is flowing, so the <u>magnetic effect</u> of the solenoid is <u>increased</u>.

7) A <u>current-carrying solenoid with an iron core</u> is an ELECTROMAGNET — a magnet with a magnetic field that can be turned <u>on</u> and <u>off</u> by turning the <u>current</u> on and off.

Electromagnets Have Many Uses

1) Magnets you can switch on and off are really <u>useful</u>. They're usually used because they're so <u>quick</u> to turn on and off or because they can create a <u>varying force</u> (like in <u>loudspeakers</u>, p.43).

2) When electromagnets were discovered in the 19th century, it led to the creation of <u>lots of devices</u>, including the <u>electromagnetic relay</u>. This led to <u>huge advances</u> in <u>communications</u> as they allowed coded messages to be sent <u>long distances</u> as electrical signals before being translated back into words (<u>telegraphs</u>). This is how relays work:

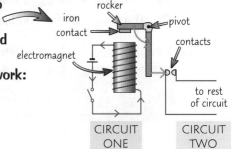

- When the <u>switch</u> in <u>circuit one</u> is <u>closed</u>, it turns on the <u>electromagnet</u>, which <u>attracts</u> the <u>iron contact</u> on the rocker.

- The <u>rocker pivots</u> and <u>pushes together</u> the contacts, <u>completing</u> circuit two and generating an electrical signal.

Strong, in uniform and a magnetic personality — I'm a catch...

Electromagnets are used in loads of everyday things from cranes to MRI machines, so learn how they work.

Q1   Draw the magnetic field for a current-carrying wire, with the current coming out of the page.   [2 marks]

The Motor Effect

Time to step into the weird and wonderful world of the motor effect — you can do this, I believe in you.

A Current-Carrying Wire in a Magnetic Field Experiences a Force

1) When a current-carrying conductor (e.g. a wire) is put near a permanent magnet (or in an external magnetic field), the two magnetic fields interact with each other. This causes a force to be exerted on both the wire and the magnet. This is called the motor effect — this usually causes the wire to move.

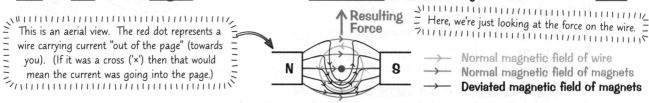

This is an aerial view. The red dot represents a wire carrying current "out of the page" (towards you). (If it was a cross ('×') then that would mean the current was going into the page.)

↑ Resulting Force

Here, we're just looking at the force on the wire.

→ Normal magnetic field of wire
→ Normal magnetic field of magnets
→ **Deviated magnetic field of magnets**

2) To experience the full force, the wire has to be at 90° (right angles) to the magnetic field. If the wire runs along the magnetic field, it won't experience any force. At angles in between, it'll feel some force.

3) The force always acts at right angles to the magnetic field of the magnets and the direction of the current in the wire.

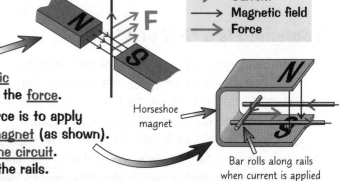

→ Current
→ Magnetic field
→ Force

4) So changing the direction of either the magnetic field or the current will change the direction of the force.

5) A good way of showing the direction of the force is to apply a current to a set of rails inside a horseshoe magnet (as shown). A bar is placed on the rails, which completes the circuit. This generates a force that rolls the bar along the rails.

Horseshoe magnet

Bar rolls along rails when current is applied

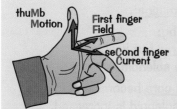

thuMb Motion
First finger Field
seCond finger Current

1) Fleming's left-hand rule is used to find the direction of the force on a current-carrying conductor that is at right-angles to a magnetic field.

2) Using your left hand, point your First finger in the direction of the magnetic Field and your seCond finger in the direction of the Current.

3) Your thuMb will then point in the direction of the force (Motion).

You can Calculate the Force Acting on a Current-Carrying Conductor

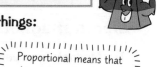

The force acting on a conductor at 90° to a magnetic field is proportional to three things:

1) The magnetic field strength — this is also called the magnetic flux density, i.e. how many magnetic field (flux) lines there are per unit area.

2) The size of the current through the conductor.

3) The length of the conductor that's in the magnetic field.

Proportional means that increasing any of these three things will increase the force on the conductor.

You can calculate the force when the current is at 90° to the magnetic field it's in using:

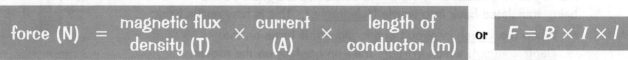

force (N) = magnetic flux density (T) × current (A) × length of conductor (m)   or $F = B \times I \times l$

A current-carrying conductor — a ticket inspector eating sultanas...

Learn the left-hand rule and use it — don't be scared of looking like a muppet in the exam.

Q1 State what the thumb, first finger and second finger each represent in Fleming's left-hand rule.   [3 marks]

Q2 A 35 cm long piece of wire is at 90° to an external magnetic field. The wire experiences a force of 9.8 N when a current of 5.0 A is flowing through it. Calculate the magnetic flux density of the field.   [3 marks]

Electric Motors

This lot might look a bit tricky, but really it's just applying the stuff you learnt on the previous page.

A Simple Electric Motor uses Magnets and a Current-Carrying Coil

1) In a d.c. motor, a rectangular current-carrying coil sits in a uniform magnetic field between two poles.

2) Because the current is flowing in different directions on each side of the coil, and each side of the coil is perpendicular to the magnetic field, each side will experience forces in opposite directions.

3) Because the coil is on a spindle, and the forces act in opposite directions on each side, it rotates.

4) The split-ring commutator is a clever way of swapping the contacts every half turn to keep the motor rotating in the same direction.

5) The direction of the motor can be reversed by either swapping the polarity of the d.c. supply (reversing the current) or swapping the magnetic poles over (reversing the field).

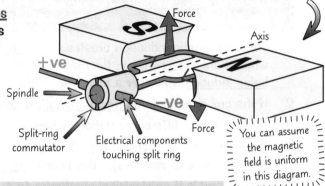

You can assume the magnetic field is uniform in this diagram.

To speed up the motor, increase the current, add more turns to the coil or increase the magnetic field strength.

You can use Fleming's left-hand rule (see the previous page) to figure out whether a coil like the one below is rotating clockwise or anticlockwise:

1) Draw in arrows to show the direction of the magnetic field lines and the current.

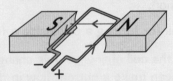

(Remember, current goes from positive to negative.)

2) Use Fleming's LHR on one side of the coil (here we've used the right-hand side).

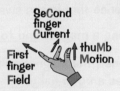

SeCond finger Current
First finger Field
thuMb Motion

3) Draw in the direction of the force (motion) for this side of the coil.

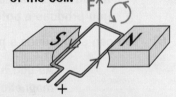

So — the coil is turning anticlockwise.

6) As a motor starts running, the current through it decreases from its initial value. As the current flows, it dissipates some energy which heats up the coil (and so increases the resistance, p.31).

7) Another reason is that the motor also behaves like a generator — as it moves, it creates a current in the opposite direction to the current originally flowing through it. See page 42 for more about this.

Electric Motors have Lots of Uses

Electric motors are found in many everyday items, both in industry and in your home. They've had a big impact on our lives — they make many processes easier (and quicker) to complete and, in some cases, have led to almost fully-automatic production of items.

1) Factories — many machines, from ones that make paper to ones that produce chewing gum, contain large electric motors to allow them to move. Motors are also used to drive conveyor belts which transport goods between machines.

2) Electric vehicles — the driving force for these cars is provided by electricity instead of petrol or diesel.

3) Household appliances — almost all household appliances that contain moving parts contain an electric motor — hair dryers, vacuum cleaners, blenders, fans, electric toothbrushes... The list goes on.

What makes the world go round? Not an electric motor. Or love...

Practise using Fleming's LHR rule on coils, so you're super confident in working out which way they will turn.

Q1 Give one everyday use of an electric motor. [1 mark]

Q2 State two properties that could be changed to decrease the speed of an electric motor. [2 marks]

Electromagnetic Induction

Electromagnetic induction — it's tough, but read this page carefully and you'll see it's not as bad as it sounds.

Cutting Field Lines Induces a Potential Difference

> **Electromagnetic Induction:** The induction of a potential difference (and current if there's a complete circuit) across a conductor which is experiencing a change in magnetic field.

Induces is a fancy word for creates.

1) Electromagnetic induction creates a potential difference (p.d.) across the ends of a conductor when there is a change in the magnetic field around the conductor. You can think of a p.d. being induced whenever a magnetic field line is 'cut' or crossed by the conductor.

2) If the coil is part of a complete circuit, it also induces a current.

3) There are two different situations where you get electromagnetic induction.

4) The first is if the magnetic field through an electrical conductor changes (changes size or reverses). This is how transformers work — p.43.

5) The second is if an electrical conductor (e.g. a coil of wire) and a magnetic field move relative to each other. You can do this by moving a magnet in a conductor OR moving a conductor in a magnetic field.

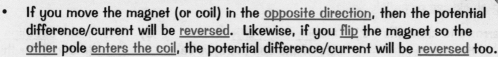

Wire 'cuts' field lines.

- If you move a magnet into a coil, it induces a potential difference across the ends of the coil.

- If you move the magnet (or coil) in the opposite direction, then the potential difference/current will be reversed. Likewise, if you flip the magnet so the other pole enters the coil, the potential difference/current will be reversed too.

- If you keep the magnet (or the coil) moving backwards and forwards, you produce a potential difference that keeps swapping direction.

6) You can also induce a p.d. by turning a magnet end to end in a coil (or turning a coil inside a field).

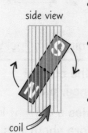
side view

coil

- As you turn the magnet, the magnetic field through the coil changes. This change in the magnetic field induces a potential difference, which can make a current flow in the wire.

- When you've turned the magnet through half a turn, the direction of the magnetic field through the coil reverses. When this happens, the potential difference reverses, so the current flows in the opposite direction around the coil of wire.

- If you keep turning the magnet in the same direction — always clockwise, say — then the potential difference will keep on reversing every half turn and you'll get an alternating current.

This is how an alternator works — see next page.

7) You can increase the induced p.d. by increasing the SPEED of the movement, increasing the STRENGTH of the magnetic field or having more TURNS PER UNIT LENGTH on the coil of wire.

Discovering Electromagnetic Induction Changed How we Live

1) After electromagnetic induction was discovered, power generators were developed and transformed the way we live. Electromagnetic induction is how most mains electricity is generated.

2) However, like all developments in new technology there can be unintended consequences to using it.

3) E.g. there is some debate over the use of pylons and overhead cables to transmit electricity across the country. The debate is whether living near to a pylon can lead to an increased risk of getting cancer.

This page induces confusion and headaches...

Take your time and make sure you really understand electromagnetic induction before moving on.

Q1   What is electromagnetic induction?   [2 marks]

Generators

Generators make use of electromagnetic induction from the previous page to induce a current. Whether this current is alternating or direct all depends on two similar sounding methods of connection.

Alternators Generate Alternating Current

1) Some alternators rotate a magnet (or electromagnet) in a coil of wire.

2) As the magnet spins, an alternating p.d. (see below) is induced across the ends of the coil.

3) This produces an alternating current (a.c.) if the coil is part of a complete circuit. This is how mains electricity (p.26) is produced.

4) You can also generate a.c. by rotating a coil in a magnetic field.

5) Slip rings at the ends of the coil remain in contact with brushes that are connected to the rest of the circuit. This means the brushes are always in contact with the same arm of the coil, so they also produce a.c..

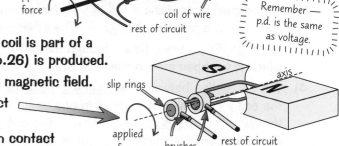

Remember — p.d. is the same as voltage.

Dynamos Generate Direct Current

1) Dynamos also rotate a coil in a magnetic field.

2) A split-ring commutator (like the one on p.40) swaps the connection every half turn to keep the current flowing in the same direction — so it produces d.c..

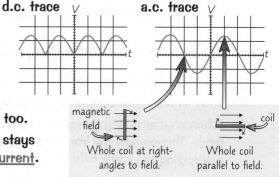

You Can Use an Oscilloscope To See the Generated p.d.

1) Oscilloscopes show how the potential difference generated in the coil changes over time.

2) The peaks of the graphs occur when the most field lines are being cut in a given time.

3) The p.d. produced is a maximum whenever the whole coil is parallel to the magnetic field (i.e. the positions shown in the diagrams above).

4) When the coil has turned 90° from this position, the induced p.d. is zero.

5) Increasing the frequency of revolutions increases the overall p.d., but it also creates more peaks in a given time too.

6) For d.c. the line isn't straight like you might expect, but it stays above the axis (p.d. is always positive) so it's still direct current. These peaks are usually smoothed out (see p.26).

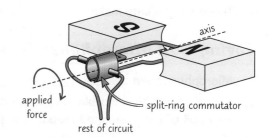

d.c. trace

a.c. trace

magnetic field

Whole coil at right-angles to field.

coil

Whole coil parallel to field.

Induced Current Opposes the Change that Made It

1) So, a change in magnetic field can induce a current in a coil. But as you saw on page , when a current flows through a wire, a magnetic field is created around the wire. (Yep, that's a second magnetic field — different to the one whose field lines were being cut in the first place.)

2) The magnetic field created by an induced current always acts against the change that made it (whether that's the movement of the coil or a change in the field it's in). Basically, it's trying to return things to the way they were.

3) This means that the induced current always creates a field that opposes the change that made it.

NO MORE CHANGES

---

a.c. from alternators, d.c. from dynamos — easy peasy...

Make sure you know the purpose of slip rings and split-ring commutators before you move on.

Q1   Explain how a dynamo generates direct current.   [3 marks]

Loudspeakers, Microphones & Transformers

And it's time for some more <u>applications</u> of <u>electromagnetic induction</u> and the <u>motor effect</u> (p.39).

Loudspeakers Use Magnets and a Coil of Wire

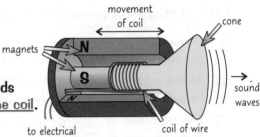

movement of coil

cone

magnets

sound waves

to electrical circuit

coil of wire

1) The force between a <u>current-carrying coil of wire</u> and a <u>magnetic field</u> (the motor effect) can be used to make things move back and forth, like in a <u>loudspeaker</u>.

2) A loudspeaker contains a <u>coil of wire</u> (solenoid) which surrounds <u>one pole</u> of a permanent <u>magnet</u>. The other pole <u>surrounds the coil</u>.

3) <u>An alternating current</u> flows through the <u>coil of wire</u>, which is wrapped around the base of a <u>cone</u>.

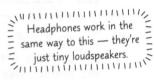

Headphones work in the same way to this — they're just tiny loudspeakers.

4) The <u>interaction</u> between the <u>magnetic fields</u> of the permanent magnet and the coil <u>forces</u> the coil to <u>move</u> in one <u>direction</u>. As it's an alternating current, the <u>current changes direction</u>, forcing the coil <u>back</u> in the <u>other direction</u>. As the current continues to alternate, the coil <u>moves back and forth</u>. The size of the <u>force</u> (and so the <u>amount</u> the coil and cone <u>moves</u>) depends on the size of the <u>current</u> in the coil.

5) These movements make the <u>cone vibrate</u>. This creates pressure variations in the air, i.e. <u>sound</u>.

Moving Coil Microphones Generate Current From Sound Waves

diaphragm attached to coil

magnet

induced current

sound waves

1) Microphones are basically <u>loudspeakers in reverse</u>.

2) <u>Sound waves</u> hit a flexible <u>diaphragm</u> that's attached to a coil of wire, wrapped around one pole of a magnet.

3) This makes the <u>diaphragm vibrate</u> and causes the <u>coil</u> of wire to <u>move</u> in the magnetic field, <u>inducing a p.d. across</u> and <u>a current</u> through the coil.

4) The <u>movement</u> of the coil (and so the <u>size</u> and <u>direction</u> of the <u>induced current</u>) depends on the properties of the sound wave (e.g. <u>louder</u> sounds make the diaphragm move <u>further</u>).

5) This is how microphones can <u>convert</u> the <u>pressure</u> variations of a sound wave into variations in <u>current</u> in an electric circuit.

Transformers Change the p.d. — but Only for Alternating Current

1) Transformers change the size of the <u>potential difference</u> of an <u>alternating</u> current.

2) They all have two coils of wire, the <u>primary</u> and the <u>secondary</u>, joined with an <u>iron core</u>.

3) When an <u>alternating</u> current is applied through the <u>primary coil</u>, it creates an <u>alternating magnetic field</u>. This causes the iron core to <u>magnetise</u> and <u>demagnetise quickly</u>. This causes there to be a changing magnetic field through the <u>secondary coil</u>, which <u>induces</u> an alternating p.d. (p.42).

4) If the second coil is part of a <u>complete circuit</u>, this causes an <u>alternating current</u> to be induced.

5) There are <u>two types</u> of transformer:

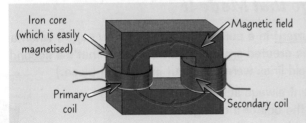

Iron core (which is easily magnetised)

Magnetic field

Primary coil

Secondary coil

<u>STEP-UP TRANSFORMERS</u> step the potential difference <u>up</u> (i.e. <u>increase</u> it). They have <u>more</u> turns on the <u>secondary</u> coil than the primary coil.

<u>STEP-DOWN TRANSFORMERS</u> step the potential difference <u>down</u> (i.e. <u>decrease</u> it). They have <u>more</u> turns on the <u>primary</u> coil than the secondary.

If a loudspeaker falls in the forest does it still make a sound...

These are three pretty common uses of the generator effect, so make sure you understand them.

Q1   Explain how a loudspeaker converts current into sound waves.   [4 marks]

Q2   State the type of transformer that has more turns on its primary coil than on its secondary coil.   [1 mark]

More on Transformers

Transformers are dead useful — we use them in the national grid to make transmitting electricity more efficient.

Transformers are Almost 100% Efficient

1) You saw on page 43 that the number of turns in a coil affects the size of the induced potential difference across it. The ratio between the potential differences across the primary and secondary coils is the same as the ratio between the number of turns in the primary and secondary coils.

$$\frac{\text{p.d. across primary coil (V)}}{\text{p.d. across secondary coil (V)}} = \frac{\text{number of turns in primary coil}}{\text{number of turns in secondary coil}} \quad \text{or} \quad \frac{V_P}{V_S} = \frac{N_P}{N_S}$$

2) You can also use this as a ratio. E.g. to boost 2 V to 10 V, the ratio is 2:10 or 1:5. So you need 5 turns on the secondary coil for every 1 turn on the primary coil.

3) Transformers are almost 100% efficient. So you can assume that energy is conserved within them, i.e. the input power is equal to the output power. Using $P = VI$ (p.33), you can write this as:

$$\text{p.d. across primary coil (V)} \times \text{current in primary coil (A)} = \text{p.d. across secondary coil (V)} \times \text{current in secondary coil (A)}$$

 **EXAMPLE:** A step-down transformer has a primary coil with 3900 turns and a secondary coil with 2400 turns. If the input voltage is 6.5 V, what is the output voltage?

1) Rearrange the ratio equation for V_s. $\quad V_S = V_P \times \dfrac{N_S}{N_P}$

2) Substitute the numbers in. $\quad V_S = 6.5 \times \dfrac{2400}{3900} = 4$ V

The input voltage is the p.d. across the primary coil and the output voltage is the p.d. across the secondary coil.

Transformers make Transmitting Mains Electricity More Efficient

Transformers are used when transmitting electricity across the country via the national grid (p.26).

1) The national grid has to transfer loads of energy each second, which means it transmits electricity at a high power (as power is the rate of energy transfer).

2) Power = potential difference × current (p.33), so to transmit the huge amounts of power needed, you either need a high potential difference or a high current.

3) But a high current makes wires heat up — there are more charges in a given time doing work (transferring energy) to travel through the cable, p.33. So loads of energy is dissipated to the thermal energy stores of the cables and the surroundings.

4) The power lost (due to resistive heating) is found using power = current² × resistance ($P = I^2R$).

5) So to reduce these losses and make the national grid more efficient, high-voltage, low-resistance cables, and transformers are used.

- Step-up transformers at power stations boost the p.d. up really high (400 000 V). This means the current is stepped down (as power = p.d. × current, see above), so energy losses through heating are low at these relatively low currents. You can use the equations above to work out the number of turns needed to increase the pd (and decrease the current) to the right levels.
- Step-down transformers then bring it back down to safe, usable levels at the consumers' end.

I once had a dream about transforming into a hamster...

...but that's a story for another time. For now, get revising what transformers do, and why they're useful. Make sure you know how transformers work and then take a stab at using those equations with this question.

Q1   a) A 100% efficient transformer has 16 turns in its primary coil, 4 turns in its secondary coil and an output potential difference of 20 V. Calculate the potential difference across the primary coil. [2 marks]

      b) Calculate the input current needed to produce an output power of 320 W.   [2 marks]

Revision Questions for Chapter P3

And you've struggled through to the end of electric circuits. Have a break, then test what you can remember.

- Try these questions and <u>tick off each one</u> when you <u>get it right</u>.
- When you've done <u>all the questions</u> for a topic and are <u>completely happy</u> with it, tick off the topic.

Static Electricity (p.28) ☑

1) How does the rubbing together of materials cause static electricity to build up? ☑
2) True or false? Two positive charges attract each other. ☑
3) Describe what is meant by an electric field. ☑

Circuits (p.29-36) ☑

4) Define current and state an equation that links current, charge and time, with units for each. ☑
5) Draw the circuit symbols for: a cell, a filament lamp, a diode, a thermistor and an LDR. ☑
6) What is the equation that links potential difference, current and resistance? ☑
7) Describe an experiment you could do to investigate how the length of a wire affects its resistance. ☑
8) Name one linear component and one non-linear component. ☑
9) Explain how the resistance of an LDR varies with light intensity. ☑
10) What happens to the resistance of a thermistor as it gets hotter? ☑
11) True or false? Power is the rate of energy transfer. ☑
12) Write down the equation linking power, current and resistance. ☑
13) True or false? The potential difference of a battery is shared between components in a series circuit. ☑
14) How does the current through each component vary in a series circuit? ☑
15) How does potential difference vary between components connected in parallel? ☑

Magnets and The Motor Effect (p.37-40) ☑

16) Describe how you could use a compass to show the direction of a bar magnet's magnetic field lines. ☑
17) Describe the behaviour of a compass that is far away from any magnets. ☑
18) What happens to an induced magnet when it is moved far away from a permanent magnet? ☑
19) Describe an electromagnet and give one example of where it could be used. ☑
20) What is Fleming's left-hand rule? ☑
21) Name three ways you could increase the force on a current-carrying wire in a magnetic field. ☑
22) Explain how a basic d.c. motor works. ☑

Electromagnetic Induction (p.41-42) ☑

23) Explain how moving a permanent magnet inside a coil of wire can generate an electric current. ☑
24) What type of generator produces an alternating current? ☑
25) Draw a graph of potential difference against time for the current produced by an alternator. ☑
26) True or false? Induced currents create magnetic fields that oppose the change that made them. ☑

Loudspeakers, Microphones & Transformers (p.43-44) ☑

27) Briefly describe how headphones produce sound waves. ☑
28) Explain how microphones translate sound waves into electrical signals. ☑
29) What kind of current do transformers use? ☑
30) Explain how using transformers improves efficiency when transmitting electricity. ☑

Forces and Newton's Third Law

Clever chap Isaac Newton — he came up with three handy laws about motion. Let's start with the third...

Forces can be Contact or Non-Contact

1) A force is a push or a pull on an object that is caused by it interacting with another object.

2) Sometimes, objects need to be touching for forces to act. These are contact forces.

3) Normal contact forces are the 'push' forces that two touching objects always exert on each other. E.g. a cat on a chair — the cat pushes down on the chair and the chair pushes up on the cat.

4) Friction is a contact force between two objects that tend to slide past each other. E.g. a book resting on a slope — friction acts on both the slope and the book in the direction that tries to prevent motion.

5) Non-contact forces are forces between two objects that aren't touching. The forces are instead caused by fields around the objects interacting. Some examples of non-contact forces are:

- Gravitational forces — e.g. the attractive forces between the Earth and the Sun.
- Electrostatic forces — the attraction or repulsion of charges when their electric fields (p.28) interact.
- Magnetic forces — the attraction or repulsion between two magnets due to their magnetic fields (p.37).

Newton's Third Law — Reaction Forces are Equal and Opposite

1) Whenever two objects interact, they both feel a force. This pair of forces is called an interaction pair.

2) You can represent an interaction pair with a pair of vectors (see page 48) — arrows showing the relative size and direction of the forces.

3) The forces which make up an interaction pair are the same type of force and are the same size, but they each act in the opposite direction and on a different object to the other. This is Newton's third law:

Newton's Third Law: When two objects interact, the forces they exert on each other are equal and opposite.

4) The trouble with Newton's third law is understanding how anything ever goes anywhere. The important thing to remember is that although the forces are equal and opposite, they act on different objects.

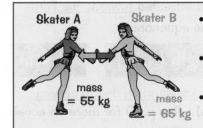

- When skater A pushes on skater B, she feels an equal and opposite force from skater B's hand (the 'normal contact' force).
- Both skaters feel the same sized force, in opposite directions, and so accelerate away from each other.
- Skater A will be accelerated more than skater B, though, because she has a smaller mass, (see Newton's Second Law on page 59).

5) It's a bit more complicated for an object in equilibrium (see page 55). Imagine a book sat on a table:

The weight (p.47) of the book pulls it down, and the normal reaction force from the table pushes it up. This is **NOT** Newton's Third Law as there are two interaction pairs of forces at work — normal contact forces and gravitational forces. Each interaction pair is different and they're both acting on the book.

Each interaction pair due to Newton's Third Law in this case are:

- The weight of the book is pulled down by gravity from Earth (W_B) and the book also pulls back up on the Earth (W_E).
- The normal contact force from the table pushing up on the book (N_B) and the normal contact force from the book pushing down on the table (N_T).

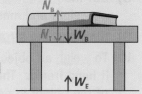

Newton's fourth law — revision must be done with cake...

For every action there is an equal and opposite reaction. Like the despair of revision and the joy of acing the exam.

Q1   Using Newton's third law of motion, explain why a ball bounces back when it hits a wall.   [2 marks]

Mass and Weight

The weight is finally over, it's time to talk about mass. And where there's mass, there's gravity.

Everything Made of Matter Has a Mass

1) Mass is just the amount of matter in an object
   — a measure of the total number of atoms that make it up (see page 69).
2) Mass is measured in kilograms, kg.
3) A given object will have the same mass anywhere in the universe.

Gravity is the Force of Attraction Between All Masses

1) Everything that has mass has a gravitational field around it. Everything.
2) There will be gravitational forces on objects whose gravitational fields interact.
   These forces are always attractive.
3) Isaac Newton made a link between the forces on falling objects on Earth and the forces needed
   to keep the Moon in orbit around the Earth. He realised that gravity was a universal
   law of nature — i.e. everything with mass always attracts everything else with mass.
4) The more massive the object is, the greater the strength of its gravitational field.
5) The attraction due to gravity only becomes noticeable when the mass of one object is very large
   — e.g. there is a noticeable attraction between you and the Earth, but not between you and this book.
6) The attractive forces between the Earth and other objects with mass is what makes
   the objects fall towards the Earth's surface — and keeps them there when they land.

Weight is a Downwards Force

1) When an object is on a planet (or other massive body) a downwards force acts on
   the object due to gravitational attraction between the object and the planet.
2) This force is called its weight.
3) In most situations, weight is the force acting on an object as it is attracted towards the Earth.
4) It's measured in newtons (N). You can calculate weight using the equation:

$$\text{weight (N)} = \text{mass (kg)} \times \text{gravitational field strength (N/kg)} \qquad W = m \times g$$

5) g is called the gravitational field strength. It's also known as the acceleration due to gravity
   (i.e. it's the acceleration an object will have when falling to Earth). See p.50 for more on acceleration.
6) Near the surface of the Earth, a 1 kg mass has a weight of roughly 10 N.
   This means that g has a value of about 10 N/kg near the Earth's surface.
   The value of g is different on other planets, so an identical
   object on another planet will have a different weight.

   You'll need to remember that g = 10 N/kg on Earth for your exam.

7) Remember, mass is not the same as weight — an object's mass is the same everywhere.
8) But the more massive an object is, the larger its weight will be
   — weight and mass are directly proportional.
9) Similarly, the stronger the gravitational field an object is in, the larger the object's weight.
10) To weigh an object, hold a force meter level and attach the object to force meter's spring, letting
    it hang freely. The weight of the object will extend the spring and the meter will show the weight
    of the object in newtons. You could also use a top pan balance (p.103) to measure weight.

Drag yourself away from the TV and force yourself to revise...

A common mistake is thinking that mass and weight are the same thing. They are not. Learn the difference.

Q1   A person has a weight of 820 N on Earth. Calculate their mass.   [3 marks]

Scalars and Vectors

The stuff on this page is pretty darn important. <u>Learn it</u>, don't forget it, and <u>do the question</u> at the end.

Scalars are Just Numbers, but Vectors Have Direction Too

1) Everything you <u>measure</u> in physics is either a <u>scalar quantity</u>, or a <u>vector quantity</u>.

2) <u>Scalar quantities</u> are <u>just numbers</u> — they simply tell you the '<u>size</u>' (or '<u>magnitude</u>') of the thing you're measuring, and nothing more.

3) <u>Mass</u> is a <u>scalar</u> quantity, as it only has a size. Other scalar quantities include: ⟶ <u>Scalar quantities</u>: speed, distance, time, etc.

4) <u>Vector quantities</u> tell you both the <u>size</u> of the thing AND its <u>direction</u>.

5) <u>Force</u> is a <u>vector</u> quantity, because it is applied in a particular <u>direction</u>, e.g. <u>10 N to the right</u>. Other vector quantities include: ⟶ <u>Vector quantities</u>: velocity, displacement, acceleration, etc.

6) Vectors are usually represented by an <u>arrow</u> — the <u>length</u> of the arrow shows the <u>magnitude</u>, and the <u>direction</u> of the arrow shows the <u>direction of the quantity</u>.

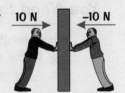

> When we use <u>vectors</u>, we talk about there being a <u>positive</u> and a <u>negative direction</u>. 10 N −10 N
>
> E.g. a <u>force</u> applied in one direction could be a <u>force</u> of <u>10 N</u>, but if it were applied in the <u>opposite direction</u> it would be a force of <u>−10 N</u>.
>
> In either direction the <u>size</u> of the force is <u>10 N</u>.
>
> You can often <u>pick</u> a positive direction that makes the <u>calculations easier</u>.

The Motion of an Object can be Described in Three Ways

1) A <u>moving object</u> can be described by its <u>speed</u>, <u>direction</u> of travel and whether its <u>speed is changing</u>.

2) <u>Distance</u>, <u>displacement</u>, <u>speed</u> and <u>velocity</u> are all terms used to <u>describe</u> an object's motion.

Distance is Scalar, Displacement is a Vector

1) <u>Distance</u> is <u>scalar</u>. It's <u>how far</u> an object has moved <u>along the path</u> it has taken at a <u>given moment</u>.

2) <u>Displacement</u> is a <u>vector</u> quantity. At a given moment, it measures the <u>net distance</u> and <u>direction</u> in a <u>straight line</u> from an object's <u>starting point</u> to its <u>finishing point</u> — e.g. the plane flew 5 metres <u>north</u>. The direction could be <u>relative to a point</u>, e.g. <u>towards the school</u>, or a <u>bearing</u> (a <u>three-digit angle measured clockwise from north</u>) e.g. <u>035</u>°.

3) If you walk 5 m <u>north</u>, then 5 m <u>south</u>, your <u>displacement</u> is <u>0 m</u> but the <u>distance</u> travelled is <u>10 m</u>.

Speed and Velocity are Both How Fast You're Going

1) <u>Speed</u> is a <u>scalar</u> and <u>velocity</u> is a <u>vector</u>. For an object at a given moment:

> <u>Speed</u> is <u>how fast</u> the object's going (e.g. 30 mph or 20 m/s) with no regard to the direction.
> <u>Velocity</u> is speed of the object in a given <u>direction</u>, (e.g. 30 mph north or 20 m/s, 060°).

2) This means you can have objects travelling at a <u>constant speed</u> with a <u>changing velocity</u>. This happens when an object is <u>changing direction</u> whilst staying at the <u>same speed</u>. An object moving in a <u>circle</u> at a <u>constant speed</u> has a <u>constantly changing</u> velocity, as the direction is <u>always changing</u> (e.g. a <u>car</u> going around a <u>roundabout</u>).

3) Objects <u>rarely</u> travel at a <u>constant speed</u>. E.g. when you <u>walk</u>, <u>run</u> or travel in a <u>car</u>, your speed is <u>always changing</u>. Generally the speed referred to is the <u>average (mean)</u> speed.

Whoever left their cat on this top tip please pick it up...

Important things to know in life: how to correctly pronounce 'scone' and the difference between scalars and vectors.

Q1   Describe the difference between scalar and vector quantities. Give an example of each.   [2 marks]

Calculating Speed

Are you ready for a super speedy page? Get set... goooooooooo!!

Speed, Distance and Time — the Formula

You really ought to get pretty slick with this equation, it pops up a lot...

$$\text{average speed (m/s)} = \text{distance (m)} \div \text{time (s)}$$

> The equation for calculating velocity is:
> velocity (m/s) = displacement (m) ÷ time (s).

EXAMPLE: A cat skulks 20 m in 50 s. Find: a) its average speed, b) how long it takes to skulk 32 m.

1) Use the equation above to calculate the average speed.
2) Now rearrange the equation for time.
3) Stick in the value you calculated for average speed and the distance you've been given.

average speed = distance ÷ time
= 20 ÷ 50 = 0.4 m/s

time = distance ÷ average speed
= 32 ÷ 0.4 = 80 s

You Need to be Able to Convert Between Units

1) When using any equation, it's important to have your quantities in the right units. E.g. in the speed equation above, the speed must be in m/s (metres per second), the distance must be in m (metres) and the time must be in s (seconds).

2) You may need to convert between units, and you need to understand prefixes — see page 97.

> To convert 8 h (hours) into s:
> Multiply 8 by 60 to find the number of minutes — 8 × 60 = 480 minutes.
> Then multiply 480 minutes by 60 to find the number of seconds — 480 × 60 = 28 800 s.

3) In the real world speeds are often measured in kilometres per hour, (km/h). Make sure you can convert between km/h and m/s.

> Convert km/h into m/s:
> Divide by 3600 (i.e. 60 × 60) to turn h into s.
> Then multiply by 1000 to change from km to m. (Or just divide by 3.6).
> So 48 km/h = 48 ÷ 3.6 = 13.33... ~ 13 m/s (to 2 s.f.).

> To get from m/s to km/h, divide by 1000 and multiply by 3600.

> The ~ symbol just means it's an approximate value (or answer).

4) Some speeds (and other quantities) that you're given may be in standard form. It's a way of writing very big or very small numbers. Numbers in standard form always look like this:

A is always a number between 1 and 10.

$$A \times 10^n$$

n is the number of places the decimal point would move if you wrote the number out fully. It's negative for numbers less than 1, and positive for numbers greater than 1.

Learn these Typical Speeds

You also need to know the usual speeds of some everyday objects. This is handy when you make estimates.

1) Walking — 1.4 m/s (5 km/h)
2) Running — 3 m/s (11 km/h)
3) Cycling — 5.5 m/s (20 km/h)
4) Average wind speed — 7 m/s (25 km/h)
5) Cars in a built-up area — 13 m/s (47 km/h or 30 mph)
6) Cars on a motorway — 31 m/s (112 km/h or 70 mph)
7) Trains — up to 55 m/s (200 km/h)
8) Speed of sound in air — 340 m/s (1220 km/h)

I feel the need, the need for calculating speed...

This stuff is pretty dull, but it's important for the next few pages, so make sure you know it all.

Q1   Calculate the average speed of a cyclist who cycles 660 m in 2.0 minutes.   [3 marks]

Q2   Find the distance travelled in 24 s by a car with a constant speed of 54 km/hr.   [3 marks]

Acceleration

Acceleration is all about <u>speeding up</u> and <u>slowing down</u>. So let's pick up the pace, and dive straight in.

Acceleration is How Quickly You're Speeding Up

1) Acceleration is the <u>change in velocity</u> of an object in a certain amount of <u>time</u>.
2) In <u>most</u> everyday situations, this change in velocity is a <u>change of speed</u> but <u>not</u> a change in <u>direction</u>. This means you can <u>simplify</u> acceleration to be the <u>change of speed</u> of an object <u>in a given time</u>.
3) If an object <u>speeds up</u>, it must be <u>accelerating</u>.
4) If an object <u>slows down</u>, it's <u>decelerating</u> (deceleration is just <u>negative</u> acceleration).
5) You can find the <u>average acceleration</u> of an object using:

> **acceleration (m/s²) = change in speed (m/s) ÷ time taken (s)**

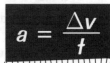

$$a = \frac{\Delta v}{t}$$

You can use this equation with velocities, as long as they're in the same direction.

6) You might have to <u>estimate</u> the <u>acceleration</u> (or <u>deceleration</u>) of an object. To do this, you might need to use the <u>typical speeds</u> from p.49 or <u>estimate a time</u>:

> **EXAMPLE:** A woman begins cycling from rest. Estimate her acceleration.
>
> 1) First <u>estimate</u> the cyclist's <u>typical speed</u>.   typical speed ~ 5.5 m/s
> 2) Find the <u>change in speed</u>.   change in speed = 5.5 − 0 = 5.5 m/s
> 3) Make an <u>estimate</u> of <u>how long</u> it would take a cyclist to get from rest to a typical cycling speed.   estimated time ~ 5 s
> 4) Then <u>substitute</u> this into the acceleration equation.   acceleration = change in speed ÷ time taken = 5.5 ÷ 5 = 1.1 m/s²

There's a Useful Equation for Constant Acceleration

For any object that is travelling with <u>constant acceleration</u> (which you might sometimes be called uniform acceleration), you can use the following <u>equation</u>:

This equation is really handy, so make sure you're comfortable with rearranging it and using it.

> **(final speed)² − (initial speed)² = 2 × acceleration × distance**
> **(m/s)²   (m/s)²   (m/s²)   (m)**

It might <u>help</u> you to remember the equation in symbols, as $v^2 - u^2 = 2 \times a \times s$.

Objects in <u>free fall</u> near the Earth's surface are <u>common</u> examples of objects that have a <u>constant acceleration</u> — they undergo an acceleration due to gravity of roughly <u>10 m/s²</u> (the same value as g, p.47).

These Equations Can be Used to Form a Computational Model

The <u>equations</u> on this page, and on page 49, can be used to form a simple <u>computational model</u> — a computer based model that can be used to <u>predict</u> the motion of an object. The computer does lots of <u>calculations</u>, and can be used to work out, e.g. the <u>position</u> or <u>speed</u> of an object after a certain amount of time. This can be done for objects travelling at a <u>constant speed</u> or with a <u>constant acceleration</u>.

CAUTION! Accelerating through pages means you miss key info...

Get those equations firmly stuck in your head and make sure you're totally happy rearranging and using them.

Q1   A ball is dropped from a height, h, above the ground.
The speed of the ball just before it hits the ground is 5.00 m/s.
Calculate the height the ball is dropped from. (Acceleration due to gravity ≈ 10 m/s².)   [3 marks]

Investigating Motion

Here's a simple <u>experiment</u> you can try out to investigate the relation between <u>distance</u>, <u>speed</u> and <u>acceleration</u>.

You can Investigate the Motion of a Trolley on a Ramp

1) Set up your <u>apparatus</u> as shown in the diagram below, and mark a <u>line</u> on the ramp just before the <u>first light gate</u> — this is to make sure the trolley starts from the <u>same point</u> each time.

2) Measure the <u>distances</u> between light gates 1 and 2, and 2 and 3.

3) Hold the trolley <u>still</u> at the start line, and then <u>let go</u> of it so that it starts to roll down the slope.

4) As it rolls down the <u>ramp</u> it will <u>accelerate</u>. When it reaches the <u>runway</u>, it will travel at a <u>constant speed</u> (ignoring any friction).

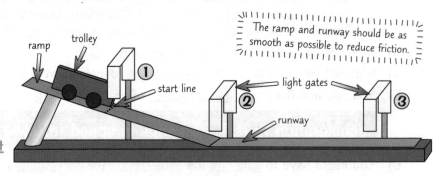

The ramp and runway should be as smooth as possible to reduce friction.

5) Each <u>light gate</u> will record the <u>time</u> when the trolley passes through it. (See page 105 for more on light gates.)

6) The time it takes to travel between <u>gates 1 and 2</u> can be used to find the <u>average speed</u> on the ramp, and between <u>gates 2 and 3</u> gives the <u>speed</u> on the <u>runway</u> (using <u>speed = distance ÷ time</u>, p.49).

7) The <u>acceleration</u> of the trolley on the ramp can be found using <u>acceleration = change in speed ÷ time</u> (p.50) with the following values:

You can also measure speed at a point using one light gate.

- the <u>initial speed</u> of the trolley (= 0 m/s),
- the <u>final speed</u> of the trolley, which equals the speed of the trolley on the <u>runway</u> (ignoring <u>friction</u>),
- the <u>time</u> it takes the trolley to travel between light gates 1 and 2.

The trolley's <u>acceleration</u> on the ramp and its final <u>speed</u> on the runway will <u>increase</u> when the <u>angle</u> of the ramp increases, or the amount of <u>friction</u> between the ramp and the trolley <u>decreases</u>. Increasing the <u>distance</u> between the <u>bottom</u> of the ramp and where the <u>trolley</u> is <u>released</u> will also increase the final speed of the trolley.

Try varying these things in your experiment to see the results for yourself.

You can use Different Equipment to Measure Distance and Time

Generally, you measure <u>speed</u> by <u>measuring distance</u> and <u>time</u>, and then <u>calculating</u> speed. You might need to use <u>different methods</u> for measuring distance and time depending on what you're investigating.

1) If possible, your <u>measuring instrument</u> should always be <u>longer</u> than the <u>distance</u> you're measuring with it — e.g. you shouldn't use a 30 cm ruler to measure something that's 45 cm long.

2) For experiments in the lab like the one above, the distances involved will generally be <u>less than a metre</u>, so you'll be able to measure them with a <u>ruler</u> or a <u>metre stick</u>.

3) If you're investigating e.g. how fast someone <u>walks</u>, you'll want to measure their speed over <u>many metres</u>, so you'll need a <u>long tape measure</u>, or a <u>rolling tape measure</u> (one of those clicky wheel things).

4) To measure time intervals longer than about <u>5 seconds</u>, you can use a <u>stopwatch</u>.

5) To measure <u>short intervals</u>, like in the experiment above it's best to use <u>light gates</u> connected to a <u>computer</u>. Using a stopwatch involves <u>human error</u> (p.94) due to, for example, <u>reaction times</u>. This is more of a problem the shorter the interval you're timing, as the reaction time makes up a <u>larger proportion</u> of the interval.

If you want to investigate motion you'll need to invest in gates...

Think about it this way — say you were measuring the height of an elephant, you wouldn't use a 30 cm ruler, that would be daft. You'd be there forever. What experiment are you doing with an elephant anyway?

Q1 Explain how the speed of an object can be found using two light gates. [3 marks]

Q2 Explain why using light gates to measure short time intervals is more accurate than a stopwatch. [2 marks]

Distance-Time Graphs

A <u>graph</u> speaks a thousand words, so they make life a lot easier on your vocal cords...

Distance-Time Graphs Tell You How Far Something has Travelled

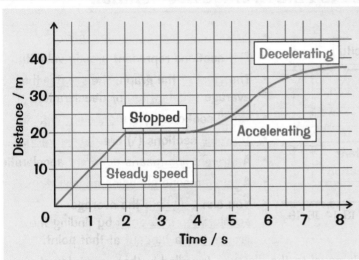

The different parts of a <u>distance-time graph</u> describe the <u>motion</u> of an object:

- The <u>slope</u> (<u>gradient</u>) at <u>any</u> point gives the <u>average speed</u> of the object.
- A <u>steeper</u> graph means it's going <u>faster</u>.
- <u>Flat</u> sections are where it's <u>stopped</u>.
- <u>Straight uphill</u> sections mean it is travelling at a <u>steady speed</u>.
- <u>Curves</u> represent <u>acceleration</u>.
- A <u>steepening</u> curve means it's <u>speeding up</u> (increasing gradient).
- A <u>levelling off</u> curve means it's <u>slowing down</u>.

The Average Speed of an Object can be Found From a Distance-Time Graph

1) The <u>gradient</u> of a distance-time graph at any point is equal to the <u>average speed</u> of the object at that time.

2) If the graph is a <u>straight line</u>, the gradient at any point along the line is equal to $\dfrac{\text{change in the vertical}}{\text{change in the horizontal}}$.

> <u>Example</u>: In the graph above, the average speed at any time between 0 s and 2 s is:
>
> $$\text{Average speed} = \text{gradient} = \frac{\text{change in the vertical}}{\text{change in the horizontal}} = \frac{20}{2} = \underline{10 \text{ m/s}}$$

A tangent is a line that is parallel to the curve at that point.

3) If the graph is <u>curved</u>, to find the average speed at a certain time you need to draw a <u>tangent</u> to the curve at that point, and then find the <u>gradient</u> of the <u>tangent</u>.

> The graph shows the <u>distance-time graph</u> for a bike <u>accelerating</u> for 30 seconds and then travelling at a <u>steady speed</u> for 5 s.
>
> The average <u>speed</u> of the bike at <u>25 s</u> can be found by drawing a <u>tangent</u> to the <u>curve</u> (red line) at 25 s and then finding the <u>gradient</u> of the tangent:
>
> $$\text{gradient} = \frac{\text{change in the vertical}}{\text{change in the horizontal}} = \frac{170}{20} = \underline{8.5 \text{ m/s}}$$
>
> You can also use distance-time graphs to calculate the <u>average acceleration</u> between two points. First, find the <u>speed</u> at <u>both points</u> (draw a tangent or find the gradient of the line) then <u>divide</u> the <u>difference in speed</u> by the <u>time taken</u> to accelerate.
>
> For example, the average acceleration after <u>25 s</u> can be calculated as:
>
> $$\text{average acceleration} = \frac{\text{difference in speed}}{\text{time taken to accelerate}} = \frac{(8.5 - 0)}{25} = \underline{0.34 \text{ m/s}^2}$$

Tangent — a man who's just come back from holiday...

For practice, try sketching distance-time graphs for different scenarios. Like cycling up a hill or running from a bear.

Q1 Sketch a distance-time graph for an object that first accelerates, then travels at a constant speed. [2 marks]

Velocity-Time Graphs

Huzzah, more graphs. And they're <u>velocity-time graphs</u> too, you lucky thing. And just like distance-time graphs, these beauties are also brilliant ways to <u>describe the motion</u> of an object.

Velocity-Time Graphs can Be Used to Find Average Acceleration

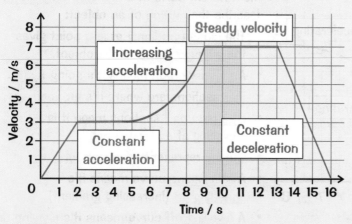

- <u>Gradient = average acceleration</u>.
- <u>Flat</u> sections represent <u>steady</u> velocity.
- The <u>steeper</u> the graph, the <u>greater</u> the average <u>acceleration</u> or deceleration.
- <u>Uphill</u> sections (/) are <u>acceleration</u>.
- <u>Downhill</u> sections (\) are <u>deceleration</u>.
- A <u>straight line</u> means <u>constant</u> acceleration.
- A <u>curve</u> means <u>changing acceleration</u>.
- You can <u>calculate</u> the average <u>acceleration at a point</u> by finding the <u>gradient</u> of a <u>tangent</u> at that point.

- The <u>area</u> under any section of the graph is equal to the <u>distance</u> travelled in that <u>time</u> interval.
- If the graph is a <u>straight line</u>, you can calculate the <u>distance travelled</u> using <u>geometry</u> — e.g. the <u>distance travelled</u> between <u>9 s and 11 s</u> is equal to the area of the <u>shaded rectangle</u>.
- If the graph is <u>curved</u>, you may have to use <u>other methods</u> to calculate the area beneath it, see below.
- <u>Velocity-time graphs</u> are sometimes called <u>speed-time graphs</u> if the object's moving in a <u>straight line</u>. You can find the <u>average acceleration</u> of the object by finding the <u>gradient</u> of a <u>speed-time graph</u>. And the <u>distance travelled</u> is the <u>area</u> under the graph — just like for <u>velocity-time graphs</u>.

You can Use the Counting Squares Method To Find the Area Under the Graph

1) If an object has an <u>increasing</u> or <u>decreasing acceleration</u>, the graph is <u>curved</u>. You can estimate the <u>distance travelled</u> from the <u>area under the graph</u> by <u>counting squares</u>.

2) First you need to find out how much distance <u>one square</u> of the graph paper <u>represents</u> (in metres). To do this, multiply the <u>width</u> of square (in <u>seconds</u>) by the <u>height</u> of one square (in <u>metres per second</u>).

3) Then you just <u>multiply</u> this by the <u>number of squares</u> under the graph. If there are squares that are <u>partly</u> under the graph, you can <u>add them together</u> to make <u>whole squares</u> (see below).

The graph below is a <u>velocity-time graph</u>. You can estimate the <u>distance travelled</u> in the <u>first 10 s</u> by <u>counting</u> the number of squares <u>under</u> the graph (shown by the shaded area).

Total number of shaded squares = <u>32</u>

Distance represented by one square
 = width of square × height of square
 = 1 s × 0.2 m/s = <u>0.2 m</u>

So total distance travelled in 10 s
 = 32 × 0.2 = <u>6.4 m</u>

As you go through and count the squares, it helps to put a dot in the square once it's been counted. That way you don't lose track of what's been counted and what hasn't.

These two partially shaded squares add up to make one square.

Anyone up for a game of squares?

Remember — the acceleration of an object on a velocity-time graph is the gradient of the curve at that time.

Q1 Sketch a velocity-time graph for a car that initially travels at a steady speed and then decelerates constantly to a stop. It is then stationary for a short time before accelerating with increasing acceleration. [3 marks]

Free Body Diagrams and Forces

A <u>free body diagram</u> is really useful to understanding how and why a object is moving or not moving.

Free Body Diagrams Show All the Forces Acting on an Object

drag

weight

1) You need to be able to <u>describe</u> all the <u>forces</u> acting on an <u>isolated object</u> or a <u>system</u> (p.20) — i.e. <u>every</u> force <u>acting on</u> the object or system but <u>none</u> of the forces the object or system <u>exerts</u> on the rest of the world.

2) For example, a skydiver's <u>weight</u> acts on him pulling him towards the ground. <u>Drag</u> (air resistance) also acts on him, in the <u>opposite direction</u> to his motion.

3) This can be shown using a <u>free body diagram</u> like the one on the right.

4) The <u>sizes</u> of the arrows show the <u>relative magnitudes</u> of the forces and the <u>directions</u> show the directions of the forces acting on the object.

A Resultant Force is the Overall Force on a Point or Object

1) In most <u>real</u> situations there are at least <u>two forces</u> acting on an object along any line.

2) If you have a <u>number of forces</u> acting at a single point, you can replace them with a <u>single force</u> that takes into account the <u>sizes</u> and <u>directions</u> of all of the forces. The single force has the <u>same effect</u> as all the individual forces <u>added together</u>.

3) This single force is called the <u>resultant force</u>.

4) If the forces all act along the <u>same line</u> (they're all parallel), the <u>overall effect</u> is found by <u>adding</u> those going in the <u>same</u> direction and <u>subtracting</u> any going in the opposite direction.

5) If you have two forces that are <u>perpendicular</u> (at 90°) to each other, the resultant force can be found using <u>scale drawings</u> (see next page).

EXAMPLE: For the following force diagram, calculate the resultant force acting on the van.

1) Consider the <u>horizontal</u> and <u>vertical</u> directions <u>separately</u>.

2) State the <u>size</u> and <u>direction</u> of the <u>resultant</u> force.

Vertical: 1500 – 1500 = 0 N

Horizontal: 1200 – 1000 N = 200 N

The resultant force is 200 N to the left.

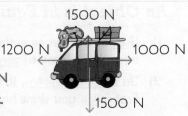
1500 N
1200 N 1000 N
1500 N

The diagram shows an apple sat on a table.

The <u>force</u> due to <u>gravity</u> (its <u>weight</u>, see p.47) is acting <u>downwards</u>. The <u>normal contact force</u> from the table top is pushing <u>up</u> on the apple.

These two forces are equal in size and act in opposite directions. This is a special case where the forces are balanced and cause a <u>zero resultant force</u>. The object is said to be in <u>equilibrium</u> (p.55).

normal contact force

weight

There are <u>four</u> forces acting on an <u>accelerating</u> block.

The <u>weight</u> and <u>normal contact force</u> are equal in size and act in the opposite direction, so the resultant <u>vertical</u> force is <u>zero</u> (like the apple above).

The <u>pushing force</u> on the block is <u>larger</u> than the <u>friction</u>, so there <u>is</u> a <u>resultant horizontal force</u>. This force is equal to the <u>pushing force minus the friction</u>.

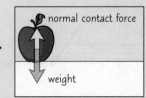
resultant force = 10 N forwards

normal contact force = 100 N

driving force = 19 N

friction = 9 N

weight = 100 N

Consolidate all your forces into one easy-to-manage force...

Free body diagrams make most force questions easier, so start by sketching one. Then get to work.

Q1   Draw a free body diagram for a book resting on a table.   [2 marks]

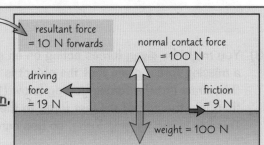

Chapter P4 — Explaining Motion

Forces and Scale Drawings

<u>Scale drawings</u> are useful things — they can help you <u>work out</u> the <u>resultant force</u>.

Use Scale Drawings to Find Resultant Forces

1) Draw all the <u>forces</u> acting on an object, to scale, '<u>tip-to-tail</u>'.

2) Then draw a <u>straight line</u> from the start of the <u>first force</u> to the <u>end</u> of the <u>last force</u> — this is the <u>resultant force</u>.

3) Measure the <u>length</u> of the <u>resultant force</u> on the diagram to find the <u>magnitude</u> and measure the <u>angle</u> to find the <u>direction</u> of the force.

EXAMPLE: A man is on an electric bicycle that has a driving force of 4 N north. However, the wind produces a force of 3 N east. Find the magnitude and direction of the resultant force.

1) Start by drawing a <u>scale drawing</u> of the forces acting.

2) Make sure you choose a <u>sensible scale</u> (e.g. 1 cm = 1 N).

3) Draw the <u>resultant</u> from the tail of the first arrow to the tip of the last arrow.

4) Measure the <u>length</u> of the resultant with a <u>ruler</u> and use the <u>scale</u> to find the force in N.

5) Use a <u>protractor</u> to measure the direction as a <u>bearing</u>.

A bearing is an angle measured clockwise from north, given as a 3 digit number, e.g. 10° = 010°.

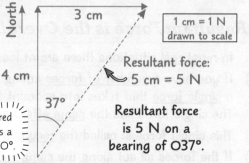

Resultant force:
5 cm = 5 N

Resultant force is 5 N on a bearing of 037°.

4) Putting forces <u>tip-to-tail</u> to find the resultant force <u>works</u> for <u>any</u> number of forces. So don't worry if you have more than one force acting in the same direction, just <u>draw them all</u>.

An Object is in Equilibrium if the Forces Acting on it are Balanced

1) If <u>all</u> of the forces acting on an object <u>combine</u> to give a resultant force of <u>zero</u>, the object is in <u>equilibrium</u>.

2) On a <u>scale diagram</u>, this means that the <u>tip</u> of the <u>last</u> force you draw should end where the <u>tail</u> of the first <u>force</u> you drew begins. E.g. for the <u>four</u> forces below, the scale drawing will form a <u>square</u>.

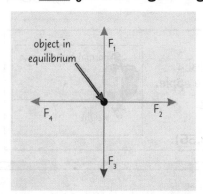

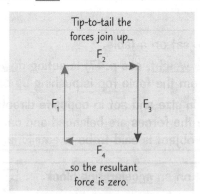

Tip-to-tail the forces join up...

...so the resultant force is zero.

3) You might be <u>given</u> forces acting on an <u>object</u> and told to <u>find</u> a missing force, given that the object is in <u>equilibrium</u>. To do this, draw out the forces you <u>do</u> know (to <u>scale</u> and <u>tip-to-tail</u>), then <u>join</u> the <u>end</u> of the <u>last force</u> to the <u>start</u> of the <u>first force</u>. This line is the <u>missing force</u>, so you can measure its <u>size</u> and <u>direction</u>.

Make sure you draw the last force in the right direction. It's in the opposite direction to how you'd draw a resultant force.

Don't blow things out of proportion — it's only scale drawings...

Keep those pencils sharp and those scale drawings accurate — or you'll end up with the wrong answer.

Q1 A toy boat crosses a stream. The motor provides a 12 N driving force to the north. The river's current causes a force of 5 N west to act on the boat. Find the magnitude of the resultant force. [2 marks]

Newton's First Law and Circular Motion

You met Newton's third law on page 46, and now it's time for the first of Newton's incredibly useful laws.

Newton's First Law — A Force is Needed to Change Motion

1) Newton's first law says that a resultant force is needed to change the motion of an object.

2) So for an object travelling in a straight line, Newton's first law says:

> If the resultant force on a moving object is zero, it will just carry on moving at a constant speed in a straight line.

And for stationary objects:

> If the resultant force on a stationary object is zero, the object will remain stationary.

3) If a non-zero resultant force acts on an object, three things can happen:

- the object will speed up (accelerate) if the force is in the same direction as the object's motion (see page 50).
- the object will slow down if the force is in the opposite direction to the object's motion.
- the object will change direction if the force isn't parallel to the object's motion (i.e. the force doesn't act entirely along the line of motion of the object). This usually leads to a change of speed as well.

If there's a non-zero resultant force on an object, it will have unequal arrows on its free body diagram, p.54.

4) If a non-zero force acts at 90° (perpendicular) to an object's direction of motion, then the object will travel in a circle at a constant speed. There's more on this below.

Objects in Circular Motion have Constant Speed but Changing Velocity

1) If an object is travelling in a circle it's constantly changing direction. As you saw above, this means that a resultant force is acting on the object.

2) This force always acts towards the centre of the circle and is always perpendicular to the line of motion of the object.

3) So the object never changes speed because the force doesn't act in the same or opposite direction to the object's motion.

4) However, the velocity of the object is constantly changing, as its direction is constantly changing and velocity is a vector.

5) A good example of this in action is planets orbiting the Sun (see page 86). The force acting along the radius of the orbit is provided by gravity and it acts at right angles to the path the planet takes around the Sun.

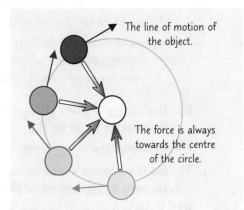

The line of motion of the object.

The force is always towards the centre of the circle.

Now you've started revising, you won't need a push to keep going...

Newton's first law means that an object at a steady speed doesn't need a net force to keep moving. Remember that.

Q1   A car is moving at a constant velocity. State the resultant force acting on it.   [1 mark]

Q2   A student attaches a stone to the end of a piece of string. She swings it around her head in a circular motion at a constant speed. Describe the resultant force acting on the stone.   [2 marks]

Momentum and Newton's Second Law

All moving objects have momentum. Like this book when I throw it across the room.

Momentum = Mass × Velocity

The greater the mass of an object and the greater its velocity, the more momentum the object has. They're linked by this equation:

> momentum (kg m/s) = mass (kg) × velocity (m/s)   or $p = m \times v$

Momentum is a vector — it has size and direction.

 A 65 kg kangaroo is moving in a straight line at 12 m/s.
Calculate its momentum.

momentum = mass × velocity = 65 × 12 = **780 kg m/s**

Forces Cause Changes of Momentum

1) When a resultant force acts on an object, it causes a change in the object's velocity (see previous page). As momentum = mass × velocity, this means that the resultant force also causes a change of momentum in the direction of the force.

2) Newton's second law says that this change of momentum is proportional to the size of the resultant force and the time over which the force acts on the object.

3) Newton's second law in terms of momentum can be written as:

> change of momentum (kg m/s) = resultant force (N) × time for which it acts (s)

4) You can also write Newton's second law as: $\Delta p = F \times t$

 A rock of mass 1.0 kg is travelling through space at 15 m/s. A comet hits
the rock, applying a force of 2500 N for 0.60 seconds. Calculate:
a) the rock's initial momentum
b) the rock's change of momentum resulting from the impact.

a) Substitute into the equation for momentum.   momentum = mass × velocity = 1.0 × 15 = **15 kg m/s**

b) Use the equation for force and   change of momentum = resultant force × time for which it acts
momentum to find what happens
when the comet hits the rock.   = 2500 × 0.60 = **1500 kg m/s**

5) The slower a given change of momentum happens, the smaller the average force causing the change must be (i.e. if t gets bigger in the equation above, F gets smaller).

6) Similarly, the faster a change of momentum happens, the larger the average force must be.

7) So if someone's momentum changes very quickly, like in a car crash, the forces on the body will be very large, and more likely to cause injury. There's more about this on page 64.

8) Newton's second law can also be expressed in terms of force, mass and acceleration. There's more on this on page 59.

Learn this stuff — it'll only take a moment... um.

Make sure you remember that momentum equation at the top of the page and practise using both equations.

Q1   Calculate the momentum of a 220 000 kg aeroplane that is travelling at 250 m/s.   [2 marks]

Q2   Calculate the force a golf club needs to apply to a 45 g golf ball
to accelerate it from rest to 36 m/s in 10.8 ms.   [5 marks]

Conservation of Momentum

Momentum is always <u>conserved</u>. Easy peasy. Go squeeze some lemons.

Momentum Before = Momentum After

Make sure you learn the <u>law of conservation of momentum</u>:

> In a collision when no other external forces act, <u>momentum is conserved</u>
> — i.e. the total momentum <u>after</u> a collision is the <u>same</u> as it was <u>before</u> it.

- Imagine a <u>white</u> snooker ball rolls towards a <u>stationary yellow</u> snooker ball with the <u>same mass</u>. At the point of collision, the <u>yellow ball</u> has a momentum of <u>0</u>, and the <u>white ball</u> has a momentum equal to <u>its mass × its velocity</u> (p.57).
- If after the collision, the white ball <u>stops</u> and the yellow ball <u>moves off</u>, then the yellow ball will have the <u>same velocity</u> as the original velocity of the white ball (assuming there's no friction).
- This is because the <u>white ball</u> will now have a momentum of <u>0</u>, so by conservation of momentum, the <u>yellow ball's momentum</u> must <u>equal</u> the momentum of the white ball <u>before</u> the collision. Since the <u>mass</u> of the balls are the <u>same</u>, the yellow ball must now move with the <u>same velocity</u> as the white ball moved at when it hit the yellow ball.

You can use the idea of conservation of momentum to find the <u>velocity</u> of an object <u>after</u> a <u>collision</u>:

Ball A (mass, m_A = 0.08 kg) is moving with an initial velocity (u_A) of 9 m/s towards ball B (mass, m_B = 0.36 kg). Ball B is moving at an initial velocity (u_B) of 3 m/s in the same direction as ball A. The two balls collide. After the collision, ball A is stationary (v_A = 0 m/s) and ball B moves away with a velocity of v_B. Calculate the velocity of ball B after the collision.

Before

u_A = 9 m/s u_B = 3 m/s

After

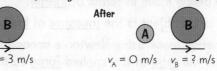

v_A = 0 m/s v_B = ? m/s

1) First, calculate the <u>total momentum</u> before the collision.

total momentum before = ball A's momentum + ball B's momentum
$$= (m_A \times u_A) + (m_B \times u_B)$$
$$= (0.08 \times 9) + (0.36 \times 3) = 1.8 \text{ kg m/s}$$

2) The total momentum <u>before</u> the collision is <u>equal</u> to the total momentum <u>after</u> the collision.

total momentum before = total momentum after = 1.8 kg m/s

3) Write out the equation for the total momentum <u>after</u> the collision, and substitute in the values you know.

total momentum after = $(m_A \times v_A) + (m_B \times v_B)$
$$1.8 = (0.08 \times 0) + (0.36 \times v_B)$$
$$1.8 = 0 + (0.36 \times v_B)$$

4) Rearrange and <u>solve</u> the equation.

$$v_B = 1.8 \div 0.36 = 5 \text{ m/s}$$

If two objects collide and <u>join together</u>, then the total momentum of <u>both</u> objects <u>before</u> the collision is equal to the momentum of the <u>combined</u> objects <u>after</u> the collision. So in the example above, if the balls had <u>joined together</u> and moved away at a <u>steady speed</u>, you would have ended up with <u>total momentum after = (mass of A + mass of B) × velocity of the combined balls</u>.

Homework this week — play pool to investigate momentum...

sigh if only. It's probably best to practise questions instead. Much less fun, but definitely useful for your exams.

Q1   A 2.0 kg trolley travelling at 1.5 m/s collides with a 3.0 kg stationary trolley. They then stick together and move off together at a constant speed. Calculate the final velocity of the two trolleys.   [4 marks]

Q2   A 20 kg object is travelling to the right at 3 m/s. It hits another 20 kg object travelling to the left at 2 m/s. Following the collision the two objects bounce off each other, and one object moves at a speed of 1 m/s to the left. Calculate the velocity of the other object, assuming that momentum is conserved.   [4 marks]

Newton's Second Law and Inertia

In the interests of keeping things moving, this page is on <u>inertia</u>...

Inertial Mass Can be Used in Newton's Second Law

1) When Newton was coming up with his laws of motion, he wrote about how a <u>force applied</u> to an object over a given time affects its <u>amount of motion</u>. He was referring to what we now call <u>momentum</u>.

2) Newton's second law in terms of momentum is:
   <u>change of momentum = resultant force × time for which it acts</u> (p.57).
   But you can also express it in terms of <u>acceleration</u>:

   You need to be able to show how to get from one version of Newton's second law to the other.

   • (Resultant) force = change of momentum ÷ time (for which the force acts).
   • You know that <u>momentum = mass × velocity</u> from page 57.
   • Substituting this into Newton's 2nd law, you get force = (mass × change in velocity) ÷ time.
   • <u>Acceleration</u> is the <u>change of velocity ÷ time</u>, so you can write this as <u>force = mass × acceleration</u>.

3) So <u>Newton's second law</u> in terms of <u>acceleration</u> is:

$$\text{force (N)} = \text{mass (kg)} \times \text{acceleration (m/s}^2) \qquad \text{or} \qquad F = m \times a$$

Inertia Explains Why it's Harder to Move a Hammer Than a Feather

1) <u>Inertia</u> is the tendency for an object's <u>motion</u> to <u>remain unchanged</u> — i.e. <u>stationary</u> objects tend to <u>remain stationary</u> and <u>moving</u> objects tend to <u>keep moving</u>.

2) You learnt that an object's <u>mass</u> is the <u>amount of matter</u> in an object on p.47. But you can <u>also</u> define mass in terms of <u>inertia</u>.

3) The <u>inertial mass</u> of an object is the <u>measure</u> of <u>how difficult</u> it is to <u>change the velocity</u> of the object.

4) You can define inertial mass using Newton's second law. <u>Inertial mass = force ÷ acceleration</u>, i.e. inertial mass is the <u>ratio</u> of the applied <u>force</u> to the <u>acceleration it causes</u>.

> Imagine that a <u>bowling ball</u> and a <u>golf ball</u> roll towards you with the <u>same velocity</u>. You would find it <u>more difficult</u> to stop the <u>bowling ball</u> than the <u>golf ball</u> — a <u>larger force</u> would be required to <u>stop</u> the bowling ball in a <u>given time</u>.
>
> This is because the bowling ball has a <u>larger inertial mass</u> than the golf ball, so it is <u>more difficult</u> to change its motion (velocity).

Newton's Three Laws Required Creativity

Some people think that Newton's creation of the laws of motion was one of the major intellectual advances in our understanding of the world.

So now you've met all of Newton's laws of motion. They're some of the most important laws in physics and are brilliant <u>examples</u> of needing lots of <u>imagination</u> to come up with a <u>scientific explanation</u> to observations.

Before Newton, lots of scientists had <u>observed</u> and <u>discussed</u> many different ideas about how objects moved. But Newton was the one who managed to <u>link them all together</u>. Newton expressed the laws in a way that meant they could be applied to <u>any</u> scenario, which meant that they could be <u>tested</u> over many years.

Over the years, <u>observations</u> and <u>discussions</u> have <u>agreed</u> with Newton's three laws of motion. His three laws are considered <u>scientific knowledge</u> (p.91).

Accelerate your learning — force yourself to revise...

A lot to get your head around on this page, but the physics is dead useful. $F = ma$ crops up all over the place.

Q1   A full shopping trolley and an empty one are moving at the same speed. Explain why it is easier to stop the empty trolley than the full trolley over the same amount of time.   [2 marks]

Moments

Moments sound a lot like momentum, but they're two different things. Moments are all about turning objects.

A Moment is the Rotational Effect of a Force

1) If a resultant force acts on an object with a pivot (a fixed point about which the object can turn) it can cause the object to rotate around the pivot — like pushing open a door on a hinge.

2) This rotational (or turning) effect is called the moment of the force.

3) The size of the moment of a force is given by:

moment of a force (Nm) = force (N) × distance (m)   or $M = F \times d$

The distance here is the normal (perpendicular) distance between the pivot and the direction of the force.

EXAMPLE:
A 50 N force applied perpendicular to a door produces a moment of 5 Nm. Calculate the distance from the door's hinges (the pivot) that the force is applied.

Moment of a force = force × distance,
so distance = moment of a force ÷ force = 5 ÷ 50 = 0.1 m.

4) The greater the applied force or the further the force acts from the pivot, the larger the turning effect.

1) The force on the spanner causes a turning effect or moment on the nut (which acts as a pivot). A larger force would mean a larger moment.

Force = 10 N   Distance = 0.1 m   Tough nut

Moment of a force = force × distance
= 10 × 0.1 = 1 Nm

2) By using a longer spanner, the same force can exert a larger moment because the distance from the pivot is greater.

Pivot
10 N   0.2 m

Moment of a force = force × distance
= 10 × 0.2 = 2 Nm

3) To get the maximum moment you need to push at right angles (perpendicular) to the spanner.

4) Pushing at any other angle means a smaller moment because the perpendicular distance between the direction of the force and the pivot is smaller.

Pivot
Force   Direction of force   Perpendicular distance

Moments can Act on Both Sides of the Pivot

Pivots aren't always at the end of objects — e.g. for a seesaw, the pivot is in the middle of the object. The applied force can cause an object to rotate clockwise or anticlockwise. The direction of the rotation depends on the direction of the force and which side of the pivot the force is on. If the anticlockwise moments are equal to the clockwise moments, an object won't turn. The object is then said to be balanced.

I'll think of a joke soon, give me a moment...

The distance in the equation at the top of this page is the perpendicular distance between the pivot and the direction of the force — not the point at which the force is applied. Make sure you remember that, it's pretty important.

Q1 A 15 N force is applied to a spanner fit around a nut. The moment of the force is 2.4 Nm. Calculate the perpendicular distance between the pivot and the direction of the force. [3 marks]

Levers and Gears

I have good news — there are <u>no equations</u> to learn on this page. Savour this moment because it won't last.

Levers can Transmit Rotational Effects

1) <u>Levers</u> transfer the <u>rotational effect</u> of a force — push one end of a lever <u>down</u> and the <u>rotation</u> around the <u>pivot</u> causes the other end to <u>rise</u>.

2) You saw on p.60 that the moment of a force depends on the <u>distance</u> of the force from the pivot.

3) Levers <u>increase</u> the <u>distance</u> from the pivot that the <u>force</u> is applied.
This <u>increases</u> the size of the <u>moment</u> created by a <u>given input force</u>.

4) Usually, the <u>load</u> is placed a <u>short distance</u> from the pivot. This means that the moment created by the input force exerts an <u>output force</u> that is much <u>larger</u> than the <u>original input force</u>.

5) Levers are <u>useful</u> because they make <u>lifting</u> and <u>moving</u> things <u>easier</u> (they reduce the input force needed to provide a large output force). Some <u>examples</u> of levers in everyday life are:

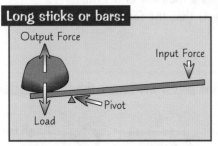

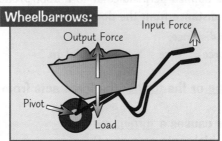

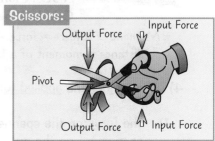

Gears Fit Together to Transfer Turning Effects

1) Gears are <u>circular discs</u> with '<u>teeth</u>' around their edge.

2) The teeth of different gears can <u>interlock</u> so that turning one gear causes another to turn as well. Because of how they are <u>linked</u> together, a gear spinning <u>clockwise</u> will make the <u>next</u> gear spin <u>anticlockwise</u>. This then <u>alternates</u> as you go from gear to gear.

3) A <u>force</u> applied to a <u>small gear</u> creates a <u>small moment</u>. The small gear applies this <u>force</u> to the gear <u>next to it</u>. If this second gear is <u>larger</u>, the force is being applied <u>further</u> from the <u>pivot</u> (of the larger gear), so the <u>moment</u> of the second gear is <u>larger</u>.

4) A series of gears that get <u>bigger</u> from gear to gear will <u>multiply</u> the <u>moment</u> of the first, smallest gear.

5) <u>Interlocked</u> gears will rotate at <u>different speeds</u>, depending on their size — the <u>larger</u> the gear, the <u>slower</u> it spins. (Think of a <u>large gear</u> and a <u>small gear</u> turning together. For every <u>complete</u> turn of the small gear, the large gear has only turned a <u>small amount</u>.)

<u>Clocks</u> are a common example of an object that uses gears.
Inside a clock, <u>different sized</u>, <u>interlocking</u> gears are <u>connected</u> to the <u>different hands</u> on the clock.

The <u>sizes</u> of the gears are arranged so that the <u>gear</u> attached to the <u>hour hand</u> only moves by a <u>small amount</u> (the <u>hour divisions</u> on the clock) in the <u>time</u> it takes for the <u>gear</u> attached to the <u>minute hand</u> to <u>fully rotate</u>.

What did one gear say to the other? Gear we go again...

Make sure you can explain how levers make it easier to do work, they're a common example of using moments.

Q1 A 30 cm diameter gear is interlocked with a 20 cm diameter gear. The 30 cm gear turns clockwise. State:
   a) the direction the 20 cm gear will turn. [1 mark]
   b) whether the 20 cm gear will turn quicker or slower than the 30 cm gear. [1 mark]

Reaction Times

Go long! You need fast <u>reaction times</u> to avoid getting hit in the face when playing catch.

You can Measure Reaction Times with the Ruler Drop Test

<u>Everyone's</u> reaction time is different and many different <u>factors</u> affect it (see next page).
<u>Typical</u> human reaction times are between <u>0.2 s and 0.6 s</u>.
You can do a <u>simple experiment</u> to investigate your reaction time.
As reaction times are <u>so short</u>, you haven't got a chance of measuring one with a <u>stopwatch</u>.
One way of measuring reaction times is to use a <u>computer-based test</u> (e.g. <u>clicking a mouse</u> when the screen changes colour). Another is the <u>ruler drop test</u>:

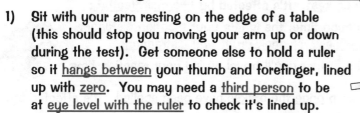

1) Sit with your arm resting on the edge of a table (this should stop you moving your arm up or down during the test). Get someone else to hold a ruler so it <u>hangs between</u> your thumb and forefinger, lined up with <u>zero</u>. You may need a <u>third person</u> to be at <u>eye level with the ruler</u> to check it's lined up.

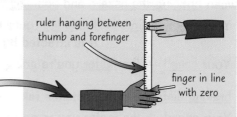

ruler hanging between thumb and forefinger

finger in line with zero

2) Without giving any warning, the person holding the ruler should <u>drop it</u>. Close your thumb and finger to try to <u>catch the ruler as quickly as possible</u>.

3) The measurement on the ruler at the point where it is caught is <u>how far</u> the ruler fell in the time it took for you to react.

4) The <u>longer</u> the <u>distance</u>, the <u>longer</u> your <u>reaction time</u>.

5) You can calculate <u>how long</u> the ruler falls for (your <u>reaction</u> time) because <u>acceleration due to gravity is constant</u> (roughly 10 m/s^2).

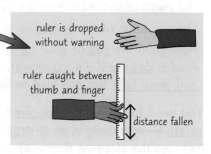

ruler is dropped without warning

ruler caught between thumb and finger

distance fallen

E.g. say you catch the ruler at 20 cm. From p.50 you know:

(final speed)^2 – (initial speed)^2 = 2 × acceleration × distance

Initial speed = 0, acceleration = 10 m/s^2 and distance = 0.2 m, so:

final speed = $\sqrt{2 \times \text{acceleration} \times \text{distance} + (\text{initial speed})^2}$ = $\sqrt{2 \times 10 \times 0.2 + 0}$ = <u>2 m/s</u>

As initial speed is zero, final speed is equal to the <u>change in speed</u> of the ruler.

From page 50 you also know: acceleration = change in speed ÷ time, so

time = change in speed ÷ acceleration = 2 ÷ 10 = <u>0.2 s</u>

This gives your <u>reaction time</u>.

6) It's <u>pretty hard</u> to do this experiment <u>accurately</u>, so you should do a lot of <u>repeats</u>. The results will be better if the ruler falls <u>straight down</u> — you might want to add a <u>blob of modelling clay</u> to the bottom to stop it from waving about.

7) Make sure it's a <u>fair test</u> — use the <u>same ruler</u> for each repeat and have the <u>same person</u> dropping it.

8) You could try to investigate some factors affecting reaction time, e.g. you could introduce <u>distractions</u> by having some <u>music</u> playing or by having someone <u>talk to you</u> while the test takes place.

Test a friend's reaction time by throwing this book at them...

Not really. Instead re-read this page and make sure you can describe the experiment. Much more fun.

Q1   Briefly describe one method other than the ruler drop test that can be used to
      investigate reaction times.   [2 marks]

Q2   Mark's reaction time is tested using the ruler drop test.
      He catches the ruler after it has fallen a distance of 16.2 cm. Calculate Mark's reaction time.   [4 marks]

Stopping Distances

Knowing what affects stopping distances is useful for everyday life, as well as the exam.

Stopping Distance = Reaction Distance + Braking Distance

1) In an emergency (e.g. a hazard ahead in the road), a vehicle driver may perform an emergency stop. This is where maximum force is applied by the brakes in order to stop the vehicle in the shortest possible distance. The longer it takes to perform an emergency stop, the higher the risk of crashing.

2) The distance it takes to stop a vehicle in an emergency (its stopping distance) is the sum of the reaction distance and the braking distance, i.e. stopping distance = reaction distance + braking distance.

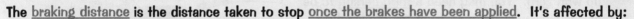

The reaction distance is the distance the vehicle travels in the driver's reaction time (the time between noticing the hazard and applying the brakes). It's affected by two main factors:
- Your reaction time — the longer your reaction time, the longer your reaction distance. It is affected by tiredness, alcohol, drugs and distractions.
- Your speed — the faster you're going, the further you'll travel during your reaction time.

The braking distance is the distance taken to stop once the brakes have been applied. It's affected by:
- Your speed — the faster you're going, the further it takes to stop (see next page).
- The mass of the vehicle — a vehicle full of people and luggage won't stop as quickly as an empty one.
- The condition of the brakes — worn or faulty brakes won't be able to brake with as much force.
- How good the grip of your tyres is — you're more likely to skid when the road is dirty or if it's icy or wet. If the tyres are bald (they don't have any tread left) this can lead to them skidding on top of the water.

3) You need to be able to describe the factors affecting a vehicle's stopping distance and how this affects safety — especially in an emergency. E.g. icy conditions increase the chance of skidding (and so increase the stopping distance) so driving too close to other cars in icy conditions is unsafe. The longer your stopping distance, the more space you need to leave in front in order to stop safely.

Braking Relies on Friction Between the Brakes and Wheels

1) When the brake pedal is pushed, this causes brake pads to be pressed onto the wheels. This contact causes friction, which causes work to be done. The work done (p.20) between the brakes and the wheels transfers energy away from the kinetic energy stores (p.66) of the wheels.

2) You can write this as work done by the brakes = energy transferred away from kinetic energy store, or: braking force × braking distance = 0.5 × mass of vehicle × (speed of vehicle)^2.

3) So the faster a vehicle is going, the more energy it has in its kinetic energy stores, and the more work needs to be done to stop it. In an emergency stop, where the maximum braking force is applied, this means that the faster the vehicle is going before the emergency stop, the longer its braking distance.

4) As speed increases, reaction distance increases at the same rate as the speed. The driver's reaction time will stay fairly constant, but the higher the speed, the further you go in that time (p.49).

5) However, because of that (speed)^2 in the equation for energy in kinetic energy stores, braking distance and speed have a squared relationship — e.g. if speed doubles, braking distance increases 4-fold (2^2).

6) You need to be able to use these relationships between speed, reaction distance and braking distance to make estimates of stopping distances over a range of speeds. For example, you may have to estimate how the stopping distance changes if the speed of a car doubles. Typical car stopping distances are: 23 m at 30 mph, 73 m at 60 mph and 96 m at 70 mph, but you could be asked about other vehicles.

Stop right there — and learn this page...

Bad visibility also causes accidents — if it's foggy, it's harder to notice a hazard, so there's less room to stop.

Q1   A 1000 kg car travelling at 25 m/s makes an emergency stop. It brakes with a force of 5000 N.
      Estimate the braking distance of the car, using ideas about energy in the car's kinetic store.   [5 marks]

Chapter P4 — Explaining Motion

More Stopping Distances

You need to know about <u>large decelerations</u> and be able to make some estimations of <u>forces</u> and <u>accelerations</u>.

Large Decelerations can be Dangerous

1) The <u>faster</u> an object is going, the <u>more momentum</u> it has. A <u>force</u> is needed to <u>change</u> this momentum (p.57). The <u>larger</u> the <u>change of momentum</u>, or the <u>quicker</u> this change happens, the <u>larger</u> the <u>force</u> on the object. So for events like <u>car crashes</u>, where the momentum changes a lot in a short amount of time, the <u>forces</u> acting on the <u>car</u> and its <u>passengers</u> are very <u>large</u>.

2) The <u>large forces</u> required for <u>large decelerations</u> (e.g. in car crashes) can cause <u>injuries</u>. They may also cause the brakes to <u>overheat</u> (so they don't work as well) or they could cause the vehicle to <u>skid</u>.

3) The <u>force</u> on an object can be <u>lowered</u> by <u>slowing</u> the object down over a <u>longer time</u>.

4) <u>Safety features</u> in cars are designed to <u>increase collision times</u>, which <u>reduces</u> the <u>deceleration</u> and <u>forces</u>, and so reduces the risk of injury. For example, <u>seat belts stretch</u> slightly and <u>air bags</u> slow passengers down over a <u>longer period of time</u>. <u>Crumple zones</u> are areas at the front and back of a car which <u>crumple up easily</u> in a collision, increasing the time taken to stop.

5) <u>Motorbike</u> and <u>bicycle helmets</u> contain a <u>crushable layer</u> of foam which increases the <u>time taken</u> for your head to stop and so reduces the force on your head if you're in an accident.

6) It's thanks to our understanding of <u>Newton's laws of motion</u> that we have been able to <u>improve technologies</u> like these, as well as <u>develop new materials</u> that have improved the <u>safety</u> of travelling.

You May Need to Estimate Forces and Accelerations

You need to be able to <u>estimate</u> the <u>forces</u>, <u>accelerations</u> and <u>decelerations</u> involved in <u>everyday</u> road situations and <u>emergencies</u>. To do this, you'll need to know the <u>typical speeds</u> from page 49 and some vehicle masses: <u>Car</u> ~1000 kg. <u>Single decker bus</u> ~10 000 kg. <u>Loaded lorry</u> ~30 000 kg.

EXAMPLE:
A loaded lorry brakes as it slows down before reaching a junction. It experiences a braking force of −39 000 N. Estimate the deceleration of lorry.

1) Recall the <u>typical mass</u> of a loaded lorry.　mass of lorry ~30 000 kg
2) Use <u>force = mass × acceleration</u> (p.59) to find the deceleration.　force = mass × acceleration, so:
acceleration = −39 000 ÷ 30 000
3) <u>Round</u> your answer to <u>1 s.f.</u> (since it's an estimate).　= −13 m/s²
deceleration ~10 m/s² (to 1 s.f.)

Remember, deceleration is just negative acceleration.

EXAMPLE:
A car is travelling through a built-up area. The car comes off the road and collides with a street lamp. Estimate the force on the car during the crash.

1) <u>Estimate</u> the <u>speed</u> of the car and the <u>time</u> it took the car to stop once it hit the street lamp.　speed of car ~ 13 m/s, time taken to stop ~ 0.1 s
2) Calculate the <u>acceleration</u> of the car (p.50).　acceleration = change in speed ÷ time taken
= (0 − 13) ÷ 0.1 = −130 m/s²
3) <u>Estimate</u> the mass of the car.　mass of car ~1000 kg
4) <u>Calculate</u> the <u>force</u> acting on the car.　force = mass × acceleration = 1000 × −130
= −130 000 N
5) <u>Round</u> your answer to 1 s.f. The negative sign just means the force acted in the <u>opposite</u> direction to the <u>motion</u> of the car.
So the force on the car ~ (−)100 000 N (to 1 s.f.)

It's enough to put you off learning to drive, isn't it...

This is quite a tough page, but it's important, so head back to the top and read it again.

Q1　Estimate the size of the force needed to stop a loaded lorry travelling at 16 m/s within 50 m.　[5 marks]

Work Done and Energy Transfers

This page is all about <u>work</u>. But not the kind you're already doing by reading this book.
Oh no, this is all about our old friends <u>energy transfers</u> (have a look over at page 20 for more about these).

Work is Done When a Force Moves an Object

> When a <u>FORCE</u> makes an object <u>MOVE</u>, <u>ENERGY IS TRANSFERRED</u> and <u>WORK IS DONE</u>.

1) Whenever something begins to <u>move</u>, or <u>changes</u> how it's moving (e.g. speeds up, slows down or changes direction), something is providing some sort of <u>effort</u> (force) to move it.

See Chapter P2 for lots more about energy.

2) If a <u>force</u> is exerted <u>on</u> the object, you can say that <u>work is done on the object</u> by the force. Energy is transferred <u>to</u> the object's energy stores.

3) Similarly, if the <u>object</u> itself exerts the force (or transfers energy in a different way, see page 20), work is done <u>by the object</u> and energy is transferred <u>from</u> the object's energy stores.

4) Whether this energy is <u>transferred usefully</u> (e.g. by <u>lifting a load</u>) or <u>wasted</u> (e.g. dissipated by <u>heating</u> from <u>friction</u>), you still say that '<u>work is done</u>'. '<u>Work done</u>' and '<u>energy transferred</u>' are <u>the same</u>.

5) The <u>formula</u> to calculate the <u>amount of work done</u> (energy transferred) when an object is moved through a distance by a force is:

> work done (Nm or J) = force (N) × distance (m)   or $W = F \times d$

The <u>distance</u> here is the distance moved <u>along</u> the <u>line of action</u> of the <u>force</u> (i.e. the distance moved in the <u>direction</u> of the force).

6) Work done is sometimes given in newton-metres, <u>Nm</u>, but it's the same as joules, <u>J</u>. <u>1 Nm = 1 J</u>. You need to be able to <u>convert</u> between the two, e.g. 5 Nm = 5 J.

They said joule, Dave.

Energy is Always Conserved

1) You saw back on page 21 that for <u>any</u> event or process, <u>energy is always conserved</u>.

2) So if in the process you're looking at, the <u>energy before doesn't equal the energy after</u>, you know that process <u>can't happen</u>.

3) If a process <u>can</u> happen, the formulas for <u>work done</u> (above) and the <u>energy</u> in certain <u>stores</u> (the next page) can be used to <u>calculate what will happen</u>. But they <u>cannot</u> explain <u>why</u> a process happens.

4) In situations where there are <u>no frictional forces</u> acting (i.e. no <u>friction</u>, no <u>air resistance</u> etc.), the <u>work done</u> on an object will be <u>equal</u> to the energy transferred to <u>useful energy stores</u>.

> If a force does work on an object and <u>increases</u> its <u>velocity</u> (along the line of action of the force), <u>energy is transferred</u> to the object's <u>kinetic energy store</u> (p.66). <u>If there's no friction</u>, the energy in the kinetic energy store will <u>equal</u> the <u>work done</u> on the object by the force.

5) In most processes in the <u>real world</u>, some work must be done <u>against</u> resistive forces.

6) This causes some energy to be <u>dissipated</u> (p.21), usually through <u>heating</u>.

7) So if there are <u>frictional forces</u> and work is done <u>to</u> an object, the <u>energy transferred</u> to the object's <u>useful</u> energy store (p.22) <u>won't equal</u> the <u>work done</u> to cause the energy transfer.

> <u>Work is done</u> on an object to <u>increase</u> its <u>velocity</u>. <u>Frictional forces</u> act on the object. The energy in the <u>kinetic</u> energy store of the object will be <u>less than</u> the <u>work done</u> by the <u>force applied to move the object</u>. <u>Some</u> energy will be transferred to <u>thermal stores</u>. The <u>work done</u> to move the object will <u>equal</u> the energy in the objects <u>kinetic energy store</u> + the energy in thermal energy stores.

8) If work is done <u>by</u> the object, work done = energy transferred <u>from</u> the object's <u>useful energy store</u>.

Energy transfers can be a lot of work...

Work done is just energy transferred. Make sure you remember how work done is related to motion and forces.

Q1   A book sliding across a table has 1.25 J of energy in its kinetic energy store. Friction from the table provides a constant force of 5.0 N. Calculate the distance travelled by the book before it stops.   [3 marks]

Kinetic and Potential Energy Stores

This page covers two types of energy stores (p.20) and how to calculate how much energy is in them.

An Object at a Height has Energy in its Gravitational Potential Energy Store

1) When an object is at any height above the Earth's surface, it will have energy in its gravitational potential energy (g.p.e.) store.

2) When an object is raised, energy is transferred to its gravitational potential energy store.

3) When it is lowered, or falls, energy is transferred away from its gravitational potential energy store.

4) You need to be able to describe the energy transfers in terms of work done when these things happen.

> When an object is lifted above the ground, work is done by the lifting force (against gravity) to move the object. Energy is transferred to the object's gravitational potential energy store. Assuming there's no friction or air resistance, when the object stops moving, the work done to lift the object will be equal to the energy transferred to its gravitational potential energy store.

5) You can calculate the amount of energy in the gravitational potential energy store using the equation:

> Here, h is the height of the object above the ground. You can find the change in energy in the g.p.e. store with a change in height, h.

$$\text{gravitational potential energy (J)} = \text{mass (kg)} \times \text{gravitational field strength (N/kg)} \times \text{height (m)}$$

or $GPE = m \times g \times h$

A Moving Object has Energy in its Kinetic Energy Store

1) When an object is moving, it has energy in its kinetic energy store.

2) This energy depends on both the object's mass and speed.

3) The greater its mass and the faster it's going, the more energy it has in its kinetic energy store.

4) You need to remember and know how to use the formula:

$$\text{kinetic energy (J)} = 0.5 \times \text{mass (kg)} \times \text{(speed)}^2 \text{ (m/s)}^2$$

or $KE = \frac{1}{2} \times m \times v^2$

EXAMPLE: A car of mass 1450 kg is travelling at 28 m/s. Calculate the energy in its kinetic energy store, giving your answer to 2 s.f.

kinetic energy = 0.5 × mass × (speed)²
= 0.5 × 1450 × 28²
= 568 400 = 570 000 J (to 2 s.f.)

> Watch out for the (speed)², that's where people tend to make mistakes and lose marks.

5) You need to be able to use this equation and the one above to calculate energy transfers in a given process or event (e.g. a falling object).

6) Remember, energy is always conserved. So if you assume there are no frictional forces, energy lost/gained by the kinetic store = energy gained/lost by the gravitational potential store.

There's potential for a joke here somewhere...

More equations to learn here. Look on the bright side, at least you don't have to learn something like $G_{\mu\nu} = 8\pi G (T_{\mu\nu} + \rho_\Lambda g_{\mu\nu})$. And we all know what that equation is — altogether now, it's... erm...*

Q1 Calculate the energy in the gravitational potential energy store of a 0.80 kg ball at a height of 1.5 m above the Earth's surface. [2 mark]

Q2 An otter is swimming with a speed of 2.0 m/s. It has a mass of 4.9 kg. Calculate the energy in the otter's kinetic energy store. [2 mark]

*don't panic, you really don't need to know what this is.

Energy Transfers and Power

Whenever I think of <u>power</u>, I have to stop myself from plotting world domination whilst stroking a cat.

You Might Need to Describe How Energy is Transferred

<u>Transfers of energy</u> result in a change in the <u>system</u> (p.20). If you understand a few different <u>examples</u>, it'll be easier to think through whatever they ask you about in the exam.

<u>A BALL THROWN UPWARDS OR ROLLING UP A SLOPE:</u> energy is transferred <u>mechanically</u> from the <u>kinetic energy store</u> of the ball to its <u>gravitational potential energy store</u>.

<u>A BAT HITTING A (STATIONARY) BALL:</u> some energy in the <u>kinetic energy store</u> of the bat is transferred <u>mechanically</u> to the <u>thermal energy stores</u> of the bat, the ball and their surroundings. Some energy is transferred <u>mechanically</u> from the <u>kinetic energy store</u> of the bat to the <u>kinetic energy store</u> of the ball. The <u>rest</u> of the energy is carried away by <u>sound</u>.

<u>A CAR SLOWING DOWN:</u> when you apply the brakes in a car, <u>work is done</u> and energy is transferred <u>mechanically</u> from the <u>kinetic</u> energy store of the <u>car</u> to the <u>thermal</u> energy stores of the <u>brakes</u>. Energy is also transferred <u>by heating</u> to the <u>thermal</u> energy store of the <u>environment</u> and some energy is carried away by <u>sound</u>.

<u>A SKYDIVER FALLING TO EARTH:</u> energy is transferred <u>mechanically</u> from the <u>gravitational potential energy</u> store of the skydiver to his <u>kinetic energy store</u>. The rest of the energy would be <u>dissipated</u> through <u>heating</u> and <u>sound</u> due to air resistance.

Power is the 'Rate of Energy Transfer' — i.e. How Much per Second

<u>Power</u> is the <u>rate</u> at which <u>energy is transferred</u> (or work is done) in a system.

1) The proper unit of power is the <u>watt (W)</u>. <u>1 W = 1 J of energy transferred per second</u> (J/s).

2) So, the power of a <u>machine</u> is the <u>rate</u> at which it <u>transfers energy</u>. For example, if an <u>electric drill</u> has a power of <u>700 W</u> this means it can transfer <u>700 J</u> of energy (or do 700 J of work) <u>every second</u>.

3) This is the <u>very easy formula</u> for power:

$$\text{power (W)} = \text{energy transferred (J)} \div \text{time (s)} \quad \text{or} \quad P = E \div t$$

EXAMPLE:

A motor transfers 4.8 kJ of useful energy in 2 minutes. Find its power output.

1) <u>Convert</u> the values to the <u>correct units</u> first.   4.8 kJ = 4800 J and 2 mins = 120 s
2) <u>Substitute</u> the values into the power equation.   power = energy transferred ÷ time
                                                 = 4800 ÷ 120 = 40 W

4) Electrical appliances are <u>useful</u> because they have <u>high powers</u>. If you <u>calculate</u> how much work is done to, e.g. <u>lift</u> a <u>heavy crate</u> or even just to <u>climb</u> a bunch of <u>stairs</u>, you'll see that it requires a <u>lot</u> of energy.

5) Machines can often transfer energy <u>much quicker</u> than people — their <u>power output</u> is much larger than a person's. This makes them dead handy as it <u>reduces</u> the <u>time</u> taken to do loads of <u>everyday tasks</u>.

Watt's power? Power's watts...

Phew, you've reached the end of the chapter. Well done — do these questions then have a break. You've earned it.

Q1   Describe the energy transfers for a falling ball landing on the ground without bouncing.   [3 marks]

Q2   Calculate the energy transferred by a 12 W power supply in 5.0 minutes.   [3 marks]

Revision Questions for Chapter P4

Phew! It's the end of Chapter P4. Now it's time to see what you've got in the bag and what needs work.
- Try these questions and tick off each one when you get it right.
- When you've done all the questions for a topic and are completely happy with it, tick off the topic.

Forces (p.46-48) ☑

1) What is the definition of an interaction pair? ☑
2) What is Newton's third law of motion? Give an example of it in action. ☑
3) What is the difference between mass and weight? How can weight be calculated? ☑
4) True or false? Velocity is a scalar quantity. ☑

Speed and Acceleration (p.49-53) ☑

5) What is the equation for calculating the average speed of an object? ☑
6) Define acceleration. ☑
7) Describe an experiment to investigate the acceleration of a trolley down a ramp. ☑
8) How is the average speed of an object found from its distance-time graph? ☑
9) What does a flat section on a velocity-time graph represent? ☑
10) How is the distance travelled by an object found from its velocity-time graph? ☑

Newton's First and Second Laws (p.54-59) ☑

11) Draw a free body diagram of a remote-controlled car travelling at a constant speed. ☑
12) Explain how to use a scale drawing to find the resultant force on an object. ☑
13) What is Newton's first law of motion? ☑
14) Give the equation for momentum in terms of mass and velocity. ☑
15) Give the equation for Newton's second law in terms of momentum. ☑
16) True or false? The total momentum before a collision always equals the total momentum after it. ☑
17) What is inertial mass? ☑
18) Give the equation for Newton's second law in terms of acceleration. ☑

Moments, Levers and Gears (p.60-61) ☑

19) Give the equation for calculating the moment of a force. ☑
20) How does the size of a gear in a series of interlocked gears affect its speed compared to other gears? ☑

Reaction Times and Stopping Distances (p.62-64) ☑

21) Describe the ruler drop test which is used to measure reaction times. ☑
22) What is meant by a driver's reaction time? ☑
23) State two factors which affect the braking distance of a vehicle. ☑
24) True or false? If the speed of a car trebles, its braking distance increases by a factor of 9. ☑
25) Explain how crumple zones reduce the risk of injury in a crash. ☑

Energy Transfers (p.65-67) ☑

26) Give the equation for the work done on an object when it's moved a certain distance by a force. ☑
27) How does the energy in an object's gravitational potential energy store vary with height? ☑
28) Give the equation for the energy in the kinetic energy store of a moving object. ☑
29) What is meant by power? How is power calculated? ☑

Developing the Model of the Atom

All this started with a Greek fella called Democritus in the 5th Century BC. He thought that all matter, whatever it was, was made up of identical lumps called "atomos". And that's as far as it got until the 1800s...

Rutherford Came up with the Nuclear Model...

1) In 1804 John Dalton agreed with Democritus that matter was made up of tiny spheres ("atoms") that couldn't be broken up, but he reckoned that each element was made up of a different type of "atom".

2) Nearly 100 years later, J. J. Thomson discovered particles called electrons that could be removed from atoms. So Dalton's theory wasn't quite right. This led scientists to believe that atoms were spheres of positive matter with tiny negative electrons stuck in them like currants in a cake.

3) That theory didn't last long though. The Rutherford-Geiger-Marsden alpha particle scattering experiment fired a beam of alpha particles (see p.70) at thin gold foil. It was expected that the particles would pass straight through the gold sheet, or only be slightly deflected. But although most of the particles did go straight through the sheet, some were deflected more than expected, and a few were deflected back the way they had come — something the original model couldn't explain.

4) These results provided evidence that the gold atom was mostly empty space — most of the alpha particles weren't deflected. It also provided evidence that the atom had a central, tiny nucleus containing most of the atom's mass (as most alpha particles passed straight through, but some were deflected by large angles) which was positively charged (because it repelled positively-charged alpha particles). This led to the first nuclear model of the atom in 1910. (All models with a nucleus are called nuclear models.)

...Which Developed into the Modern Nuclear Model of the Atom

1) Rutherford, Geiger and Marsden's nuclear model described the atom as a positively charged nucleus orbited by a cloud of negative electrons.

2) Scientists realised that electrons in a 'cloud' around the nucleus of an atom like this would be attracted to the nucleus, causing the atom to collapse. Niels Bohr got round this by adapting the initial model to show that electrons orbiting the nucleus can only do so at certain distances.

Take a look at p.6 for more on electrons around the nucleus and how they can move within the atom.

3) This means that electrons can move within (or sometimes leave) the atom.

The Modern Model of the Atom

Each atom has a tiny nucleus at its centre that makes up almost all of the mass of the atom. It contains protons (which are positively charged — they have a $+1$ relative charge) and neutrons (which are neutral, with a relative charge of 0) — which gives it an overall positive charge. It is about 100 000 times smaller than the diameter of the atom.

The rest of the atom is mostly empty space.
Negative electrons (relative charge -1) whizz round the outside of the nucleus really fast. They give the atom its overall size — the diameter of an atom is about 1×10^{-10} m (which is also quite tiny).

Atoms can join together to form molecules.
Small molecules are roughly the same size as an atom (1×10^{-10} m).

The number of protons = the number of electrons, as protons and electrons have an equal but opposite charge and atoms have no overall charge.
If atoms lose or gain electrons and become charged, they become ions (p.6).

Our current nuclear model of the atom has evolved over time. At every stage, scientists had to use logic and reasoning to create a model which would be able to explain all the available evidence. Old models were rejected, and either old models were modified or new ones created or adapted to explain all the evidence.

These models don't have anything on my miniature trains...

That's a whole lot of history, considering this is a book about physics. It's all good, educational fun though.

Q1   a) Describe the modern model of the atom.   [4 marks]

      b) State the diameter of an atom and describe how this compares to the size of its nucleus.   [2 marks]

Isotopes and Radioactive Decay

Understanding what <u>isotopes</u> are is important for learning about <u>radioactive decay</u>. So let's get cracking.

Isotopes are Different Forms of the Same Element

1) The <u>atomic or proton number</u> is the <u>number of protons</u> in an atom's <u>nucleus</u>.

2) This can also be thought of as the <u>charge</u> of the nucleus, as all protons have the <u>same positive charge</u> (<u>+1</u>) and all neutrons are <u>neutral</u>.

3) The <u>identity</u> of an <u>element</u> is <u>defined</u> by the <u>number of protons</u> in the atom. <u>Nuclei</u> of an element <u>always</u> have the <u>same number of protons</u>, (e.g. a carbon atom <u>always</u> has <u>6 protons</u>) but they can have <u>different amounts</u> of <u>neutrons</u>.

4) This means that the nucleus of <u>each element</u> has a <u>particular</u> positive <u>charge</u> (e.g. carbon <u>always</u> has a charge of <u>+6</u>).

5) The <u>mass number</u> is the <u>number of protons</u> plus the <u>number of neutrons</u> in an atom. It tells you the <u>mass</u> of the <u>nucleus</u> (the <u>nuclear mass</u>).

6) You can <u>represent</u> atoms using this <u>notation</u>:

7) <u>Isotopes</u> of an element are atoms that have the <u>same</u> number of <u>protons</u> as each other but a <u>different</u> number of <u>neutrons</u>. E.g. $^{12}_{6}C$, $^{13}_{6}C$ and $^{14}_{6}C$ are all <u>isotopes of carbon</u>. So different isotopes of an element have <u>different nuclear masses</u> but the <u>same nuclear charge</u>.

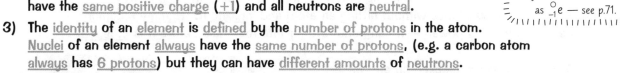

> Remember, electrons have a charge of −1. They are sometimes written as $^{0}_{-1}e$ — see p.71.

Mass number ——— A
Atomic number ——— Z **X** ——— Chemical symbol

8) <u>Most elements</u> have different isotopes, but there are usually only one or two <u>stable</u> ones.

9) The nuclei of other <u>unstable isotopes</u> tend to <u>decay</u> into <u>other elements</u> and give out <u>radiation</u> as they try to become more stable. This process is called <u>radioactive decay</u>.

10) Substances containing unstable isotopes are <u>radioactive</u> — they <u>always</u> emit one or more types of <u>ionising radiation</u> from their <u>nucleus</u> — <u>alpha particles</u>, <u>beta particles</u>, <u>gamma rays</u> or <u>neutrons</u>.

11) <u>Ionising radiation</u> is radiation that knocks <u>electrons</u> off atoms, creating <u>positive ions</u>. The ionising <u>power</u> of radiation is how <u>easily</u> it can do this.

You Need to Know These Four Types of Ionising Radiation

- An <u>alpha</u> particle (α) is <u>two neutrons</u> and <u>two protons</u> — the same as a <u>helium nucleus</u>. They have a <u>relative mass of 4</u> and a <u>relative charge of +2</u>.
- They are relatively <u>big</u>, <u>heavy</u> and <u>slow moving</u>.

- A <u>beta</u> particle (β) is identical to an <u>electron</u>, with <u>virtually no mass</u> and a <u>relative charge of −1</u>.
- <u>Beta particles</u> move <u>quite</u> fast and are <u>quite</u> small.
- For every <u>beta particle</u> emitted, a <u>neutron</u> turns into a <u>proton</u> in the nucleus.

- <u>After</u> spitting out an alpha or beta particle, the nucleus might need to get rid of some <u>extra energy</u>. It does this by emitting a <u>gamma ray</u> — a type of <u>electromagnetic radiation</u> with a <u>high frequency</u>.
- Gamma rays (γ) have <u>no mass</u> and <u>no charge</u>. They <u>just transfer energy</u>, so they <u>don't</u> change the element of the nucleus that emits them.

- If a nucleus contains <u>a lot</u> of <u>neutrons</u>, it may just <u>throw out</u> a neutron.
- The <u>number of protons</u> stays the <u>same</u>, but it now has a <u>different nuclear mass</u>, so it becomes a <u>different isotope</u> of the <u>same element</u>.

Isotopes of an outfit — same dress, different accessories...

I'd learn those alpha, beta, gamma and neutron radiations if I were you. They'll be coming up again, mark my words.

Q1 An oxygen atom has 8 protons and 8 neutrons.
Which one of the following represents an isotope of this oxygen atom?

A: $^{17}_{9}O$ B: $^{16}_{7}O$ C: $^{17}_{8}O$ D: $^{16}_{9}O$ [1 mark]

Penetration Properties and Decay Equations

Time to learn a bit <u>more</u> about some of the types of radiation before putting them in <u>equations</u>. How thrilling.

Different Types of Radiation Have Different Penetration Properties

1) How <u>far</u> radiation can travel through a material before it's <u>absorbed</u> (how far it can <u>penetrate</u> a material) depends on the <u>ionising power</u> of the radiation and <u>material</u> it's travelling through.

2) <u>Alpha particles</u> have the <u>highest</u> ionising power — this means that they <u>can't</u> travel <u>very far</u> through a substance without hitting an atom and <u>ionising</u> it. <u>Gamma radiation</u> has the <u>lowest</u> ionising power — it can penetrate <u>far</u> into materials before it is <u>stopped</u>.

- <u>Alpha particles</u> are blocked by e.g. <u>paper</u>.
- <u>Beta particles</u> are blocked by e.g. thin <u>aluminium</u>.
- <u>Gamma rays</u> are blocked by e.g. <u>thick lead</u>.

> The alpha and beta particles would also be blocked by the lead, and the alpha particles would also be blocked by the aluminium.

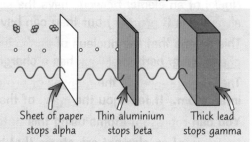

Sheet of paper stops alpha   Thin aluminium stops beta   Thick lead stops gamma

You Need to be Able to Balance Nuclear Equations

You can write nuclear decays as <u>nuclear equations</u>. You need to be able to <u>balance</u> these equations for <u>alpha</u>, <u>beta</u>, <u>gamma</u> and <u>neutron</u> decays by balancing the total <u>masses (mass numbers)</u> and <u>charges</u> (atomic numbers) on each side.

Emitting an Alpha Particle

- The <u>mass decreases by 4</u> — it <u>loses</u> two protons and two neutrons.
- The <u>charge decreases by 2</u> — because it has <u>two less</u> protons.

Radium decaying to radon:	$^{226}_{88}Ra \rightarrow {}^{222}_{86}Rn + {}^{4}_{2}He$			
mass number:	226	$\rightarrow$	222	+ 4 (= 226)
atomic number:	88	$\rightarrow$	86	+ 2 (= 88)

> You can also write the alpha particle as $^{4}_{2}\alpha$ and the beta particle as $^{0}_{-1}\beta$ in equations.

Emitting a Beta Particle

A neutron changes into a proton, so:

- The <u>mass doesn't change</u> — as it has <u>lost</u> a neutron but <u>gained</u> a proton.
- The <u>nuclear charge increases by 1</u> — because it has <u>one more</u> proton.

Carbon decaying to nitrogen:	$^{14}_{6}C \rightarrow {}^{14}_{7}N + {}^{0}_{-1}e$			
mass number:	14	$\rightarrow$	14	+ 0 (= 14)
atomic number:	6	$\rightarrow$	7	+ (−1) (= 6)

> In both alpha and beta emissions, a new element will be formed, as the number of protons changes.

Emitting a Gamma Ray

- The <u>mass doesn't change</u>.
- And the charge <u>doesn't change</u>.

Iodine decaying to a more stable atom of iodine:	$^{130}_{53}I \rightarrow {}^{130}_{53}I + {}^{0}_{0}\gamma$

Emitting a Neutron

- The <u>mass decreases by 1</u> — because it has one less neutron.
- The <u>nuclear charge doesn't change</u>.

Helium decaying to a different isotope of helium:	$^{5}_{2}He \rightarrow {}^{4}_{2}He + {}^{1}_{0}n$

I think balancing equations is more fun than anything ever...

Right? Right?? *cough* I can't see your face, but I'm going to take a wild guess and say you don't believe me.

Q1   A uranium nucleus (U), with an atomic number of 238 and a mass number of 92, decays into a thorium (Th) atom by emitting an alpha particle. Write a balanced equation to show this decay. [3 marks]

Activity and Half-life

Radioactive decay is <u>totally random</u>, so how can we know how an isotope will decay? I give you, <u>half-lives</u>.

The Radioactivity of a Sample Always Decreases Over Time

1) <u>Radioactive decay</u> is a <u>random process</u> — you <u>can't predict</u> exactly <u>which</u> nucleus in a sample will decay next, or <u>when</u> any one of them will decay.

2) But each <u>nucleus</u> of a given <u>isotope</u> has a <u>fixed chance</u> of decaying. You can use this to work out the <u>time</u> it takes for the <u>amount of radiation</u> emitted by a source to <u>halve</u> — known as the <u>half-life</u>. It can be used to make <u>predictions</u> about radioactive sources, even though their decays are <u>random</u>.

3) The <u>number of unstable nuclei</u> that <u>decay</u> in a given time is called the <u>activity</u> and is measured in <u>becquerels (Bq)</u> — the number of nuclei that decay each second. So you can define half-life as:

> The half-life of a source is the average time taken for its activity to halve.

4) It's also the <u>average time taken</u> for <u>half</u> of the remaining <u>unstable nuclei</u> of a given <u>isotope</u> to <u>decay</u>.

5) Each time a radioactive nucleus <u>decays</u> to become a <u>stable nucleus</u>, the activity of the sample will <u>decrease</u>. So over time, the activity <u>always decreases</u>.

6) A <u>short half-life</u> means the <u>activity falls quickly</u>, because <u>lots</u> of the nuclei decay in a <u>short time</u>. A <u>long half-life</u> means the activity <u>falls more slowly</u> because <u>most</u> of the nuclei don't decay <u>for a long time</u>.

7) A <u>Geiger-Muller tube</u> can detect <u>radiation</u> that has been emitted from a decaying nucleus. It measures the <u>count rate</u> — the number of radiation counts that reach a Geiger-Muller tube in a <u>given time</u>.

Half-life can be Calculated from Numbers or from a Graph

You could be asked to <u>calculate</u> how you'd expect the <u>activity</u> of a source to <u>change over time</u>:

A <u>sample</u> of a radioactive isotope has an <u>activity of 1000 Bq</u> and a <u>half-life of 5 years</u>:

- After <u>1 half-life</u> (<u>5 years</u>) the activity will be 1000 ÷ 2 = <u>500 Bq</u>.

- After <u>2 half-lives</u> (<u>10 years</u>) the activity will be 500 ÷ 2 = <u>250 Bq</u>.

You can also find the <u>net decline of a sample</u> — <u>how much</u> the activity (or the number of undecayed nuclei) decreases by over a period of time — normally a <u>ratio</u>.

For this example, the <u>net decline of the sample after 2 half-lives</u> (10 years) is 1000 − 250 = 750 Bq. Or as a <u>ratio</u>: decrease in activity/ original activity = 750/1000 = <u>3/4</u>.

You also need to be able to find the half-life of a sample from a <u>graph</u>...

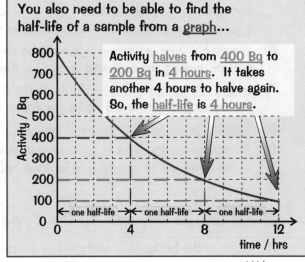

Activity <u>halves</u> from <u>400 Bq</u> to <u>200 Bq</u> in <u>4 hours</u>. It takes another 4 hours to halve again. So, the <u>half-life is 4 hours</u>.

If you're given count rates rather than activity, you can find the half-life in exactly the same way.

EXAMPLE: The half-life of a radioactive sample is 30 minutes. Calculate how long it will take for the activity of the radioactive sample to fall to one quarter of its initial value, A.

1) Find how many <u>half-lives</u> it will take for the activity to fall to <u>one quarter</u> of its <u>initial value</u>.

2) Calculate <u>how long</u> this is using the value for the half-life.

Initially: A after 1 half-life: $(\div 2) \rightarrow \dfrac{A}{2}$ after 2 half-lives: $(\div 2) \rightarrow \dfrac{A}{4}$

2 × 30 minutes = 60 minutes (or 1 hour)

Half-life of a box of chocolates — about five minutes...

To measure half-life, you time how long it takes for the activity to halve. This can be in seconds, days, years...

Q1   The half-life of a radioactive source is 60 hours. There are initially N radioactive nuclei in the sample. Calculate the fraction of the initial radioactive nuclei that will have decayed after 10 days.   [3 marks]

Dangers of Radioactivity

Time to find out about the hazards of <u>ionising radiation</u> — it <u>damages</u> living cells when it ionises atoms in them.

Ionising Radiation Harms Living Cells

1) Ionising radiation can <u>enter living cells</u> and <u>interact with molecules</u>.

2) These interactions cause <u>ionisation</u> (see p.6).

3) <u>Lower doses</u> of ionising radiation <u>damage living cells</u> by causing <u>mutations</u> in the <u>DNA</u>. This can cause the cell to <u>divide uncontrollably</u> — which is <u>cancer</u>.

4) <u>Higher doses</u> tend to <u>kill cells completely</u>, which causes <u>radiation sickness</u> if a lot of cells <u>all get blasted at once</u>.

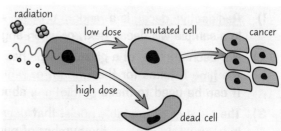

All Radioactive Sources Have Irradiation and Contamination Risks

1) Whenever your body is <u>exposed</u> to radiation, there is a risk that your cells will be <u>damaged</u>.

2) If <u>radiation</u> from a <u>radioactive source</u> reaches your body, you are being <u>irradiated</u>.

3) As the <u>distance</u> between you and the source <u>increases</u>, the amount of radiation reaching your body decreases. So standing <u>far</u> from a source is one way to <u>reduce irradiation</u>. Other ways to reduce irradation are to <u>not point</u> sources <u>directly at people</u> and to store them in <u>lead-lined boxes</u> when not in use.

4) If a radioactive source ends up <u>on</u> or <u>inside</u> your body, your body is <u>contaminated</u>.

5) How <u>likely</u> you are to be contaminated <u>depends on the source</u>. If it's a <u>solid</u>, but you <u>don't touch</u> it, there's <u>very little</u> chance of contamination. However, radioactive <u>gases</u> can spread and be <u>inhaled</u>, so contamination is much more <u>likely</u>.

6) Wearing <u>gloves</u> or using <u>tongs</u> reduces the chance of particles getting stuck to you or under your nails and so <u>reduce</u> the chance of <u>contamination</u>.

7) <u>Irradiation is temporary</u> — if the source is <u>taken away</u>, any irradiation it's causing stops, and it no longer poses a risk to your health.

8) <u>Contamination lasts longer</u> — if the <u>original source</u> is taken away, the contaminating atoms are <u>left behind</u>.

9) So contamination by a <u>given</u> source poses a <u>higher risk</u> of harm than irradiation as cells in the body will be <u>exposed</u> to ionising radiation until the source <u>leaves the body</u>.

The Hazards Depend on the Type of Radiation

1) <u>Outside</u> the body, <u>beta</u> and <u>gamma</u> sources are the most dangerous.

2) This is because <u>beta particles</u> and <u>gamma rays</u> can both <u>penetrate the body</u> and get to delicate <u>organs</u>. <u>Gamma rays</u> can <u>penetrate further</u>, so they are <u>more dangerous</u> than beta particles.

3) Alpha particles are the <u>least dangerous</u> because they <u>can't penetrate the skin</u> and are easily blocked by a <u>small air gap</u>.

4) <u>Inside the body</u>, <u>alpha</u> particles are the <u>most</u> dangerous, because they do all their damage in a <u>very localised area</u>.

5) <u>Beta</u> particles are <u>less damaging</u> inside the body, as radiation is absorbed over a <u>wider area</u>, and some <u>passes out</u> of the body altogether.

6) <u>Gamma</u> rays are the <u>least dangerous</u> inside the body, as they mostly <u>pass straight out</u> without doing any damage — they have the <u>lowest ionising power</u>.

Top tip number 364 — if something is radioactive, don't lick it...

If you're working with radioactive sources, read about the safety risks and make experiments as safe as possible.

Q1   Give two effects that ionisation caused by radiation can have on living cells.   [2 marks]

Chapter P5 — Radioactive Materials

Half-life and Uses of Radiation

Ionising radiation is very <u>dangerous</u> stuff, but used in the <u>right way</u> it can be so useful that it <u>saves lives</u>.

The Hazards Associated with a Radioactive Source Depend on its Half-Life

1) The <u>lower</u> the <u>activity</u> of a <u>radioactive source</u>, the <u>safer</u> it is to be around.

2) If two sources that emit the <u>same type</u> of radiation start off with the <u>same activity</u>, the one with the <u>longer</u> half-life will be <u>more dangerous</u>. This is because, after <u>any period</u> of time, the activity of the source with a <u>short half-life</u> will have <u>fallen more</u> than the activity of the source with a <u>long half-life</u>.

3) If those two sources have <u>different initial activities</u>, the danger associated with them changes over time. Even if its <u>initial activity</u> is lower (so it is <u>initially safer</u>), the source with the <u>longer half-life</u> will be <u>more dangerous</u> after a certain period of time because its <u>activity</u> falls <u>more slowly</u>.

4) The <u>half-life</u> can be used to work out <u>how long</u> it is before a radioactive source becomes <u>relatively safe</u>.

Tracers in Medicine — Short Half-life Gamma Emitters

1) Certain <u>radioactive isotopes</u> that emit <u>gamma</u> radiation are used as <u>tracers</u> in the body.

2) They can be <u>injected</u> or <u>ingested</u> (<u>drunk</u> or <u>eaten</u>) to see how parts of the body, e.g. organs, are <u>working</u>.

3) They <u>spread</u> through the body and their progress is followed on the outside using a <u>radiation detector</u>.

4) They need a relatively <u>short half-life</u> — i.e. <u>a few hours</u>, so that the source becomes relatively safe <u>quite quickly</u>, but long enough that it still emits <u>enough radiation</u> by the time it reaches the correct place.

5) <u>Medical tracers</u> are <u>GAMMA</u> (never alpha) sources. Gamma radiation <u>penetrates tissue</u>, so can <u>pass out the body</u> and be <u>detected</u>. Alpha and beta <u>can't</u> and cause more damage <u>in the body</u> compared to gamma.

Radiotherapy — the Treatment of Cancer Using Radiation

1) Since high doses of radiation will <u>kill living cells</u>, they can be used to <u>treat cancers</u>.

2) The radiation is <u>directed carefully</u> and at a specific <u>dosage</u> (depending on the <u>size</u> and <u>type of tumour</u>, and <u>size and age of patient</u>), so it kills the <u>cancer cells</u> without damaging too many <u>normal cells</u>.

3) Radiation can be used to <u>remove</u> tumours completely or to <u>control</u> and <u>stop</u> them <u>spreading further</u>.

4) However, a <u>fair bit of damage</u> is often done to <u>normal cells</u>, which makes the patient feel <u>very ill</u>.

5) Before ionising radiation is used as part of any medical treatment, both the <u>patient</u> and <u>doctor</u> need to make an <u>informed decision</u> on whether the <u>benefits outweigh the risks</u>.

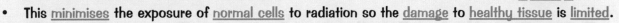

<u>To treat cancer externally</u> (using <u>gamma rays</u>):

- The gamma rays are <u>focused</u> on the tumour using a <u>wide beam</u>.
- The patient stays <u>still</u> and the beam is <u>rotated</u> round them with the tumour at the centre.
- This <u>minimises</u> the exposure of <u>normal cells</u> to radiation so the <u>damage</u> to <u>healthy tissue</u> is <u>limited</u>.
- The treatment is given in doses with <u>time between</u> for the healthy cells to be <u>repaired or replaced</u>.

γ rays focused on tumour

Source rotated outside the body.

<u>To treat cancer internally</u>:

- <u>Implants</u> containing <u>beta-emitters</u> are placed <u>next to</u> or <u>inside</u> the tumour. The beta particles damage the cells in the tumour, but have a <u>short enough range</u> that the <u>damage</u> to <u>healthy tissue</u> is <u>limited</u>.
- An implant with a <u>long half-life</u> should be <u>removed</u> to stop the radiation killing healthy cells once the cancerous cells have been killed. If the half-life is <u>short</u> enough, the implant can be <u>left in</u>.
- <u>Alpha-emitters</u> can be injected into a tumour. Alpha particles are <u>strongly ionising</u>, so they do lots of damage to the cancer cells. But as they have a <u>short range</u>, damage to normal tissue is <u>limited</u>.

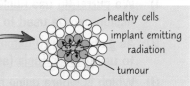

healthy cells
implant emitting radiation
tumour

So radiation is pretty handy in medicine...

Try making lists of when and why the different types of radiation are used in medicine to see what you've learnt.

Q1 Explain why radioactive sources that emit gamma radiation are used as medical tracers. [2 marks]

Fission and Fusion

Nuclear fuels give out lots of energy when their nuclei change — they're used in fission and fusion reactions.

Nuclear Fission — the Splitting Up of Big Atomic Nuclei

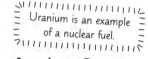
Uranium is an example of a nuclear fuel.

1) If a large unstable nucleus, e.g. uranium, absorbs a slow moving neutron, it can split into two smaller nuclei of roughly the same size. This is nuclear fission.

2) This change in the nucleus gives out a lot of energy — some of this energy is transferred to the kinetic energy stores of the fission products. There is also a lot of extra energy which is carried away by gamma radiation.

3) Each time a uranium nucleus splits up, it spits out two or three neutrons, some of which might be absorbed by other nuclei, causing them to split too, and thus causing a chain reaction.

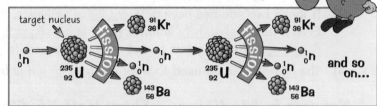

4) Nuclear power stations generate electricity from chain reactions, using uranium or plutonium as fuel.

5) The nuclear equation for the fission of uranium is:

$$^{235}_{92}\text{U} + ^{1}_{0}\text{n} \rightarrow ^{143}_{56}\text{Ba} + ^{91}_{36}\text{Kr} + 2^{1}_{0}\text{n}$$

Having the 2 in front of $^{1}_{0}$n shows that there are two neutrons produced. It saves time, rather than writing out $^{1}_{0}$n + $^{1}_{0}$n.

6) Every neutron released from a nuclear fission has the potential to cause another fission reaction. As two or more neutrons are released from every fission of uranium, this means a chain reaction could release an increasing amount of energy as the number of unstable nuclei undergoing fission increases rapidly. This massive release of energy from the nuclear energy store is similar to the release of energy from the chemical energy store of TNT when it explodes — only much, much larger.

7) Not every neutron will necessarily cause another nuclear fission though — if one neutron from each nuclear reaction causes another fission, then the rate of nuclei splitting won't increase or decrease. The smallest amount of nuclear fuel needed for this steady reaction is called the critical mass.

Nuclear Fusion — the Joining of Small Atomic Nuclei

1) Two light nuclei can join to create a larger nucleus if they're brought close enough together — this is called nuclear fusion. For example, two hydrogen nuclei can fuse to form a helium nucleus.

2) Fusion releases a lot of energy (more than fission for a given mass of fuel).

3) The energy is due to a difference in mass between the original nuclei and the new nucleus. This extra mass is converted into energy and released. The mass of the nuclei before fusion will always be larger than the mass of the nucleus after fusion. (You don't need to understand why the masses are different.)

Energy From Nuclear Reactions can be Used to Generate Electricity

1) We currently use nuclear fission to generate some of our electricity — the energy released from nuclear fission can be used to heat water to make steam, which goes on to generate electricity (see p.23).

2) As global energy demands are continually increasing (see p.25), we need to find alternatives to using fossil fuels (as they will one day run out and are bad for the environment, p.23).

3) Which is where using nuclear fuels come in. Nuclear power stations are more reliable than some renewable energy resources (p.25), they're clean, and fuel costs are relatively cheap.

4) However, they produce harmful nuclear waste which is hard to store and could leak, there's the risk of a major disaster and the overall cost of nuclear power plants is quite high. These risks need to be weighed up against the benefits when considering what resources should be used to generate electricity.

Ten million degrees — that's hot...

Fission — splitting up big nuclei for energy. Fusion — combining small nuclei for energy. Nowt else to it. Well...

Q1   Explain how nuclear fission can lead to a chain reaction.   [2 marks]

Revision Questions for Chapter P5

So that's it for <u>Chapter P5</u> — not long, but full of really important information.

- Try these questions and <u>tick off each one</u> when you <u>get it right</u>.
- When you've done <u>all the questions</u> for a topic and are <u>completely happy</u> with it, tick off the topic.

<u>The Model of the Atom (p.69)</u> ☑

1) Briefly explain how the model of the atom has changed over time. ☑
2) True or false? Atoms have no overall charge. ☑
3) What happens to an atom if it loses one or more of its electrons? ☑

<u>Isotopes, Radioactive Decay and Half-life (p.70-72)</u> ☑

4) What is the atomic number of an atom equal to: the nuclear charge or the nuclear mass? ☑
5) What number is equal to the number of protons + the number of neutrons in the nucleus? ☑
6) What defines the identity of an element: the nuclear charge or the nuclear mass? ☑
7) What is an isotope? Are they usually stable? ☑
8) True or false? Gamma radiation can be stopped by a thin sheet of aluminium. ☑
9) Draw the symbols for both alpha and beta radiation in nuclear equations. ☑
10) What type of radioactive decay doesn't change the mass or charge of the nucleus? ☑
11) What is the activity of a source? What are its units? ☑
12) Define half-life. ☑
13) True or false? A short half-life means a small proportion of unstable nuclei are decaying per second. ☑
14) Explain how you would find the half-life of a source, given a graph of its activity over time. ☑

<u>Dangers and Uses of Radiation (p.73-74)</u> ☐

15) Explain how exposure to radiation can lead to cancer. ☑
16) What is meant by irradiation? ☑
17) What is meant by contamination? ☑
18) Compare the hazards of being irradiated and contaminated by:
    a) an alpha source,   b) a gamma source. ☑
19) Give one example of how to protect against: a) contamination,   b) irradiation. ☑
20) Explain the dangers of a radioactive source with a long half-life. ☑
21) Explain what sort of half-life a source must have in order to be used as a medical tracer. ☑
22) Apart from medical tracers, give one other way that radiation is used in medicine. ☑

<u>Fusion and Fission (p.75)</u> ☑

23) What is nuclear fission? ☑
24) Describe the energy transfers that occur as a nucleus has undergone nuclear fission. ☑
25) True or false? Nuclear fusion typically involves unstable, heavy nuclei. ☑
26) Explain the benefits and disadvantages of using nuclear power stations to generate electricity. ☑

Density

Time for some <u>maths</u> I'm afraid. But at least it comes with a fun experiment, so it's not all bad...

Density is Mass per Unit Volume

<u>Density</u> is a measure of the '<u>compactness</u>' (for want of a better word) of a substance.
<u>Mass</u> (the <u>amount of matter</u> in a substance) depends on the <u>density</u> of the substance,
and its <u>volume</u> (the amount of <u>space</u> it takes up).

Density is <u>defined</u> by:

$$\text{density (kg/m}^3) = \frac{\text{mass (kg)}}{\text{volume (m}^3)}$$

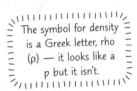
The symbol for density is a Greek letter, rho (ρ) — it looks like a p but it isn't.

The <u>units</u> of density are g/cm³ or kg/m³.
The density of an object depends on what it's <u>made</u> of. Density <u>doesn't vary</u> with <u>size</u> or <u>shape</u>.

You Can Measure the Density of Solids and Liquids

1) To <u>measure</u> the density of a substance, measure the <u>mass</u> and <u>volume</u> of a sample of the substance and use the formula above.

2) You can measure the <u>mass</u> of a solid or liquid using a <u>mass balance</u> (see page 103).

3) To measure the volume of a <u>liquid</u>, you can just pour it into a <u>measuring cylinder</u>.

4) <u>1 ml = 1 cm³</u>. If you need to convert a volume into other units, e.g. m³, you get the <u>scaling factor</u> by <u>cubing</u> the scaling factor that you'd use for converting the <u>distance</u> units. For example, to convert 50 cm³ into m³, you need to divide by 100³ = 1 000 000 (as there are 100 cm in 1 m). So <u>50 cm³</u> = 50 ÷ 1 000 000 = <u>5 × 10⁻⁵ m³</u>.

5) If you want to measure the volume of a <u>solid cuboid</u>, measure its <u>length</u>, <u>width</u>, and <u>height</u>, then <u>multiply</u> them together. The volume of <u>any prism</u> is the <u>area</u> of its <u>base</u> multiplied by its <u>height</u>.

6) An object <u>submerged</u> in water will displace a volume of water <u>equal</u> to its <u>own volume</u>. You can use this to find the volume of <u>any object</u>. It is particularly useful in finding the volume of objects with <u>irregular shapes</u> which can't be easily calculated mathematically. You can do this, for example, using a <u>eureka (Archimedes) can</u>:

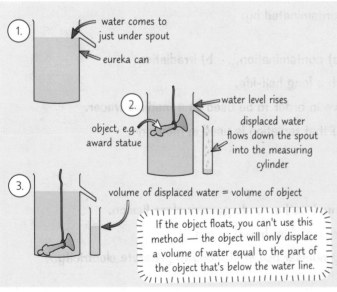

1. water comes to just under spout
eureka can

2. water level rises
displaced water flows down the spout into the measuring cylinder
object, e.g. award statue

3. volume of displaced water = volume of object

If the object floats, you can't use this method — the object will only displace a volume of water equal to the part of the object that's below the water line.

PRACTICAL

1) You need the eureka can to be filled so that the water level is <u>just under</u> the spout. The best way to do this is to <u>slightly over-fill</u> the can then let the extra water <u>drain away</u>.

2) Place a measuring cylinder under the spout, then <u>gently lower</u> your object in the can, using a <u>thin</u>, <u>strong thread</u>. The displaced water will start to <u>come out</u> of the spout.

3) Wait for the spout to <u>stop dripping</u>, then measure the <u>volume</u> of water collected in the <u>cylinder</u>. This is the volume of water displaced by the object, which is equal to the <u>volume of the object</u>.

4) Repeat three times and calculate a <u>mean</u>.

I'm feeling a bit dense after that lot...

Converting between volume units catches people out all the time, so be careful.

Q1   Describe an experiment to calculate the density of an irregular solid object.   [4 marks]

Q2   An object has a mass of 4.5 × 10⁻² kg and a volume of 75 cm³. Calculate its density in kg/m³.   [3 marks]

The Particle Model of Matter

According to the particle model, everything's made of tiny little balls. The table, this book, your Gran...

The Particle Model is a Way of Modelling Matter

The particle model of matter explains how the particles (atoms and molecules) that make up matter behave.

1) In the particle model, matter is made up of tiny particles. You can think of them as tiny balls.

2) There's nothing in between the tiny balls — they make up all matter (e.g. air is made up of tiny particles, and in between there is nothing).

3) A substance is made up of identical particles, and particles of any other substance have different masses.

4) There are attractive forces between the particles. The size of the force differs for different substances.

5) The particles are always moving — how much they can move depends on what state they are in.

The particle model is a key example of how scientists use models to explain observations (see page 91).

The Particle Model Explains the Properties of the States of Matter...

The three states of matter are solid (e.g. ice), liquid (e.g. water) and gas (e.g. water vapour). The particles of a substance in each state are the same — only the arrangement and energy of the particles are different.

SOLIDS — strong forces of attraction hold the particles close together in a fixed, regular arrangement. The particles don't have much energy so they can only vibrate about their fixed positions and can't move away from neighbouring particles. The density is generally highest in this state as the particles are closest together.

LIQUIDS — there are weaker forces of attraction between the particles. The particles are close together, but can slide past each other, and form irregular arrangements. They have more energy than the particles in a solid — they can vibrate and jostle around in random directions at low speeds. Liquids are generally less dense than solids.

GASES — there are no noticeable forces of attraction between the particles. The particles have more energy than in liquids and solids — they're free to move and travel in random directions at high speeds. Gases are generally less dense than liquids — they have low densities.

...and the Effects of Heating a System

1) The particles in a system vibrate or move around — they have energy in their kinetic energy stores.

2) They also have energy in their potential energy stores due to their positions.

3) The energy stored in a system is stored by its particles. The internal energy of a system is the total energy that its particles have in their kinetic and potential energy stores.

4) Experiments combined with mathematical analysis have shown a link between the temperature of a substance and the amount of energy in the kinetic energy stores of its particles — the higher the temperature, the higher the average energy. The particle model can explain this.

5) Heating the system transfers energy to its particles, increasing the internal energy.

6) As the substance is heated, the particles gain energy in their kinetic stores and move faster. The hotter a substance is, the more its particles can move around.

7) If the system is heated to a high enough temperature, the substance will change state (see page 79). During a change in state, energy is transferred by heating to the particles' potential energy stores instead of their kinetic energy stores.

8) So heating a system will either lead to a change in temperature or a change in state.

Particles can't be trusted — they make everything up...

The particle model explains a lot of what's coming up, so make sure you know it inside out.

Q1   Describe how the density of solids, liquids and gases generally varies and explain why this is.   [3 marks]

More on the Particle Model of Matter

The particle model explains all sorts... so why stop after just one page? Read on for more particle model fun...

In a Change of State, Mass is Conserved But Density Changes

1) When you heat a liquid, it boils (or evaporates) and becomes a gas. When you heat a solid, it melts and becomes a liquid. These are both changes of state.

2) The state can also change due to cooling.

3) The changes of state are:

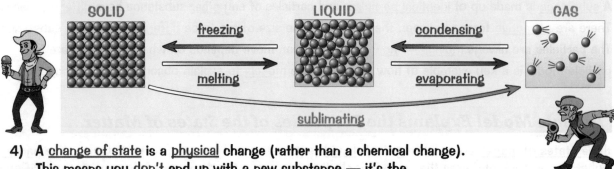

4) A change of state is a physical change (rather than a chemical change). This means you don't end up with a new substance — it's the same substance as you started with, just in a different form.

5) If you reverse a change of state (e.g. freeze a substance that has been melted), the substance will return to its original form and get back its original properties.

6) The number of particles doesn't change — they're just arranged differently. This means mass is conserved — none of it is lost when the substance changes state.

7) Although the mass stays the same, the space that the particles take up (their volume) changes. Since density = mass ÷ volume (p.77) this means the density changes.

8) Generally, the change in density is very small between a solid and a liquid, but very large between a liquid and a gas. This is why a small volume of liquid produces a large volume of gas.

The Particle Model Explains Gas Pressure Too

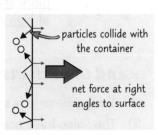

particles collide with the container

net force at right angles to surface

1) As gas particles move about, they randomly bang into each other and whatever else gets in the way, like the walls of their container.

2) Particles are light, but they still have a mass and so a momentum (p.57).

3) When the particles collide with something they change direction, and so change momentum. This exerts a force on the thing they collided with.

4) All these collisions cause a net force at right angles to the inside surface of the container.

5) The force per unit area is the pressure, so the gas exerts a pressure on its container.

6) As you know from the previous page, increasing the temperature of a substance makes its particles move faster. Faster particles exert a larger net force on their container for two reasons:

   - As the particles are travelling faster, they hit the sides of the container more often in a given amount of time.

   - Faster particles also have a larger momentum. This means the change in momentum, and so the force exerted, is larger when they collide with the container.

7) A larger force means a larger pressure, so as temperature goes up, so does pressure. Temperature and pressure for a gas at a constant volume are proportional to each other.

Gas particles need to watch where they're going...

Remember, the higher the temperature of a gas, the faster the particles travel, and the higher the pressure. Simple.

Q1   Explain what happens to the pressure of a gas in a sealed container with a fixed volume
      when the particles move slower due to a decrease in temperature.   [3 marks]

Specific Heat Capacity

The <u>energy needed</u> to <u>change the temperature</u> is <u>different</u> for <u>every material</u>...

Heating and Mechanical Work Done are the Same as 'Energy Transferred'

1) In the 18th and 19th centuries, a number of scientists noticed that <u>heating</u> and <u>mechanical work done</u> were both forms of <u>energy transfer</u>. Joule devised experiments that showed that the <u>same amount</u> of <u>mechanical work</u> would always produce the <u>same increase</u> in temperature in a given substance.

> In an electric kettle, energy is transferred <u>electrically</u> from the mains to the <u>thermal energy store</u> of the kettle's <u>heating element</u>. It is then transferred <u>by heating</u> to the <u>thermal energy store</u> of the water (the <u>kinetic energy stores</u> of the particles) — the water's <u>temperature</u> rises.

> When an object <u>slows down</u>, there is a <u>resultant force</u> on it (see page 56). Energy is transferred <u>mechanically</u> (<u>work is done</u> by the force) from the <u>kinetic energy stores</u> of the object to its <u>thermal energy store</u>. This causes a <u>rise in the temperature</u> of the object. Similarly, if an object hits an <u>obstacle</u>, the object (and the obstacle) <u>heats</u> up (p.67).

2) An <u>increase</u> in temperature of a substance is <u>always</u> caused by <u>energy being transferred</u>. It can be transferred by <u>burning a fuel</u>, using an <u>electric heater</u>, or doing <u>mechanical work</u> on the substance. The <u>size</u> of the <u>temperature rise</u> depends on the <u>mass</u> and <u>material</u> of the substance and the <u>energy supplied</u>.

3) It takes <u>more energy</u> to <u>increase the temperature</u> of some materials than others. These materials also <u>release</u> more energy when they <u>cool down</u>. They <u>store</u> more energy for a <u>given</u> temperature change.

4) The <u>energy stored</u> by <u>1 kg</u> of a material for a <u>1 °C</u> temperature rise is its <u>specific heat capacity</u>.

$$\text{Change in Internal Energy (J)} = \text{Mass (kg)} \times \text{Specific Heat Capacity (J/kg°C)} \times \text{Change in Temperature (°C)}$$

5) You could be asked to find the energy transferred <u>to</u> or <u>from</u> a system that's <u>changed temperature</u> using this equation. The energy transferred will be equal to the change in the <u>internal energy</u> of the system.

> *This equation can only be used if there's no change of state.*

You can Find the Specific Heat Capacity of a Substance | PRACTICAL |

You can use this experiment to find the specific heat capacity of a <u>liquid</u> or a <u>solid</u>.

1) Use a <u>mass balance</u> to measure the <u>mass</u> of your substance.

2) Set up the experiment shown below. Make sure the <u>joulemeter</u> reads <u>zero</u>.

> *The joulemeter measures the energy supplied.*

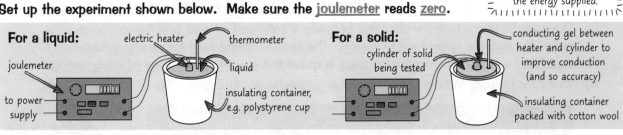

For a liquid: joulemeter, electric heater, thermometer, liquid, to power supply, insulating container, e.g. polystyrene cup

For a solid: cylinder of solid being tested, conducting gel between heater and cylinder to improve conduction (and so accuracy), insulating container packed with cotton wool

3) Make sure that the apparatus is set up <u>correctly</u> and used <u>safely</u> — e.g. make sure not to <u>burn</u> yourself when handling the heater and that there is no chance of the liquid <u>spilling</u> out of the polystyrene cup.

4) Measure the <u>temperature</u> of the substance you're investigating, then turn on the power. Keep an eye on the <u>thermometer</u>. When the temperature has increased by e.g. <u>ten degrees</u>, stop the experiment and record the <u>energy</u> on the joulemeter and the <u>increase in temperature</u>.

> *You could also use a voltmeter and ammeter instead of a joulemeter — time how long the heater is on for, then calculate the energy supplied (see p.33).*

5) Use your results to calculate the specific heat capacity of your substance. <u>Repeat</u> the whole experiment at least <u>three</u> times, then calculate an <u>average</u> specific heat capacity (see p.95).

I wish I had a high specific fact capacity...

Make sure you fully understand that equation — it's a bit of a tricky one.

Q1 If a metal has a specific heat capacity of 420 J/kg°C, calculate how much the temperature of a 0.20 kg block of the metal will increase by if 1680 J of energy are supplied to it. [3 marks]

Specific Latent Heat

If you heat up a pan of water on the stove, the water never gets any hotter than 100 °C. You can <u>carry on heating it up</u>, but the <u>temperature won't rise</u>. How come, you say? It's all to do with <u>latent heat</u>...

You Need to Put In Energy to Break Bonds Between Particles

1) Remember, when you <u>heat</u> a solid or liquid and the temperature rises, you're transferring <u>energy</u> to the kinetic energy stores of the particles in the substance, making the particles <u>vibrate</u> or <u>move faster</u>.

2) If you heat a substance <u>enough</u>, it will reach its <u>melting</u> or <u>boiling point</u>, and start to <u>change state</u>.

3) When a substance is <u>melting</u> or <u>boiling</u>, energy is transferred to the potential energy stores of the particles as the energy is used to <u>break bonds between particles</u> and move the particles <u>further apart</u>. So the temperature <u>doesn't</u> change but the <u>internal energy increases</u>.

4) There are <u>flat spots</u> on the heating graph at the <u>melting</u> and <u>boiling points</u> where energy is being transferred but the temperature does not change.

5) When a substance is <u>condensing</u> or <u>freezing</u>, bonds are <u>forming</u> between particles, which <u>releases</u> energy. This means the <u>internal energy decreases</u> but the <u>temperature doesn't go down</u> until all the substance has turned into a liquid (condensing) or a solid (freezing).

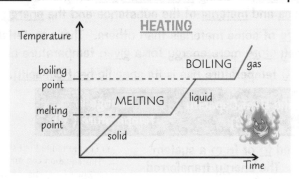

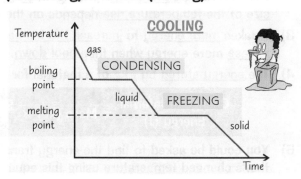

Specific Latent Heat is the Energy Needed to Change State

1) The <u>specific latent heat</u> of a <u>change of state</u> for a substance is the <u>change of energy</u> when <u>1 kg</u> of the substance <u>changes state without changing its temperature</u> (i.e. the substance has got to be at the right temperature already).

2) Specific latent heat is <u>different</u> for <u>different materials</u>, and for different <u>changes of state</u>.

3) The specific latent heat for changing between a solid and a liquid (melting or freezing) is called the <u>specific latent heat of fusion</u>. The specific latent heat for changing between a liquid and a gas (boiling or condensing) is called the <u>specific latent heat of vaporisation</u>.

4) There's a <u>formula</u> to help you with all the <u>calculations</u>. And here it is:

> Be careful not to get this confused with specific heat capacity (p.80).

$$\text{Energy to cause a Change of State (J)} = \text{Mass (kg)} \times \text{Specific Latent Heat (J/kg)}$$

this is specific latent heat

EXAMPLE: The specific latent heat of vaporisation for water is 2.26×10^6 J/kg. 2.825×10^6 J of energy is used to boil dry a pan of water at 100 °C. What was the mass of water in the pan?

Energy to cause a change of state = mass × specific latent heat,
so mass = energy to cause a change of state ÷ specific latent heat
= $2.825 \times 10^6 \div 2.26 \times 10^6 = 1.25$ kg

> You came across standard form on page 49, e.g. $2.26 \times 10^6 = 2\,260\,000$.

Breaking Bonds — Blofeld never quite manages it...

Remember, whilst there's a change of state, there's no change in temperature.

Q1 Sketch a graph showing how the temperature of a sample of water will change over time as it is constantly heated from –5 °C to 105 °C. [3 marks]

Pressure

You've seen why gases <u>exert a pressure</u> on any container they are in.
In fact, <u>all fluids</u> do this, and you need to know all about this pressure and what can cause it to <u>change</u>.

Pressure is the Force per Unit Area

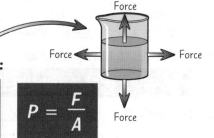
A fluid is either a liquid or a gas.

1) <u>Fluids</u> are substances that can '<u>flow</u>' because their particles are able to <u>move around</u>.
2) Fluids exert a <u>pressure</u> on any surface they are in contact with due to <u>particle collisions</u>.
3) The <u>pressure</u> of a fluid means a <u>force</u> is exerted at <u>right angles</u> (<u>normal</u>) to any <u>surface</u> in contact with the fluid.
4) You can calculate the <u>pressure</u> at the <u>surface</u> of a fluid by using:

$$\text{Pressure (Pa)} = \frac{\text{Force normal to a surface (N)}}{\text{Area of that surface (m}^2)} \qquad P = \frac{F}{A}$$

5) An object <u>submerged</u> in a <u>fluid</u> also experiences a force due to the <u>fluid pressure</u>. The forces act at <u>right angles</u> to <u>every surface</u> of the object.

Gas Pressure and Volume are Inversely Proportional

1) You saw on p.79 that the <u>pressure</u> of a <u>gas</u> depends on the number of <u>collisions</u> in a certain time with the container walls, and the <u>momentum</u> of the particles (and so the <u>temperature</u> of a gas is <u>proportional</u> to the <u>pressure</u>).
2) If <u>temperature is constant</u>, increasing the <u>volume</u> of the container means the particles get <u>more spread out</u> and hit the walls of the container <u>less often</u>. The gas <u>pressure decreases</u>. And if you <u>decrease the volume</u>, the <u>pressure increases</u>.
3) Pressure and volume are <u>inversely proportional</u> — when volume goes <u>up</u>, pressure goes <u>down</u> (and when <u>volume</u> goes <u>down</u>, <u>pressure</u> goes <u>up</u>). For a gas of <u>fixed mass</u> at a <u>constant temperature</u>, the relationship is:

> pressure × volume = constant

4) This equation <u>only works</u> for a <u>fixed mass</u> of gas at a <u>constant temperature</u>. When a gas is <u>compressed</u>, for example in a bicycle pump, <u>mechanical work</u> is done on the gas. Energy is transferred to the <u>internal energy</u> of the gas. If the change in volume is <u>too fast</u>, the gas doesn't have chance to <u>transfer</u> energy away to the environment, so the temperature increases — '<u>pressure × volume = constant</u>' will not be true.

A Change in External Pressure can Cause a Change in Volume

1) The <u>pressure</u> of a gas causes a <u>net outwards force</u> at right angles to the surface of its container.
2) There is also a force on the <u>outside</u> of the container due to the pressure of the gas <u>around it</u>.
3) If a container can easily <u>change its size</u> (e.g. a balloon), then any change in these pressures will cause the container to <u>compress</u> or <u>expand</u>, due to the overall force.

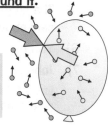

E.g. if a <u>helium balloon</u> is released, it rises. Atmospheric pressure <u>decreases</u> with height (p.83), so the pressure <u>outside</u> the balloon <u>decreases</u>. This causes the balloon to <u>expand</u> until the pressure inside <u>drops</u> to the same as the atmospheric pressure.

'Under Pressure — dun dun dun dundundun dun'...

Lots of facts to get into your head here I'm afraid, but you can do it, I believe in you.

Q1   Explain why compressing a gas at a constant temperature results in an increase in gas pressure.   [2 marks]

Atmospheric Pressure and Liquid Pressure

Just like the looming threat of exams, the air in the atmosphere puts <u>pressure</u> on us all the time.

Liquid Pressure Depends on Density and Depth

1) Liquids <u>can't be compressed</u> (or not very much), so their <u>density is the same</u> everywhere (unlike gases).

2) Liquid pressure <u>increases with depth</u>, due to the <u>weight</u> of the 'column' of liquid <u>directly above</u> the object.

3) The <u>more dense</u> a given liquid is, the <u>more particles</u> it has in a certain space, and so the more often particles will <u>collide</u>. A more <u>dense liquid</u> also has more particles in a <u>column</u> above a certain point, meaning a <u>larger weight</u> above that point. So a <u>higher density</u> means a <u>higher pressure</u> at a given depth.

4) The <u>pressure due to the liquid</u> at a certain point can be found using:

> pressure (Pa) = density (kg/m^3) × gravitational field strength (N/kg) × depth (m)

5) On Earth, the <u>gravitational field strength</u> (or g) is equal to about <u>10 N/kg</u>.

6) As <u>pressure</u> in a liquid <u>increases with depth</u>, the force <u>pushing upwards</u> on the bottom of an object due to the liquid pressure is <u>greater</u> than the force <u>pushing down</u> on the top of the object.

> You might also see this equation as 'pressure due to a column of liquid = height of column × density × g', where the 'height' of the column is equal to the depth of the object.

7) This causes an overall <u>upwards force</u>.

8) The upwards force acting on an object is <u>equal</u> to the <u>weight of fluid</u> it has <u>displaced</u>. If this force is <u>equal</u> to the <u>object's weight</u>, then the object will <u>float</u>. If it is <u>less</u> than the object's weight, it will <u>sink</u>.

9) An object will <u>float</u> if it is <u>less dense</u> than the liquid it is in — it displaces a volume of water with a weight <u>equal</u> to its <u>own weight</u> before it's <u>completely submerged</u>.

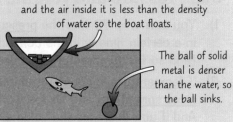

The combined density of the boat, its cargo and the air inside it is less than the density of water so the boat floats.

The ball of solid metal is denser than the water, so the ball sinks.

10) If an object is <u>more dense</u> than the liquid, it <u>sinks</u>. It displaces a volume of liquid equal to its volume, but that <u>weighs less</u> than the object. So the <u>weight of the object</u> is always <u>greater</u> than the <u>upwards force</u>.

11) This upwards force is also the reason that the <u>apparent weight</u> (the weight if measured in that substance) of an object is <u>less</u> in <u>water</u> than in <u>air</u>.

Atmospheric Pressure is All Around Us All the Time

1) The Earth's atmosphere stretches to roughly 100 km above the Earth's surface. That's <u>a lot of air</u>.

2) This air exerts '<u>atmospheric pressure</u>' at <u>right angles</u> to the <u>surface</u> of any object that's in it. This pressure acts in <u>all directions</u> and it's <u>equal in every direction</u>.

3) The <u>lower</u> you are, the <u>more atmosphere</u> there is above you, so the <u>higher</u> the atmospheric pressure is. If you <u>gain</u> height, there's <u>less atmosphere</u> above you, so the atmospheric pressure <u>decreases</u>.

4) The density of the atmosphere gets <u>higher</u> the <u>closer</u> you are to <u>sea level</u>. This is because the <u>weight</u> of the air above pushes down on the air below it, <u>compressing it</u> — the closer to sea level you are, the more air there is <u>above</u> you, so the more the air around you is <u>compressed</u>.

5) The <u>higher density</u> lower down also contributes to a <u>higher atmospheric pressure</u> — as you saw above, a <u>higher density</u> means <u>collisions more often</u>, and so a higher pressure.

6) You can <u>assume</u> the <u>density</u> of the atmosphere is <u>uniform at a given height</u>.

7) John <u>Dalton</u>'s studies of atmospheric pressures led to him noticing that gases could only be combined in <u>certain proportions</u>. This <u>quantitative</u> discovery helped develop his <u>atomic theory</u>, in which he said that all atoms of an element are the <u>same</u>. This theory became the basis for the <u>particle model of matter</u>.

This stuff really floats my boat...

The floating and sinking stuff is really hard to get your head around, so give this page another read...

Q1   A submarine dives from a depth of 120 m to a depth of 320 m. Given that the density of water is 1000 kg/m^3, calculate the increase in liquid pressure acting on the submarine. [3 marks]

Forces and Elasticity

Elasticity involves lots of physics and pinging elastic bands at people. Ok, maybe not that last one.

A Deformation can be Elastic or Plastic

1) When you <u>apply forces</u> to an object it can be <u>stretched</u>, <u>compressed</u> or <u>twisted</u> — this is <u>deformation</u>.

2) To <u>deform</u> an object, you need <u>at least two forces</u>. Think of a <u>spring</u> — if you just pull <u>one end</u> of it, and there's <u>no force</u> at the other end, you'll just <u>pull the spring along</u> rather than stretching it.

3) If an object <u>returns to its original shape</u> after the forces are removed, you can say the object is <u>elastic</u> and it has been <u>elastically deformed</u>. If the object <u>doesn't</u> return to its original shape when you remove the forces, the forces were <u>too large</u>. The object has become <u>plastic</u>, and has been <u>plastically deformed</u>.

4) You can explain both <u>elastic</u> and <u>plastic deformation</u> with the <u>particle model of matter</u> (see p.78). Woo.

5) <u>Solids</u> are held in <u>fixed shapes</u> due to the forces between their particles. During <u>elastic</u> deformation the <u>separation between particles</u> changes so the <u>forces</u> between them also change. However, once the applied force has been <u>removed</u>, the particles <u>return</u> to their <u>original positions</u> within the substance.

6) In <u>plastic</u> deformation, the <u>separation</u> and <u>forces</u> between particles change. However, the applied forces are <u>too large</u>, so when they're removed the particles <u>don't</u> return to their <u>original positions</u>. The object is <u>permanently</u> deformed.

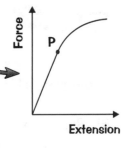

The Relationship Between Extension and Force can be Linear or Non-Linear

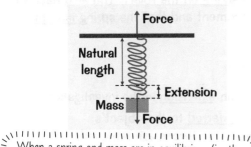

1) If a material is supported at the top and a mass is attached to the bottom, it <u>stretches</u>.

2) In some cases, e.g. a spring, this relationship is <u>linear</u>. The <u>extension</u> (or compression) of the stretched material is <u>directly proportional</u> to the load or <u>force</u> applied.

3) The relationship between the extension of a material and the force is called <u>Hooke's law</u>:

When a spring and mass are in equilibrium (i.e. the spring isn't stretching any further), the force applied on the spring (the weight of the mass) is equal to the force exerted by the spring upwards on the mass.

$$\text{force exerted by a spring (N)} = \text{extension (m)} \times \text{spring constant (N/m)}$$

$$F = x \times k$$

4) The <u>spring constant</u> depends on the <u>material</u> that you are stretching — a <u>stiffer</u> spring has a <u>greater</u> spring constant.

5) <u>Hooke's law</u> also works for <u>compression</u> (the difference between the <u>natural</u> and <u>compressed</u> lengths).

6) In other cases, the relationship is <u>non-linear</u>, e.g. <u>rubber bands</u>. Force is <u>not proportional</u> to extension.

7) Most objects behave <u>linearly</u> up to a point, and then start to behave <u>non-linearly</u>.

8) The graph shows <u>force against extension</u> for an object being stretched.

9) Up to point P, the graph is a <u>straight line</u> and <u>Hooke's law</u> applies.

10) The <u>gradient</u> of the straight line is <u>equal</u> to the <u>spring constant</u> of the object — the <u>larger</u> the spring constant, the <u>steeper</u> the gradient.

11) <u>Beyond</u> point P, the object <u>no longer</u> obeys <u>Hooke's law</u>. The relationship between force and extension has become <u>non-linear</u>, so the force-extension graph <u>curves</u> and the spring <u>stretches more</u> for each <u>unit increase in force</u>.

It's important to remember that being '<u>elastic</u>' doesn't mean an object obeys <u>Hooke's law</u>. <u>Rubber bands</u> are <u>elastic objects</u>. They return to their <u>original shape</u> when released. But they <u>DON'T</u> obey Hooke's Law.

I hope this stuff isn't stretching you too much...

The gradient of a force-extension graph for a material obeying Hooke's law is equal to its spring constant.

Q1   A spring has a natural length of 0.16 m. When a force of 3.0 N is applied to the spring, it stretches linearly and its length becomes 0.20 m. Calculate the spring constant of the spring.   [3 marks]

 **Investigating Hooke's Law**

More springs here, but now you actually get to do some experiments with them. Hip hip hooray.

You can Investigate the Extension of a Spring

1) Hang your spring from a clamp stand, as shown in the diagram (without the masses, but with the hook the masses hang from), then measure the spring's length using the ruler — this is the spring's original length.

2) Weigh your masses and add them one at a time to the hook hanging from the spring, so the force on the spring increases.

3) After each mass is added, measure the new length of the spring, then calculate the extension: → extension = new length − original length

4) Plot a graph of force (weight) against extension using your results and draw a line of best fit.

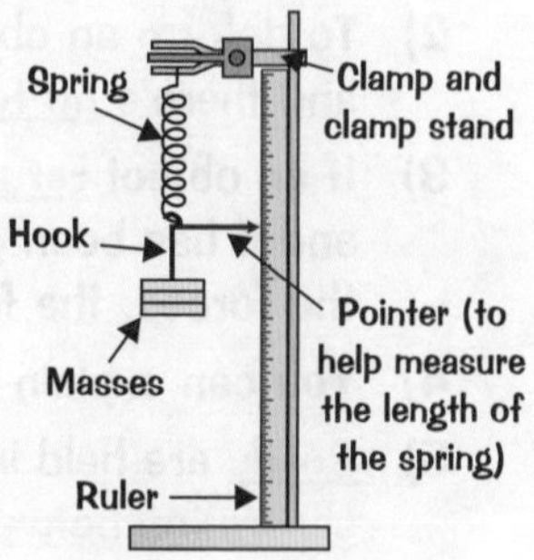

5) A straight line of best fit is where the spring obeys Hooke's law and the gradient = spring constant (see page 84). If you've loaded the spring with enough masses, the graph will start to curve.

6) Make sure you carry out the experiment safely. You should be standing up so you can get out of the way quickly if the masses fall, and wearing safety goggles to protect your eyes in case the spring snaps.

When measuring the length of the spring, you should move yourself so the pointer on the hook is at eye level. Otherwise it could look like it is next to a different marking on the ruler. You also need to make sure the ruler is exactly vertical to get an accurate measurement and that the spring isn't moving.

(Diagram labels: Spring, Clamp and clamp stand, Hook, Masses, Pointer (to help measure the length of the spring), Ruler)

You Can Find the Work Done in Stretching a Spring

1) You can also find the work done in stretching the spring by a certain extension in the investigation above.

2) When a force deforms an object, work is done and energy is transferred to the object's elastic potential energy store. This energy can be recovered when the forces are removed.

3) For linear relationships, all the energy transferred is stored by the object, so work done = energy stored.

4) The equation for the energy stored in a stretched spring (if it obeys Hooke's Law) is:

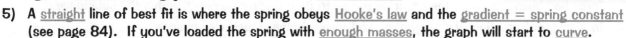

$$\text{energy stored in a stretched spring} = \tfrac{1}{2} \times \text{spring constant} \times (\text{extension})^2$$
$$\text{(J)} \qquad\qquad \text{(N/m)} \qquad\qquad \text{(m)}^2$$

5) This also works for objects obeying Hooke's law that are being compressed. Just use the compression in place of the extension in the equation.

$$E = \tfrac{1}{2} \times k \times x^2$$

EXAMPLE: A spring has a spring constant of 32 N/m. Calculate the work done on the spring if it is stretched linearly from 0.40 m to 0.45 m.

Remember: work done = energy transferred.

extension = new length − original length = 0.45 − 0.40 = 0.05 m

energy stored in a stretched spring = 0.5 × spring constant × (extension)^2 = 0.5 × 32 × 0.05^2 = 0.04 J

6) So, back to that investigation above — to find the work done or energy transferred to the spring, you can use the force-extension graph that you plotted. The work done is equal to the area under your graph. This is true for any object that is deformed linearly.

7) You can find this area by calculating the area of the triangle or by counting squares (p.53).

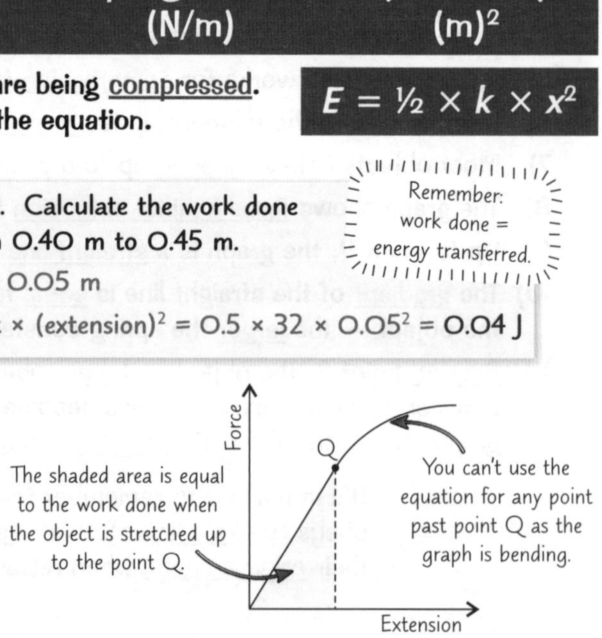

The shaded area is equal to the work done when the object is stretched up to the point Q.

You can't use the equation for any point past point Q as the graph is bending.

(Graph labels: Force, Extension, Q)

Tell your parents you need to buy a trampoline for your revision...

More energy transfers — you'd better get used to them, they'll always rear their ugly head in Physics.

Q1 A 1.2 m long spring (k = 54 N/m) extends linearly to 1.3 m. Calculate the work done. [3 marks]

The Solar System and Orbits

The <u>Sun</u> is the centre of our <u>solar system</u>. It's <u>orbited</u> by <u>eight planets</u>, along with a bunch of other objects.

Our Solar System has One Star — The Sun

The <u>solar system</u> is all the <u>stuff</u> that <u>orbits our Sun</u>. This includes things like:

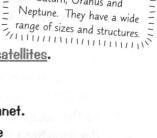

The planets are: Mercury, Venus, Earth, Mars, Jupiter, Saturn, Uranus and Neptune. They have a wide range of sizes and structures.

1) <u>Planets</u> — these are large objects that <u>orbit a star</u>. They also have to be large enough to have "<u>cleared their neighbourhoods</u>". This means that their gravity is strong enough to have <u>pulled in</u> any nearby objects apart from their <u>satellites</u>. All the planets in the solar system orbit the Sun in the <u>same direction</u>.

2) <u>Minor planets</u> (which include 'comets' and 'asteroids') — like Halley's comet. These are objects that orbit stars, but don't meet all of the rules for being a planet.

3) <u>Artificial satellites</u> are satellites that humans have built. They generally orbit the <u>Earth</u>. A satellite is just an object that orbits a second, <u>more massive</u> object.

4) <u>Moons</u> — these orbit <u>planets</u>. Most planets in the solar system have at least one. They're a type of <u>natural satellite</u> (i.e. they're not man-made).

Our solar system is a tiny part of the <u>Milky Way galaxy</u>. This is a <u>massive</u> collection of <u>billions</u> of stars that are all held together by gravity.

You are here.

Gravity Provides the Force That Creates Orbits

The planets move around the Sun in <u>almost circular</u> orbits (the same goes for <u>moons</u> or <u>artificial satellites</u> orbiting <u>planets</u>). The force that makes this happen is provided by the <u>gravitational interaction</u> (gravity) between the <u>Sun</u> and the planet (or between the <u>planet</u> and a <u>satellite</u>).

1) A <u>planet</u> that's moving <u>near</u> to a star will feel a <u>gravitational force</u> towards it.

2) This force would cause the planet to just <u>travel</u> towards whatever it is orbiting, but as the planet is <u>already moving</u>, it just causes a change in direction.

3) Although its speed remains the same, its <u>direction</u>, and so <u>velocity</u>, is <u>constantly changing</u>.

4) The planet <u>keeps accelerating</u> towards what it's orbiting but the <u>instantaneous velocity</u> (which is at a <u>right angle</u> to the <u>acceleration</u>) keeps it travelling in a <u>circle</u>.

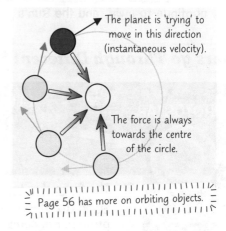

The planet is 'trying' to move in this direction (instantaneous velocity).

The force is always towards the centre of the circle.

Page 56 has more on orbiting objects.

The Force Needed for a Stable Orbit Depends on Orbital Speed and Radius

1) For an object in orbit, the <u>greater</u> its <u>speed</u>, or the <u>smaller</u> the <u>orbital radius</u>, the <u>greater</u> the <u>force</u> needed to keep it in a <u>stable orbit</u>. A <u>stable orbit</u> just means the object is orbiting with a constant speed.

2) So a planet moving at a <u>high speed</u> will need to be <u>closer</u> to a star (where the force of gravity is larger) than a slower-moving planet in order to be in a <u>stable orbit</u>.

3) If the <u>speed</u> of an orbiting object changes, the <u>orbital radius</u> also changes.

4) You <u>might expect</u> an object which <u>slows down</u> to move out to an orbit with a larger radius. But that's <u>NOT</u> what happens. Instead, the orbiting object will be <u>pulled</u> into an orbit with a <u>smaller orbital radius</u> — this causes the <u>speed</u> of the object to <u>increase</u>.

5) The opposite happens to an orbiting object that <u>speeds up</u> — it ends up in an orbit with a <u>larger radius</u>.

Revision's hard work — you've got to plan et...

Make sure you know what orbits what and how to tell a moon from a planet. Then have a go at these questions.

Q1 Two planets are in stable circular orbits round the same star. Planet 1 travels slower than Planet 2. State whether Planet 1 or Planet 2 is closer to the star they are orbiting. [1 mark]

The Formation of the Solar System

As it turns out, the solar system has gone through some <u>traumatic stages</u> in its life — just like teenagers.

The Particle Model Can Explain the Formation of the Solar System

You've seen on page 82 that doing <u>work</u> to <u>compress a gas</u> can lead to a rise in temperature. This can explain how the solar system we know and love was originally <u>formed</u>.

1) Our solar system was formed from one big <u>swirling</u> cloud of <u>dust and gas</u>.

2) All parts of the dust and gas <u>attracted</u> all other parts due to <u>gravity</u>, so over a long period of time, the force of <u>gravity</u> brought the gas and dust together.

3) As the dust and gas <u>collapsed</u> towards the centre of the cloud, the <u>density</u> of the cloud increased, particularly at the <u>centre</u>.

4) Areas of higher density had a <u>greater</u> gravitational pull, so they got <u>denser</u> and <u>denser</u>.

5) The force of gravity did <u>work</u> to <u>compress</u> the dust and gas in this way. In terms of the particle model, energy was <u>transferred</u> to the <u>kinetic energy stores</u> of the particles, increasing the <u>temperature</u> and <u>pressure</u>, so the denser regions also got <u>hotter</u> and <u>hotter</u>.

6) The region at the very <u>centre</u> of the cloud became so <u>dense</u> and <u>hot</u> that it eventually formed the <u>Sun</u> (see below).

7) Other areas of <u>high density</u> further out also got <u>denser</u> and <u>hotter</u>. Eventually, the dust and gas was compressed together enough to form <u>planets</u>. They <u>orbit</u> the Sun as any leftover bits of the cloud continue to <u>swirl</u>, and the Sun's <u>gravity</u> holds them all in place.

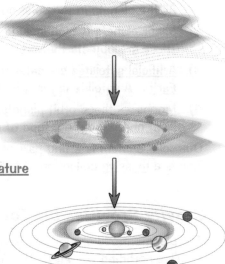

Stars go Through Different Stages During their Formation

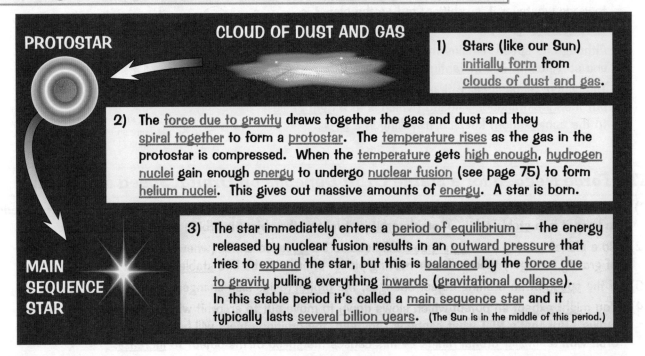

PROTOSTAR

CLOUD OF DUST AND GAS

1) Stars (like our Sun) <u>initially form</u> from <u>clouds of dust and gas</u>.

2) The <u>force due to gravity</u> draws together the gas and dust and they <u>spiral together</u> to form a <u>protostar</u>. The <u>temperature rises</u> as the gas in the protostar is compressed. When the <u>temperature</u> gets <u>high enough</u>, <u>hydrogen nuclei</u> gain enough <u>energy</u> to undergo <u>nuclear fusion</u> (see page 75) to form <u>helium nuclei</u>. This gives out massive amounts of <u>energy</u>. A star is born.

3) The star immediately enters a <u>period of equilibrium</u> — the energy released by nuclear fusion results in an <u>outward pressure</u> that tries to <u>expand</u> the star, but this is <u>balanced</u> by the <u>force due to gravity</u> pulling everything <u>inwards</u> (<u>gravitational collapse</u>). In this stable period it's called a <u>main sequence star</u> and it typically lasts <u>several billion years</u>. (The Sun is in the middle of this period.)

MAIN SEQUENCE STAR

The formation of stars — hot stuff...

Pretty neat, seeing how stars like our Sun — which all of us rely on — were made all those years ago. Lots of details to learn here, so make sure you've got a handle on them all before you move on.

Q1   Describe how the Sun was formed from a cloud of dust and gas.   [4 marks]

Q2   Explain, using the particle model, why the temperature of a star increases as it starts to form.   [2 marks]

Red-Shift and Big Bang

'How it all began' is a tricky question that we just can't answer. Our best guess at the minute is the Big Bang.

The Universe Seems to Be Expanding

The Universe is enormous. Yet, as big as the Universe already is, it looks like it's getting even bigger. The thousands of millions of galaxies in the Universe seem to be moving away from each other. There's good evidence for this...

1) When we look at light from the most distant galaxies, we find that the wavelengths are all longer than they should be — they're shifted towards the red end of the spectrum. This is called red-shift.

> You can think of the light wave 'stretching out' as the source moves away from us.

2) This suggests the source of the light is moving away from us. Measurements of the red-shift indicate that these distant galaxies are moving away from us (receding) very quickly — and it's the same result whichever direction you look in.

3) More distant galaxies have greater red-shifts than nearer ones. This means that more distant galaxies are moving away faster than nearer ones.

4) The inescapable conclusion appears to be that the whole universe (space itself) is expanding.

> Imagine a balloon covered with pompoms. As you blow into the balloon, it stretches. The pompoms move further away from each other.
>
> The balloon represents the Universe and each pompom is a galaxy. As time goes on, space stretches and expands, moving the galaxies away from each other.
>
> This is a simple model (balloons only stretch so far, and there would be galaxies 'inside' the balloon too) but it shows how the expansion of space makes it look like galaxies are moving away from us.

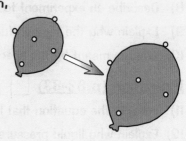

This Evidence Suggests the Universe Started with a Bang

So all the galaxies are moving away from each other at great speed — suggesting something must have got them going. Scientists' explain these observations using the Big Bang. Here's the theory...

1) Initially, all the matter in the universe occupied a very small space. This tiny space was very dense (p.77) and so was very hot.

2) Then it 'exploded' — space started expanding, and the expansion is still going on.

3) Because of this, the age of the Universe can be estimated by looking at how far a galaxy is from us, and how fast it appears to be moving. Using these values in time = distance ÷ speed (p.49), gives time as an estimate of the age of the Universe.

4) Our current observations suggest the Universe is about 14 000 million years old.

New Evidence Might Change Our Theories

1) Something important to remember is that the Big Bang theory is the best guess we have so far.

2) Whenever scientists discover new evidence which contradicts the current theory, they have to either make a new theory or change the current one to explain what they've observed (p.91). However, lots of evidence that has come to light in recent years supports the Big Bang theory, meaning it is more secure.

3) The development of improved telescopes over the last century have meant that new areas of the EM spectrum are now observable. Some of these telescopes are on satellites, outside of the Earth's atmosphere. These have increased the variety and quality of data available to scientists giving further support to the Big Bang theory.

And it all started with the Big Bang...

Well, it's what we currently think is likely. Remember — theories must change if new evidence contradicts them.

Q1   How does observed light from distant galaxies suggest that the Universe is expanding?   [4 marks]

Revision Questions for Chapter P6

Well, that wraps up <u>Chapter P6</u> — now lets see if you know it better than the back of your hand.

- Try these questions and <u>tick off each one</u> when you <u>get it right</u>.
- When you've done <u>all the questions</u> for a topic and are <u>completely happy</u> with it, tick off the topic.

<u>Density, Particles, Heating and Cooling (p.77-81)</u> ☑

1) Define 'density'? ☑

2) True or false? According to the particle model, the forces between all particles of any substance are the same. ☑

3) Describe solids, liquids and gases in terms of the movements of their particles. ☑

4) What is the relationship between the temperature of a substance and the average energy in the kinetic energy stores of its particles? ☑

5) Describe and explain the general change in density when a liquid is: a) boiled b) frozen ☑

6) Explain how the pressure of a gas at constant volume changes with a temperature rise? ☑

7) What is the specific heat capacity of a substance? ☑

8) Describe an experiment to find the specific heat capacity of water. ☑

9) Explain why the temperature of a substance doesn't change when it is melting. ☑

10) What is meant by the specific latent heat of fusion? ☑

<u>Pressure (p.82-83)</u> ☑

11) What is the equation that links pressure, force and area? ☑

12) Explain why liquid pressure increases with depth.

13) How do you calculate the pressure at different depths in a liquid? ☑

14) Explain what causes an object to sink. ☑

15) What is atmospheric pressure? ☑

16) How does atmospheric pressure change with height? Explain why. ☑

<u>Elasticity and Hooke's Law (p.84-85)</u> ☑

17) What is the difference between elastic deformation and plastic deformation? ☑

18) Give the equation that relates the force exerted by a spring with its extension and spring constant. ☑

19) Give an example of an object that doesn't obey Hooke's law. ☑

20) What value can be found by calculating the gradient of a force-extension graph for a material obeying Hooke's law? ☑

21) Describe a simple experiment to investigate Hooke's law. ☑

<u>The Solar System and The Universe (p.86-88)</u> ☑

22) What do planets orbit? ☑

23) True or false? An object in a stable orbit has a continually changing speed. ☑

24) Describe what will happen if an artificial satellite in a stable orbit slows down. ☑

25) What causes the rise in temperature that leads to nuclear fusion in a protostar? ☑

26) What is red-shift? ☑

27) True or false? Very distant galaxies are moving away faster than galaxies closer to us. ☑

28) Briefly describe the Big Bang theory. ☑

The Scientific Method

Coming up with a new scientific theory is easier said than done — it's an almost never-ending cycle of collecting data, analysing it, reaching a conclusion, improving your method, collecting more data... etc.

Scientists Come Up With Hypotheses — Then Test Them

1) Scientists try to explain things. Not only that — they try to explain things really well. There isn't a single scientific method that all scientists use to do this, but scientists do follow certain conventions and scientific principles.

2) They usually start by observing or thinking about something they don't understand. They then try to come up with a hypothesis:

   • A hypothesis isn't just a summary of their observations (e.g. a ball falls when let go from a height).

   • It's a tentative explanation for it (e.g. a ball falls when let from a height because of gravity).

   • Observations made by scientists are just that — observations. They don't show what the hypothesis should be. In order to come up with a decent explanation for their observations, scientists need to use their imaginations.

   • A good hypothesis should account for all of the observations made and any other available data (i.e. what's already been observed). If it doesn't, it's not really a very good explanation.

3) The next step is to test whether the hypothesis might be right or not. This involves making a prediction based on the hypothesis, i.e. stating how changing a particular factor will affect the outcome of a situation. The prediction is then tested by gathering evidence (i.e. data) from investigations.

   > For example, a scientist might predict that a lower count rate will be detected further from a radioactive source. This prediction could be written as a statement, or it could be presented visually as a diagram or sketch graph.

   Investigations must be designed so data can be collected in a safe, repeatable, accurate way — see pages 92-93.

4) If evidence from well-conducted experiments backs up a prediction, it increases confidence in the hypothesis — in other words, people are more likely to believe that the hypothesis is true. It doesn't prove a hypothesis is correct though — evidence could still be found that disagrees with it.

5) If the experimental evidence doesn't fit with the hypothesis, then either those results or the hypothesis must be wrong — this decreases confidence in the hypothesis.

6) Sometimes a hypothesis will account for all the data and still turn out to be wrong — that's why every hypothesis needs to be tested further (see the next page).

Different Scientists Can Come Up With Different Explanations

1) Different scientists can make the same observations and come up with different explanations for them — and both these explanations might be perfectly good ones. It's the same with data — two scientists can look at the same data and explain it differently.

2) This is because you need to interpret the thing you're observing (or your data) to come up with an explanation for it — and different people often interpret things in different ways.

3) Sometimes a scientist's personal background, experience or interests will influence the way he or she thinks. For example, one person may believe that global warming is due to burning fossil fuels, while another may put it down to natural fluctuations in the Earth's temperature.

4) So it's important to test any explanations as much as possible — to see which one is most likely to be true (or whether it's a combination of both or if neither are true).

5) Our ability to test explanations has improved as technology has developed. That's because technology allows us make new observations and find new evidence. For example, improvements in telescopes have increased the amount of evidence for the Big Bang model (p.88).

6) New data can cause scientists to modify their ideas and hypotheses to fit. E.g.

   > When Ernest Rutherford carried out his alpha scattering experiment, he expected the particles to pass straight through a thin sheet of gold foil. The results didn't match his prediction, showing that the plum pudding model of the atom was incorrect, leading to the development of the nuclear model (see p.69).

The Scientific Method

Several Scientists Will Test a Hypothesis

1) Traditionally, new scientific explanations are announced in peer-reviewed journals, or at scientific conferences.

A peer-reviewed journal is one where other scientists check results and scientific explanations before the journal is published. They check that people have been 'scientific' about what they're saying (e.g. that experiments have been done in a sensible way). But this doesn't mean that the findings are correct, just that they're not wrong in any obvious kind of way.

2) Once other scientists have found out about a hypothesis, they'll start to base their own predictions on it and carry out their own experiments.

3) When other scientists test the new hypothesis they will also try to reproduce the earlier results. Results that can't be reproduced by another scientist aren't very reliable (they're hard to trust) and scientists tend to be pretty sceptical about them. They're also doubtful about any claims based on the results.

4) When testing a hypothesis, a scientist might get some unexpected results. While these could lead to a change in the hypothesis, they tend to be treated with scepticism until they've been repeated (by the same scientist) and reproduced (by other scientists).

5) Once the results from experiments have been accepted, they become scientific knowledge.

If Evidence Supports a Hypothesis, It's Accepted — for Now

1) If a hypothesis is backed up by evidence from loads of experiments, scientists start to have a lot of confidence in it and accept it as a scientific theory — a widely accepted explanation that can be applied to lots of situations. Our current theories have been tested many times over the years and survived.

2) Once scientists have gone through this process and accepted a theory, they take a lot of persuading to drop it — even if some new data appears that can't be explained using the existing theory.

3) Until a better, more plausible explanation is found (one that can explain both the old and new data), the tried and tested theory is likely to stick around — because it already explains loads of other observations really well. And remember, scientists always question new data until it's been proven to be repeatable and reproducible (see above).

Theories Can Involve Different Types of Models

Models are used to explain ideas and test explanations. They pick out the key features of a system or process, and the rules that determine how the different features work together. This means they can be used to make predictions and solve problems. There are different types of models:

- Representational models are simplified descriptions, analogies or pictures of what's going on in real life. E.g. magnetic field lines are a simplified way of representing the interaction of magnets. They can be used to make predictions about the interaction of wires carrying current in a magnetic field.

- Spatial models represent physical space and the positions of objects within it.

- Descriptive models are used to describe how things work. For example, describing sound waves as a series of compressions and rarefactions (p.16) explains how sound can travel through materials.

- Mathematical models use patterns found in data from past events to predict what might happen in the future. They usually require lots of difficult calculations, but modern computers can do these very quickly, which is why many mathematical models are now computational.

- Computational models are mathematical models that use computers. They often involve simulations of complex real-life processes, e.g. climate change.

Models can be used to help with understanding a concept. For example, representing sound and light waves with water waves can help with understanding reflection and refraction at boundaries (see p.3).

Models sometimes allow scientists to investigate real-life situations more quickly than they could using experiments (which may also have ethical or practical limitations). However, all models have limitations on what they can explain or predict. For example, climate change models have several limitations — it's hard to take into account all the biological and chemical processes that influence the climate. It can also be difficult to include regional variations in climate.

I'm off to the zoo to test my hippo-thesis...

There's an awful lot to take in here. Make sure you understand it all before moving on as it's really important stuff.

Designing Investigations

Dig out your lab coat and dust down your badly-scratched safety goggles... it's investigation time.

Investigations Produce Evidence to Support or Disprove a Hypothesis

1) Scientists observe things and come up with hypotheses to explain them (see p.90).
   You need to be able to do the same. For example:

   > Observation: People have big feet and spots.
   > Hypothesis: Having big feet causes spots.

   Investigations include experiments and studies.

2) To determine whether or not a hypothesis is right, you need to do an investigation to gather evidence.
   To do this, you need to use your hypothesis to make a prediction — something you think will happen or
   be true that you can test. E.g. people who have bigger feet will have more spots.

3) Investigations are used to see if there are patterns or relationships between two variables,
   e.g. to see if there's a pattern or relationship between the variables 'number of spots' and
   'size of feet'. You can also carry out investigations to check someone else's data.

Evidence Needs to be Repeatable, Reproducible and Valid

1) Repeatable means that if the same person does an experiment again using
   the same methods and equipment, they'll get similar results.

2) Reproducible means that if someone else does the experiment, or a different
   method or piece of equipment is used, the results will still be similar.

   You'll need to know all the scientific terms on this page, so make sure you understand and learn them.

3) If data is repeatable and reproducible, it's reliable and scientists are more likely to have confidence in it.

4) Valid results are both repeatable and reproducible AND they answer the original question.
   They come from experiments that were designed to be a fair test.

To Make an Investigation a Fair Test You Have to Control the Variables

1) In a lab experiment you usually change one variable and measure how it affects another variable.

2) To make it a fair test, everything else that could affect the results should stay the same
   — otherwise you can't tell if the thing you're changing is causing the results or not.

3) The variable you change is called the INDEPENDENT VARIABLE.

4) The variable you measure is the DEPENDENT VARIABLE.

5) Variables that you keep the same are called CONTROL VARIABLES.

   > You could investigate how current through a circuit component affects the potential
   > difference across the component by measuring the potential difference at different currents.
   > The independent variable is the current. The dependent variable is the potential difference.
   > Control variables include the temperature of the component, the p.d. of the power supply, etc.

6) You need to be able to suggest ways to control variables in experiments. For example, you could use a
   clamp to keep the steepness of a ramp constant while investigating the acceleration of a trolley.

7) Because you can't always control all the variables, you often need to use a control experiment. This is
   an experiment that's kept under the same conditions as the rest of the investigation, but doesn't have
   anything done to it. This is so that you can see what happens when you don't change anything at all.

You Can Devise Procedures to Produce or Characterise Substances

You also need to know how to carry out experiments where you produce or characterise a substance.

For example, when you test for the spring constant (see p.85) of
different materials, you're characterising the materials.

Chapter P7 — Ideas About Science

Designing Investigations

Investigations Can be Hazardous

1) A hazard is something that can potentially cause harm. Hazards include:

- Lasers, e.g. if a laser is directed into the eye, it can cause blindness.
- Gamma radiation, e.g. a gamma-emitting radioactive source can cause cancer.
- Electricity, e.g. faulty electrical equipment could give you a shock.

2) Part of planning an investigation is making sure that it's safe.

3) You should always make sure that you identify all the hazards that you might encounter. Then you should think of ways of reducing the risks from the hazards you've identified. For example:

- If you're working with springs, always wear safety goggles. This will reduce the risk of the spring hitting your eye if the spring snaps.
- If you're using an electric heater, turn it off when it's not in use and let it cool before moving it to reduce the risk of burns.

You can find out about potential hazards by looking in textbooks, doing some internet research or asking your teacher.

The Bigger the Sample Size the Better

Sometimes, your investigation might involve sampling a population, e.g. a group of people — in which case you'll need to decide how big your sample size is going to be. There are a few things to bear in mind:

1) Data based on small samples isn't as good as data based on large samples. A sample should represent the whole population (i.e. it should share as many characteristics with the population as possible) — a small sample can't do that. It's also harder to spot outliers (see p.94) if your sample size is too small.

2) The bigger the sample size the better, but scientists (and you) have to be realistic when choosing how big. For example, if a scientist were studying how exposure to radiation affected health, it'd be great to study everyone in the UK (a huge sample), but it'd take ages and cost a bomb. It's more realistic to study a thousand people, with a mixture of ages, gender and race.

Trial Runs Help Figure out the Range and Interval of Variable Values

1) It's a good idea to do a trial run first — a quick version of your experiment. Trial runs are used to figure out the range of variable values used in the proper experiment (the upper and lower limit).

2) If you get large changes in the dependent variable in the middle of the range you're looking at, but don't get a change near to the upper or lower limit, you might narrow the range in the proper experiment. But if you still get a big change at the near the limits of your range, you might increase the range.

3) And trial runs can be used to figure out the interval (gaps) between the values too. The intervals can't be too small (otherwise the experiment would take ages), or too big (otherwise you might miss something).

For example, if you were investigating the resistance of a diode (p.32)...
- You might do a trial run with a range of voltages of 0.5 V to 1 V.
  If there was no change in current at the upper end (e.g. 0.9-1 V),
  you might narrow the range to 0.5-0.8 V for the proper experiment.
- If using 0.1 V intervals gives you big changes in the current and therefore the resistance of the diode, you might decide to use 0.05 V intervals, e.g. 0.5, 0.55, 0.60, 0.65 V...

You Need to be Able to Comment on Other People's Experiments

You should be able to look at a plan for an investigation and decide whether or not it needs improving. You'll need to say whether the improvements would make the data more accurate, precise (p.94), repeatable or reproducible.

Improving the experiment will give data of a higher quality.

This is no high street survey — it's a designer investigation...

Planning your own investigation AND improving others. Those examiners aren't half demanding.

Collecting Data

You've designed the perfect investigation — now it's time to get your hands mucky and <u>collect some data</u>.

Your Data Should be Repeatable, Reproducible, Accurate and Precise

1) To <u>check repeatability</u> you need to <u>repeat</u> the readings and check that the results are similar. You need to repeat each reading at least <u>three times</u>.

2) To make sure your results are <u>reproducible</u> you can cross check them by taking a <u>second set of readings</u> with <u>another instrument</u> (or a <u>different observer</u>).

3) Your data also needs to be ACCURATE. Really accurate results are those that are <u>really close</u> to the <u>true answer</u>. The accuracy of your results usually depends on your <u>method</u> — you need to make sure you're measuring the right thing and that you don't <u>miss anything</u> that should be included in the measurements. E.g. estimating the <u>speed</u> of a trolley by using a stop watch isn't very accurate as it is hard to stop the timer at the exactly the right point. It's <u>more accurate</u> to use <u>light gates</u> (see p.105).

4) Your data also needs to be PRECISE. Precise results are ones where the data is <u>all really close</u> to the <u>mean</u> (average) of your repeated results (i.e. not spread out).

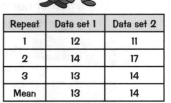

Brian's result was a curate.

Repeat	Data set 1	Data set 2
1	12	11
2	14	17
3	13	14
Mean	13	14

Data set 1 is more precise than data set 2.

Your Equipment has to be Right for the Job

The measuring equipment you use has to be <u>sensitive enough</u> to measure the changes you're looking for. For example, if you need to measure changes of 1 cm^3 you need to use a measuring cylinder that can measure in 1 cm^3 steps — it'd be no good trying with one that only has intervals of 10 cm^3.

1) The <u>smallest change</u> a measuring instrument can <u>detect</u> is called its RESOLUTION. E.g. some mass balances have a resolution of 1 g, some have a resolution of 0.1 g, and some are even more sensitive.

2) Also, equipment needs to be <u>calibrated</u> so that your data is <u>more accurate</u>. E.g. mass balances need to be set to zero before you start weighing things.

You Need to Look out for Errors and Outliers

1) The results of your experiment will always <u>vary a bit</u> because of RANDOM ERRORS — unpredictable differences caused by things like <u>human errors</u> in <u>measuring</u>. E.g. the errors you make when reading from a measuring cylinder are <u>random</u>. You have to <u>estimate</u> or <u>round</u> the level when it's <u>between</u> two marks — so sometimes your figure will be a <u>bit above</u> the real one, and sometimes it will be a <u>bit below</u>.

2) You can <u>reduce</u> the effect of random errors by taking <u>repeat readings</u> and finding the <u>mean</u>. This will make your results <u>more precise</u>.

3) If a measurement is wrong by the <u>same amount every time</u>, it's called a SYSTEMATIC ERROR. For example, if you measured from the very end of your ruler instead of from the 0 cm mark every time, all your measurements would be a bit small. Repeating the experiment in the exact same way and calculating a mean <u>won't</u> correct a systematic error.

> If there's no systematic error, then doing repeats and calculating a mean can make your results more accurate.

4) Just to make things more complicated, if a systematic error is caused by using <u>equipment</u> that <u>isn't zeroed properly</u>, it's called a ZERO ERROR. For example, if a mass balance always reads 1 gram before you put anything on it, all your measurements will be 1 gram too heavy.

5) You can <u>compensate</u> for some systematic errors if you know about them though, e.g. if your mass balance always reads 1 gram before you put anything on it you can subtract 1 gram from all your results.

6) Sometimes you get a result that <u>doesn't fit in</u> with the rest at all. This is called an OUTLIER. You should investigate it and try to <u>work out what happened</u>. If you can work out what happened (e.g. you <u>measured</u> or <u>recorded</u> something <u>wrong</u>) you can <u>ignore</u> it when processing your results — otherwise you should treat it as real <u>data</u>.

Watch what you say to that mass balance — it's very sensitive...

Weirdly, data can be really precise but not very accurate. For example, a fancy piece of lab equipment might give results that are really precise, but if it's not been calibrated properly those results won't be accurate.

Processing and Presenting Data

Once you've got your <u>data</u>, you need to <u>interpret</u> it. This means doing a bit of <u>maths</u> to make it <u>more useful</u>.

Data Needs to be Organised and Processed

1) Tables are dead useful for <u>recording results</u> and <u>organising data</u>. When you draw a table <u>use a ruler</u> and make sure <u>each column</u> has a <u>heading</u> (including the <u>units</u>).

2) When you've done repeats of an experiment you should calculate the <u>mean</u> (the <u>best estimate</u> of a value). To do this <u>add together</u> all the data values and <u>divide by</u> the total number of values in the sample.

3) You might also need to calculate the <u>range</u>. To do this find the <u>largest</u> number and <u>subtract</u> the <u>smallest</u> number from it. The range is a measure of how <u>spread out</u> the data is. The bigger the range, the less precise the data (and so the less confidence you can have in it).

EXAMPLE: The results of an experiment show the extension of a spring when a force is applied. Calculate the mean and range of the extension.

Ignore outliers when calculating these.

	Repeat (cm)					Mean (cm)	Range (cm)
	1	2	3	4	5		
Extension	18	26	22	26	28	(18 + 26 + 22 + 26 + 28) ÷ 5 = 24	28 – 18 = 10

If Your Data Comes in Categories, Present It in a Bar Chart

You should be able to draw charts and plot graphs from results in a table.

1) Once you've recorded and processed your results, you should <u>present</u> them in a nice <u>chart</u> or <u>graph</u> to help you <u>spot any patterns</u> in your data.

2) If the independent variable is <u>categoric</u> (comes in distinct categories, e.g. solid, liquid, gas) you should use a <u>bar chart</u> to <u>display</u> the data. You also use them if the independent variable is <u>discrete</u> (the data can be counted in chunks, where there's no in-between value, e.g. number of protons is discrete because you can't have half a proton). Here are the <u>rules</u> you need to follow for <u>drawing</u> bar charts:

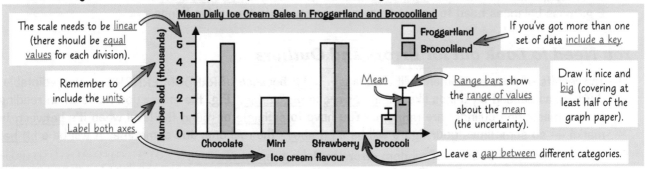

The scale needs to be <u>linear</u> (there should be <u>equal values</u> for each division).

Remember to include the <u>units</u>.

<u>Label both axes</u>.

If you've got more than one set of data <u>include a key</u>.

<u>Range bars</u> show the <u>range of values</u> about the <u>mean</u> (the uncertainty).

Draw it nice and <u>big</u> (covering at least half of the graph paper).

Leave a <u>gap between</u> different categories.

If Your Data is Continuous, Plot a Graph

If both variables are <u>continuous</u> (numerical data that can have any value within a range, e.g. length, volume, temperature) you should use a <u>graph</u> to display the data. Here are the rules for plotting points on a graph:

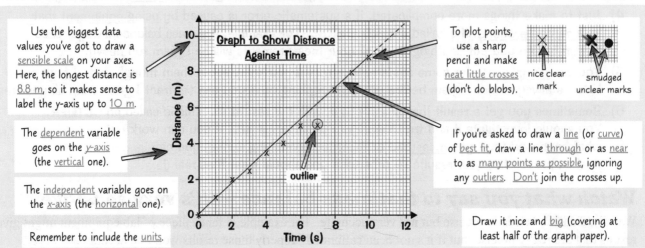

Use the biggest data values you've got to draw a <u>sensible scale</u> on your axes. Here, the longest distance is <u>8.8 m</u>, so it makes sense to label the y-axis up to <u>10 m</u>.

The <u>dependent</u> variable goes on the <u>y-axis</u> (the <u>vertical</u> one).

The <u>independent</u> variable goes on the <u>x-axis</u> (the <u>horizontal</u> one).

Remember to include the <u>units</u>.

To plot points, use a sharp pencil and make <u>neat little crosses</u> (don't do blobs). nice clear mark smudged unclear marks

If you're asked to draw a <u>line</u> (or <u>curve</u>) of <u>best fit</u>, draw a line <u>through</u> or as <u>near</u> to as <u>many points as possible</u>, ignoring any <u>outliers</u>. <u>Don't</u> join the crosses up.

Draw it nice and <u>big</u> (covering at least half of the graph paper).

Processing and Presenting Data

Graphs Can Give You a Lot of Information About Your Data

1) The <u>gradient</u> (slope) of a graph tells you how quickly the <u>dependent variable</u> changes if you change the <u>independent variable</u>.

$$\text{gradient} = \frac{\text{change in } y}{\text{change in } x}$$

If the x-axis is time, the gradient will always give you a rate of something — speed is the rate of change of distance.

This <u>graph</u> shows the <u>distance travelled</u> by a vehicle against <u>time</u>. The graph is <u>linear</u> (it's a straight line graph), so you can simply calculate the <u>gradient</u> of the line to find out the <u>speed</u> of the vehicle.

1) To calculate the gradient, pick <u>two points</u> on the line that are easy to read and a <u>good distance</u> apart.

2) <u>Draw a line down</u> from one of the points and a <u>line across</u> from the other to make a <u>triangle</u>. The line drawn down the side of the triangle is the <u>change in y</u> and the line across the bottom is the <u>change in x</u>.

Change in y = 6.8 − 2.0 = 4.8 m   Change in x = 5.2 − 1.6 = 3.6 s

Speed = gradient = $\dfrac{\text{change in } y}{\text{change in } x}$ = $\dfrac{4.8\,\text{m}}{3.6\,\text{s}}$ = <u>1.3 m/s</u> ← *The units of the gradient are (units of y)/(units of x).*

2) The <u>intercept</u> of a graph is where the line of best fit crosses one of the <u>axes</u>. The <u>x-intercept</u> is where the line of best fit crosses the x-axis and the <u>y-intercept</u> is where it crosses the <u>y-axis</u>.

3) You can use the line of best fit to <u>interpolate data</u> — this means you can find approximate values <u>in between</u> the values you <u>recorded</u>. E.g. if you recorded the distance travelled by a vehicle at <u>2 second intervals</u> and you wanted to work out how far it had travelled after <u>3 seconds</u>, you could use your graph to work it out.

<u>Read off</u> the x-axis at the value you want to know until you reach the <u>line of best fit</u>.

Then <u>read</u> <u>across</u> to find the corresponding <u>value on the</u> <u>y-axis</u>.

4) You can <u>extrapolate data</u> by <u>extending</u> the <u>line of best fit</u> (or a small part of it) to <u>predict</u> values outside of your range.

Scattergrams Show the Relationship Between Two Variables

1) You can get <u>three</u> types of <u>correlation</u> (relationship) between variables:

2) Just because there's correlation, it doesn't mean the change in one variable is <u>causing</u> the change in the other — there might be <u>other factors</u> involved (see page 99).

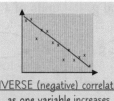

<u>POSITIVE</u> correlation: as one variable <u>increases</u> the other <u>increases</u>.

<u>INVERSE</u> (negative) correlation: as one variable <u>increases</u> the other <u>decreases</u>.

<u>NO</u> correlation: <u>no relationship</u> between the two variables.

When Doing a Calculation, Round to the Lowest Number of Significant Figures

The <u>first significant figure</u> of a number is the first digit that's <u>not zero</u>. The second and third significant figures come <u>straight after</u> (even if they're zeros). You should be aware of significant figures in calculations.

1) In <u>any</u> calculation, you should round the answer to the <u>lowest number of significant figures</u> (s.f.) given.

2) Remember to write down <u>how many</u> significant figures you've rounded to after your answer.

3) If your calculation has multiple steps, <u>only</u> round the <u>final</u> answer, or it won't be as accurate.

EXAMPLE: A car travels 15.6 m in 6.7 seconds at a steady speed. Calculate the speed of the car.

speed = 15.6 m ÷ 6.7 s = 2.328358... = **2.3 m/s (2 s.f.)** — Final answer should be rounded to 2 s.f.

3 s.f.   2 s.f.

I love eating apples — I call it core elation...

Science is all about finding relationships between things. And I don't mean that chemists gather together in corners to discuss whether or not Devini and Sebastian might be a couple... though they probably do that too.

Units and Equations

Graphs and maths skills are all very well, but the numbers don't mean much if you can't get the units right.

S.I. Units Are Used All Round the World

1) It wouldn't be all that useful if I defined volume in terms of bath tubs, you defined it in terms of egg-cups and my pal Sarwat defined it in terms of balloons — we'd never be able to compare our data.

2) To stop this happening, scientists have come up with a set of standard units, called S.I. units, that all scientists use to measure their data. Here are some S.I. units you'll see in physics:

Quantity	S.I. Base Unit
mass	kilogram, kg
length	metre, m
time	second, s

Scaling Prefixes Can Be Used for Large and Small Quantities

1) Quantities come in a huge range of sizes. For example, the volume of a swimming pool might be around 2 000 000 000 cm³, while the volume of a cup is around 250 cm³.

2) To make the size of numbers more manageable, larger or smaller units are used. These are the S.I. base unit (e.g. metres) with a prefix in front:

prefix	tera (T)	giga (G)	mega (M)	kilo (k)	deci (d)	centi (c)	milli (m)	micro (μ)	nano (n)
multiple of unit	10^{12}	10^9	1 000 000 (10^6)	1000	0.1	0.01	0.001	0.000001 (10^{-6})	10^{-9}

3) These prefixes tell you how much bigger or smaller a unit is than the base unit. So one kilometre is one thousand metres.

The conversion factor is the number of times the smaller unit goes into the larger unit.

4) To swap from one unit to another, all you need to know is what number you have to divide or multiply by to get from the original unit to the new unit — this is called the conversion factor.

- To go from a bigger unit (like m) to a smaller unit (like cm), you multiply by the conversion factor.
- To go from a smaller unit (like g) to a bigger unit (like kg), you divide by the conversion factor.

5) Here are some conversions that'll be useful for GCSE physics:

Mass can have units of kg and g.

Energy can have units of J and kJ.

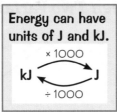

Volume can have units of m³, dm³ and cm³.

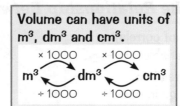

Density can have units of kg/m³ and g/cm³.

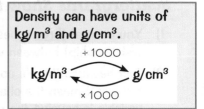

Always Check The Values Used in Equations Have the Right Units

1) Formulas and equations show relationships between variables.

2) To rearrange an equation, make sure that whatever you do to one side of the equation you also do to the other side.

> You can find the speed of a wave using the equation:
> wave speed = frequency × wavelength (see page 1). You can rearrange this equation to find the wavelength by dividing each side by the frequency: wavelength = wave speed ÷ frequency.

3) To use a formula, you need to know the values of all but one of the variables. Substitute the values you do know into the formula, and do the calculation to work out the final variable.

4) Always make sure the values you put into an equation or formula have the right units. For example, if you're calculating the speed of a wave, but the wavelength is given in nm and the frequency is in kHz, you'll have to convert both measurements into the right units (m and Hz) before you start.

5) To make sure your units are correct, it can help to write down the units on each line of your calculation.

I wasn't sure I liked units, but now I'm converted...

It's easy to get in a muddle when converting between units, but there's a handy way to check you've done it right. If you're moving from a smaller unit to a larger unit (e.g. g to kg) the number should get smaller, and vice versa.

Uncertainties and Evaluations

You can never be certain that your data is 100% correct. You need to decide how confident you are in it...

Uncertainty is the Amount of Error Your Measurements Might Have

1) When you repeat a measurement, you often get a slightly different figure each time you do it due to random error. This means that each result has some uncertainty to it.

2) The measurements you make will also have some uncertainty in them due to limits in the resolution of the equipment you use and human errors (see page 94).

3) This all means that the mean of a set of results will also have some uncertainty to it. You can calculate the uncertainty of a mean result using the equation:

4) The larger the range, the less precise your results are and the more uncertainty there will be in your results. Uncertainties are shown using the '±' symbol.

> The range is the largest value minus the smallest value (p.95).

$$\text{uncertainty} = \frac{\text{range}}{2}$$

EXAMPLE: The table below shows the results of a trolley experiment to determine the speed of the trolley as it moves along a horizontal surface. Calculate the uncertainty of the mean.

Repeat	1	2	3	mean
Speed (m/s)	2.01	1.98	2.00	2.00

1) First work out the range:

Range = 2.01 − 1.98 = 0.030 m/s

2) Use the range to find the uncertainty:

Uncertainty = range ÷ 2 = 0.030 ÷ 2 = 0.015 m/s   So the uncertainty of the mean = 2.00 ± 0.015 m/s

5) Measuring a greater amount of something helps to reduce uncertainty. For example, in a speed experiment, measuring the distance travelled over a longer period compared to a shorter period will give the same value of uncertainty, but the uncertainty will be smaller relative to the result.

You Need to Evaluate Your Data

Before you make any conclusions based on your data, you need perform an evaluation.
An evaluation is a critical analysis of the whole investigation, including the data you obtained.

1) You should comment on the method — was it valid?
Did you control all the other variables to make it a fair test?

2) Comment on the quality of the results — were the results repeatable, reproducible, accurate and precise? Were there sources of random or systematic error?

3) Were there any outliers? If there were none then say so. If there were any, try to explain them — were they caused by errors in measurement?
You should comment on the level of uncertainty in your results too.

4) All this analysis will allow you to say how confident you are that your results are good.

5) Then you can suggest any changes to the method that would improve the quality of the results, so that you could have more confidence in your data. For example, you might suggest changing the way you controlled a variable, carrying out further repeats or increasing the number of measurements you took. Taking more measurements at narrower intervals could give you a more accurate result. For example:

> I'd value this E somewhere in the region of 250-300k.

Springs have a limit of proportionality (a maximum force before force and extension are no longer proportional). Say you use several identical springs to do an experiment to find the limit of proportionality of the springs.
If you apply forces of 1 N, 2 N, 3 N, 4 N and 5 N, and from the results see that it is somewhere between 4 N and 5 N, you could repeat the experiment with one of the other springs, taking more measurements between 4 N and 5 N to get a more accurate value for the limit of proportionality.

> When suggesting improvements to the investigation, always make sure that you explain why you think this would make the results better.

Evaluation — next time, I'll make sure I don't burn the lab down...

By now you should have realised how important trustworthy evidence is (even more important than a good supply of spot cream). Evaluations are a good way to assess evidence and see how things can be improved in the future.

Drawing Conclusions

Congratulations — you're nearly at the end of the gruelling investigation process. Time to draw conclusions.

You Can Only Conclude What the Data Shows and NO MORE

1) Drawing conclusions might seem pretty straightforward — you just look at your data and say what pattern or relationship you see between the dependent and independent variables.

Potential difference (V)	Current (A)
6	4
9	5
12	6

The table on the right shows the currents through a light bulb for three different potential differences across it.

CONCLUSION: A higher potential difference across the bulb gives a higher current through the bulb.

2) But you've got to be really careful that your conclusion matches the data you've got and doesn't go any further.

You can't conclude that the current through any circuit component will be higher for a larger potential difference — the results could be totally different.

3) You also need to be able to use your results to justify your conclusion (i.e. back up your conclusion with some specific data).

The current through the bulb was 2 A higher with a potential difference of 12 V compared to a potential difference of 6 V.

4) When writing a conclusion you need to refer back to the original hypothesis and say whether the data supports it or not. You might remember from page 98 that if data backs up a prediction, it increases confidence in the hypothesis (although it doesn't prove the hypothesis is correct). If the data doesn't support the prediction, it can decrease confidence in it.

The hypothesis for this experiment might have been that a higher potential difference would increase the brightness of the bulb because there would be more energy supplied every second. The prediction may have been that a higher potential difference would give a higher current. If so, the data increases confidence in the hypothesis.

5) You could also make more predictions based on your conclusion, then further experiments could be carried out to test them.

Don't Forget, Correlation DOES NOT Mean Cause

Scientists often find correlations between variables by spotting patterns in data (like in the example above).

However, just because there's a correlation (relationship) between a factor and an outcome, it doesn't mean that the factor causes the outcome. There are several reasons for this...

1) Sometimes two things can show a correlation purely due to chance. This is why an individual case (e.g. a correlation between people's hair colour and how good they are at frisbee in a particular school) isn't enough to convince scientists that a factor is causing an outcome. Repeatable, reproducible data must be collected first.

2) A lot of the time it may look as if a factor is causing an outcome but it isn't — another, hidden factor links them both.

For example, there's a correlation between water temperature and shark attacks. This isn't because warmer water makes sharks crazy. Instead, they're linked by a third variable — the number of people swimming (more people swim when the water's hotter, and with more people in the water you get more shark attacks).

3) Sometimes a correlation is just when a factor makes an outcome more likely, but not inevitable. E.g. if you are exposed to ionising radiation, it increases your risk of cancer, but it doesn't mean you will get it. That's because there are lots of different factors interacting to influence the outcome.

4) Scientists don't usually accept that a factor causes an outcome (there is a cause-effect link) unless they can work out a plausible mechanism that links the two things.

E.g. there's a correlation between increased carbon dioxide levels in the atmosphere and global warming. Carbon dioxide can absorb thermal radiation and re-emit it back towards Earth — this is the mechanism.

I conclude that this page is a bit dull...

...although, just because I find it dull doesn't mean that I can conclude it's dull. In the exam you could be given a conclusion and asked whether the data supports it — you need to make sure the data fully justifies the conclusion.

New Technologies and Risk

By reading this page you are agreeing to the risk of a paper cut or severe drowsiness...

Scientific Technology Usually Has Benefits and Negative Impacts

Scientists have created loads of new technologies that could improve our lives. For example, discovering electromagnetic induction (p.41) and subsequently generating electricity has many benefits:

- It is used in a range of everyday appliances to make our quality of life better. We use these appliances for keeping warm, cooking, communicating with each other and for entertainment.
- It has also led to many processes in the workplace becoming automated. This reduces the physical demand of some jobs, making them more accessible to people.

However, it's not all good news. Sometimes new technology can have unintended or undesired impacts on our quality of life or the environment. For example:

- Most of our electricity is generated by burning fossil fuels. This contributes to global warming which can lead to reduced habitat for wildlife and rising sea levels.
- Burning fossil fuels also contributes to air pollution. This can have a negative effect on people's health, as well as causing damage to plants and animals.

When developing new technologies, scientists try to come up with ways to reduce negative impacts. For example, developing cleaner, renewable energy resources to generate electricity (p.24). They also try to use natural resources in a sustainable way so our resources aren't completely used up.

Nothing is Completely Risk-Free

1) Everything we do has a risk attached to it — this is the chance that it will cause harm.

2) The risks of some things seem pretty obvious, or we've known about them for a while, like the risk of causing acid rain by polluting the atmosphere, or of having a car accident when you're travelling in a car.

3) New technology arising from scientific advances can bring new risks, e.g. scientists are unsure whether nanoparticles that are being used in cosmetics and suncream might be harming the cells in our bodies. These risks need to be considered alongside the benefits of the technology, e.g. improved sun protection.

4) You can estimate the size of a risk based on how many times something happens in a big sample (e.g. 100 000 people) over a given period (e.g. a year). For example, you could assess the risk of a driver crashing by recording how many people in a group of 100 000 drivers crashed their cars over a year.

5) To make a decision about an activity that involves a risk, we need to take into account the chance of the risk happening and how serious the consequences would be if it did. So if an activity involves a risk that's very likely to happen, with serious consequences if it does, that activity is considered high-risk.

People Make Their Own Decisions About Risk

1) Not all risks have the same consequences, e.g. if you chop veg with a sharp knife you risk cutting your finger, but if you go scuba-diving you risk death. You're much more likely to cut your finger during half an hour of chopping than to die during half an hour of scuba-diving. But most people are happier to accept a higher probability of an accident if the consequences are short-lived and fairly minor.

2) People tend to be more willing to accept a risk if they choose to do something (e.g. go scuba diving), compared to having the risk imposed on them (e.g. having a nuclear power station built next door).

3) People's perception of risk (how risky they think something is) isn't always accurate. There is sometimes a big difference between perceived risk and calculated risk. People tend to view familiar activities as low-risk and unfamiliar activities as high-risk — even if that's not the case. For example, cycling on roads is often high-risk, but many people are happy to do it because it's a familiar activity. Air travel is actually pretty safe, but a lot of people perceive it as high-risk. People may also over- (or under-) estimate unfamiliar things that have long-term or invisible effects, e.g. ionising radiation.

Not revising — an unacceptable exam risk...

All activities pose some sort of risk, it's just a question of deciding whether that risk is worth it in the long run.

Communication and Issues Created by Science

Scientific developments can be great, but they can sometimes raise more questions than they answer...

It's Important to Communicate Scientific Discoveries

Scientists need to be able to communicate their findings to other scientists, and groups like the public and politicians, in a way everyone can understand. This allows people to make informed choices. For example:

> New technologies are being developed to generate renewable energy. Information about these new methods to generate power need to be communicated to politicians who decide whether to support their development with funding, and to the public, who will be affected by schemes using the technology.

1) One way discoveries can be communicated to the public is through the media. However, reports about scientific discoveries in the media (e.g. newspapers or television) aren't peer-reviewed (p.91).

2) This means that, even though news stories are often based on data that has been peer-reviewed, the data might be presented in a way that is over-simplified or inaccurate, making it open to misinterpretation.

3) People who want to make a point can sometimes present data in a biased way. (Sometimes without knowing they're doing it.) For example, a scientist might overemphasise a relationship in the data, or a newspaper article might describe details of data supporting an idea without giving any evidence against it.

Scientific Developments are Great, but they can Raise Issues

Scientific knowledge is increased by doing experiments. And this knowledge leads to scientific developments, e.g. new technologies or new advice. These developments can create issues though. For example:

Economic issues: Society can't always afford to do things scientists recommend (e.g. investing in alternative energy sources) without cutting back elsewhere.

Personal issues: Some decisions will affect individuals. For example, someone might support alternative energy, but object if a wind farm is built next to their house.

Social issues: Decisions based on scientific evidence affect people — e.g. should fossil fuels be taxed more highly? Would the effect on people's lifestyles be acceptable...

Environmental issues: Human activity often affects the natural environment. For example, building a dam to produce electricity will change the local habitat so some species might be displaced. But it will also reduce our need for fossil fuels, so will help to reduce climate change.

Science Can't Answer Every Question — Especially Ethical Ones

1) We don't understand everything. We're always finding out more, but we'll never know all the answers.

2) In order to answer scientific questions, scientists need data to provide evidence for their hypotheses.

3) Some questions can't be answered yet because the data can't currently be collected, or because there's not enough data to support a theory. Eventually, as we get more evidence, we'll answer some of the questions that currently can't be answered, e.g. what the impact of global warming on sea levels will be.

4) But there will always be the "Should we be doing this at all?"-type questions that experiments can't help us to answer...

> Think about new drugs which can be taken to boost your 'brain power'.
> - Some people think they're good as they could improve concentration or memory. New drugs could let people think in ways beyond the powers of normal brains.
> - Other people say they're bad — they could give you an unfair advantage in exams. And people might be pressured into taking them so that they could work more effectively, and for longer hours.

5) When making decisions that involve ethical dilemmas like this, a commonly used argument is that the right decision is the one that brings the greatest benefit to the most people.

Tea to milk or milk to tea? — Totally unanswerable by science...

Science can't tell you whether or not you should do something. That's for you and society to decide. But there are tons of questions science might be able to answer, like where life came from and where my superhero socks are.

Revision Questions for Chapter P7

Well, that wraps up <u>Chapter P7</u> — there's a lot of scientific know-how on these pages, so give yourself a test.

- Try these questions and <u>tick off each one</u> when you <u>get it right</u>.
- When you've done <u>all the questions</u> under a heading and are <u>completely happy</u>, tick it off.

The Scientific Method (p.90-91) ☑

1) What is a hypothesis?
2) True or false? There is only ever one way to explain data.
3) How does new technology change the way we can test explanations?
4) Briefly explain how the peer-review process works.
5) True or false? Scientific theories are explanations that still need to be accepted.
6) Give one advantage of using models.

Designing Investigations and Collecting Data (p.92-94) ☑

7) What is meant by the term 'valid result'?
8) How could a scientist try to make their investigation a fair test?
9) Why might a control experiment be used in an investigation?
10) Give one reason why it is better to use a large sample size than a small sample size in an investigation.
11) Suggest how you could work out the range of variable values to use in your experiment.
12) What are precise results?
13) What type of error is caused if a measurement is wrong by the same amount every time?

Processing and Presenting Data, Units and Equations (p.95-97) ☑

14) How would you calculate: a) the mean of a set of results, b) the range of the results?
15) What type of data would you present on a bar chart?
16) What is the intercept of a graph?
17) Sketch a graph showing: a) a positive correlation, b) a negative correlation.
18) Which of the following prefixes signifies a smaller unit: nano or micro?
19) How would you convert from grams to kilograms?

Uncertainties, Evaluations and Conclusions (p.98-99) ☑

20) Give four things you should consider when evaluating data.
21) Describe the effect data has on people's view of a hypothesis if it backs up the prediction.
22) What do scientists need to find to accept a cause-effect link between a factor and an outcome?

New Technologies and Risk (p.100) ☑

23) How might someone calculate risk?
24) True or false? People are more likely to perceive an unfamiliar situation as high-risk.

Communication and Issues Created by Science (p.101) ☑

25) Why is it important that scientists communicate their findings to the public?
26) Give an example of how information could be presented in a biased way.
27) State four types of issues that might be created by new scientific developments.
28) Describe one common argument about the best way to make decisions involving ethical dilemmas.

Apparatus and Techniques

- <u>Chapter P8</u> covers <u>practical skills</u> you'll need to know about for the course (including 15% of your exams).
- You're required to do experiments to cover at least <u>8 Practical Activity Groups</u>. These are covered in <u>Chapters P1-P6</u> earlier in the book and they're <u>highlighted</u> with <u>practical stamps</u> like this one.
- The following pages of this topic cover some <u>extra bits and bobs</u> you need to know about practical work. First up, some <u>measuring techniques</u>...

Mass Should Be Measured Using a Balance

1) For a <u>solid</u>, set the balance to <u>zero</u> and then place your object onto the scale and read off the mass.

2) If you're measuring the mass of a <u>liquid</u>, start by putting an empty <u>container</u> onto the <u>balance</u>. Next, <u>reset</u> the balance to zero.

3) Then just pour your <u>liquid</u> into the container and record the mass displayed. Easy peasy.

Measure Most Lengths with a Ruler and Use These To Calculate Area

1) In most cases a bog-standard <u>centimetre ruler</u> can be used to measure <u>length</u>. It depends on what you're measuring though — <u>metre rulers</u> or tape measures are handy for <u>large</u> distances.

2) The ruler should always be <u>parallel to</u> what you want to measure and the ruler and the object should be at <u>eye level</u> when you take a reading.

3) If you're dealing with something where it's <u>tricky</u> to measure just <u>one</u> accurately (e.g. water ripples, p.2), you can measure the length of <u>ten</u> of them and then <u>divide</u> to find the <u>length of one</u>.

4) If you're taking <u>multiple measurements</u> of the <u>same</u> object (e.g. to measure changes in length) then it's important to make sure you always measure from the <u>same point</u> on the object. It can help to draw or stick small <u>markers</u> onto the object to line up your ruler against.

> You can use <u>measurements</u> of the <u>dimensions</u> of a shape to <u>calculate its area</u>.
>
> Here are some common area formulas you might need:
>
> | square or rectangle | triangle | circle |
> |---|---|---|
> | area = length × width | area = ½ × base × height | area = π × (radius)^2 |
>
> If the area you're trying to measure is an <u>odd shape</u>, <u>split it up</u> into smaller, <u>regular</u> shapes.

Use a Protractor to Find Angles

1) First align the <u>vertex</u> (point) of the angle with the mark in the <u>centre</u> of the protractor.

2) Line up the <u>base line</u> of the protractor with one line that forms the <u>angle</u> and then measure the angle of the other line using the scale on the <u>protractor</u>.

3) If the lines creating the angle are very <u>thick</u>, align the protractor and measure the angle from the <u>centre</u> of the lines.

4) If the lines are <u>too short</u> to measure easily, you may have to <u>extend</u> them.

Using a sharp pencil to trace light rays or draw diagrams helps to reduce errors when measuring angles.

Measure Temperature Accurately with a Thermometer

bulb

1) Make sure the <u>bulb</u> of your thermometer is <u>completely submerged</u> in any substance you're measuring.

2) Wait for the temperature to <u>stabilise</u> before you take your initial reading.

3) Again, read your measurement off the <u>scale</u> on a thermometer at <u>eye level</u>.

When you're reading off a scale, use the value of the nearest mark on the scale (the nearest graduation).

You May Have to Measure the Time Taken for a Change

1) You should use a <u>stopwatch</u> to <u>time</u> most experiments — they're more <u>accurate</u> than regular watches.

2) Always make sure you <u>start</u> and <u>stop</u> the stopwatch at exactly the right time. Or alternatively, set an <u>alarm</u> on the stopwatch so you know exactly when to stop an experiment or take a reading.

3) You might be able to use a <u>light gate</u> instead (p.105). This will <u>reduce the errors</u> in your experiment.

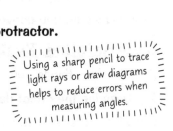

Apparatus and Techniques

Measuring Cylinders and Pipettes Measure Liquid Volume

1) <u>Measuring cylinders</u> are the most common way to measure a liquid.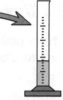

2) They come in all different <u>sizes</u>. Make sure you choose one that's the <u>right size</u> for the measurement you want to make. It's no good using a huge 1 dm³ cylinder to measure out 2 cm³ of a liquid — the graduations (markings for scale) will be <u>too big</u> and you'll end up with <u>massive errors</u>. It'd be much better to use one that measures up to 10 cm³.

3) You can also use a <u>pipette</u> to measure volume. <u>Pipettes</u> are used to suck up and <u>transfer</u> volumes of liquid between containers.

4) <u>Graduated pipettes</u> are used to transfer <u>accurate</u> volumes. A <u>pipette filler</u> is attached to the end of a graduated pipette, to <u>control</u> the amount of liquid being drawn up.

5) Whichever method you use, always read the volume from the <u>bottom of the meniscus</u> (the curved upper surface of the liquid) when it's at <u>eye level</u>.

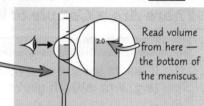

Read volume from here — the bottom of the meniscus.

Eureka Cans Measure the Volumes of Solids

1) <u>Eureka cans</u> are used in <u>combination</u> with <u>measuring cylinders</u> to find the volumes of <u>irregular solids</u> (p.77).

2) They're essentially a <u>beaker with a spout</u>. To use them, fill them with water so the water level is <u>above the spout</u>.

3) Let the water <u>drain</u> from the spout, leaving the water level <u>just below</u> the start of the spout (so <u>all</u> the water displaced by an object goes into the measuring cylinder and gives you the <u>correct volume</u>).

4) Place a <u>measuring cylinder</u> below the end of the spout. When you place a solid in the beaker, it causes the water level to <u>rise</u> and water to flow out of the spout.

5) Make sure you wait until the spout has <u>stopped dripping</u> before you measure the volume of the water in the measuring cylinder. And eureka! You know the object's volume.

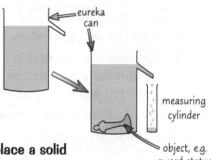

eureka can

measuring cylinder

object, e.g. award statue

Be Careful When You Do Experiments

1) There are always hazards in any experiment, so <u>before</u> you start an experiment you should read and follow any <u>safety precautions</u> to do with your method or the apparatus you're using.

2) Stop masses and equipment falling by using <u>clamp stands</u>. Make sure masses are of a <u>sensible weight</u> so they don't break the equipment they're used with.

3) When <u>heating</u> materials, make sure to let them <u>cool</u> before moving them, or wear <u>insulated gloves</u> while handling them. If you're using an <u>immersion heater</u> to heat liquids, place a <u>lid</u> on your container so they can't <u>spill</u> and let the heater <u>dry out</u> in air, just in case any liquid has leaked inside it.

4) When working with <u>springs</u>, you should wear <u>safety goggles</u> so your <u>eyes</u> are <u>protected</u> in case the spring <u>snaps</u>.

5) If you're using a <u>laser</u>, there are a few safety rules you must follow. Always wear <u>laser safety goggles</u> and never <u>look directly into</u> the laser or shine it <u>towards another person</u>. Make sure you turn the laser <u>off</u> if it's not needed to avoid any accidents.

6) When working with electronics, make sure you use a <u>low</u> enough <u>voltage</u> and <u>current</u> to prevent wires <u>overheating</u> (and potentially melting) and avoid <u>damage to components</u>, like blowing a filament bulb.

7) You also need to be aware of <u>general safety</u> in the lab — handle <u>glassware</u> carefully so it doesn't <u>break</u>, don't stick your fingers in sockets and avoid touching frayed wires. That kind of thing.

Experimentus apparatus...

Wizardry won't help you here, unfortunately. Most of this'll be pretty familiar to you by now, but make sure you get your head down and know these techniques inside out so they're second nature when it comes to any practicals.

Working with Electronics

Electrical devices are used in a bunch of experiments, so make sure you know how to use them.

You Have to Interpret Circuit Diagrams

Before you get cracking on an experiment involving any kind of electrical devices, you have to plan and build your circuit using a circuit diagram. Make sure you know all of the circuit symbols on page 29 so you're not stumped before you've even started.

There Are a Couple of Ways to Measure Potential Difference and Current

Voltmeters Measure Potential Difference

1) If you're using an analogue voltmeter, choose the voltmeter with the most appropriate unit (e.g. V or mV). If you're using a digital voltmeter, you'll most likely be able to switch between them.

2) Connect the voltmeter in parallel (p.35) across the component you want to test. The wires that come with a voltmeter are usually red (positive) and black (negative). These go into the red and black coloured ports on the voltmeter. Funnily enough.

3) Then simply read the potential difference from the scale (or from the screen if it's digital).

Ammeters Measure Current

1) Just like with voltmeters, choose the ammeter with the most appropriate unit.

2) Connect the ammeter in series (p.34) with the component you want to test, making sure they're both on the same branch. Again, they usually have red and black ports to show you where to connect your wires.

3) Read off the current shown on the scale or by the screen.

Turn your circuit off between readings to prevent wires overheating and affecting your results (p.30).

Multimeters Measure Both

1) Instead of having a separate ammeter and voltmeter, many circuits use multimeters. These are devices that measure a range of properties — usually potential difference, current and resistance.

2) If you want to find potential difference, make sure the red wire is plugged into the port that has a 'V' (for volts).

3) To find the current, use the port labelled 'A' or 'mA' (for amps).

4) The dial on the multimeter should then be turned to the relevant section, e.g. to 'A' to measure current in amps. The screen will display the value you're measuring.

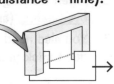

'A' stands for amps and 'mA' stands for milliamps.

Light Gates Measure Time, Velocity and Acceleration

1) A light gate sends a beam of light from one side of the gate to a detector on the other side. When something passes through the gate, the beam of light is interrupted. The light gate then measures how long the beam was undetected.

2) You can use two or more light gates connected together to work out the time it takes an object to travel between them (like on page 51).

3) You can also use light gates to find the velocity of an object at a point. First, connect it to a computer. Measure the length of the object and input this using the software. It will then automatically calculate the velocity of the object as it passes through the beam (using average speed = distance ÷ time).

4) To measure acceleration, use an object that interrupts the signal twice in a short period of time, e.g. a piece of card with a gap cut into the middle.

5) The light gate measures the velocity for each section of the object and uses this to calculate its acceleration. This can then be read from the computer screen.

Light gate

Beam of light

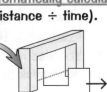

A light gate is better than a heavy one...

After finishing this page, you should be able to take on any electrical experiment that they throw at you... ouch.

Answers

Page 1 — Waves
Q1 7.5 ÷ 100 = 0.075 m *[1 mark]*
wave speed = frequency × wavelength,
so frequency = wave speed ÷ wavelength
= 0.15 ÷ 0.075 *[1 mark]* = 2 Hz *[1 mark]*

Page 2 — Wave Experiments
Q1 E.g. attach a variable power supply to a dipper and place it in a ripple tank filled with water to create waves *[1 mark]*. Place a cork in the water and time how long it takes to bob up 10 times *[1 mark]*. Divide this time by 10 to give the period of the wave *[1 mark]*. 1 ÷ the period gives the frequency of the wave *[1 mark]*.

Page 3 — Reflection and Refraction
Q1 $v = f\lambda$ *[1 mark]* and the frequency of the wave cannot change (it stays the same) *[1 mark]*. So the wavelength must decrease if speed decreases *[1 mark]*.

Page 4 — Reflection and Refraction Experiments
Q1 Draw around one prism on a piece of paper and trace the path of a light ray as it enters and leaves the prism *[1 mark]*. Draw the refracted ray by connecting the ends of the other two rays with a straight line *[1 mark]*. Draw the normals at the points where the ray enters and leaves the prism *[1 mark]*. Mark and measure the angles of incidence and refraction for the ray entering and leaving the prism *[1 mark]*. Repeat with the second prism using the same initial angle of incidence *[1 mark]*.

Page 5 — The Electromagnetic Spectrum
Q1 X-rays, visible light, microwaves *[1 mark]*.
Q2 A change in the nucleus / radioactive decay *[1 mark]*.

Page 6 — Energy Levels and Ionisation
Q1 An electron/electrons can move up to a higher energy level / leave the atom` *[1 mark]*.
Q2 Gamma radiation is ionising *[1 mark]*, which can lead to mutations of cells and their abnormal growth *[1 mark]*.

Page 7 — Uses of EM Radiation
Q1 An alternating current of a set frequency in an electric conductor causes charges to oscillate *[1 mark]*, creating an oscillating electric and magnetic field (an EM wave) of the same frequency — a radio wave *[1 mark]*.

Page 8 — More Uses of EM Radiation
Q1 Any two from: e.g. sterilising medical instruments / sterilising food / cancer treatment / medical imaging *[1 mark for each correct answer]*.

Page 9 — Absorbing and Emitting Radiation
Q1 Star A is hotter *[1 mark]*. The hotter an object it is, the higher its principal frequency *[1 mark]*.

Page 10 — The Greenhouse Effect
Q1 E.g. carbon dioxide / methane / water vapour *[1 mark for each correct answer]*.
Q2 E.g. they add more greenhouse gases to the atmosphere *[1 mark]*. The extra greenhouse gases increase the amount of radiation absorbed *[1 mark]* and re-emitted back towards Earth *[1 mark]*. This causes the temperature of the Earth's surface to gradually increase *[1 mark]*.

Page 11 — Reflection and Ray Diagrams
Q1 E.g.   red   violet

[1 mark for drawing two rays with parallel incident and reflected rays, 1 mark for the angle of reflection being equal to the angle of incidence for each ray and ~45°, 1 mark for drawing both normals correctly]

Page 12 — Refraction, Ray Diagrams and Prisms
Q1 a) E.g.

[1 mark for drawing normal correctly, 1 mark for showing ray refracting towards normal, 1 mark for indicating direction of ray, 1 mark for correctly labelled angles]

b) Green light has a different wavelength *[1 mark]*, so its speed changes by a different amount *[1 mark]*.

Page 13 — Lenses
Q1

[1 mark for all rays passing through principal focus, 1 mark for the outer rays bending towards the normal as they enter the lens, 1 mark for them bending away from the normal as they leave the lens]

Page 14 — Ray Diagrams of Lenses
Q1

[1 mark for light ray refracted through principal focus, 1 mark for unrefracted light ray through centre of lens, 1 mark for an inverted image at the point where the two rays meet]

Page 15 — Visible Light and Colour
Q1 a) A cucumber looks green because it reflects green light *[1 mark]*, but absorbs all other colours of light *[1 mark]*.
b) black *[1 mark]*

Page 16 — Sound Waves
Q1 Because sound travels by causing the vibration of particles *[1 mark]* and space is a vacuum, so there are no particles to vibrate *[1 mark]*.
Q2 Sound waves reach the eardrum causing it to vibrate *[1 mark]*. These vibrations are passed to the small bones in the middle ear (ossicles) and through the semi-circular canals on to the cochlea *[1 mark]*, which converts them into electrical signals that your brain interprets as sound *[1 mark]*.

Page 17 — Ultrasound and SONAR
Q1 When ultrasound waves reach a boundary between two different media, some of the wave is reflected and some is transmitted (and refracted) *[1 mark]*. This happens to the ultrasound waves when scanning a foetus (e.g. at the boundary between the fluid in the womb and the skin of the foetus) *[1 mark]*. The time it takes for the reflected rays to reach the detector, along with their distribution, can be used to determine how far away a boundary is and create an image using a computer *[1 mark]*.

Page 18 — Seismic Waves
Q1 S-waves can only travel through solids *[1 mark]*. The S-waves don't travel though the centre of the Earth, so at least part of the Earth's core must be liquid *[1 mark]*.

Page 20 — Energy Stores and Transfers
Q1 Energy is transferred electrically *[1 mark]* from the chemical energy store of the battery *[1 mark]* to the kinetic energy store of the motor *[1 mark]*.

Some energy will also be wasted to thermal energy stores.

Page 21 — Conservation of Energy and Power
Q1 $E = P \times t = 4.8 \times 1000 = 4800$ J *[1 mark]*
$t = 2 \times 60 = 120$ s *[1 mark]*
Rearrange $E = P \times t$ for P:
$P = E \div t = 4800 \div 120$ *[1 mark]* = 40 W *[1 mark]*
Q2 $t = 45$ minutes $= 45 \div 60 = 0.75$ hours *[1 mark]*
Calculate energy in kWh:
$E = P \times t = 4.0 \times 0.75$ *[1 mark]* = 3 kWh *[1 mark]*
At 14p per kWh, a load of drying costs:
$3 \times 14p = 42p$ *[1 mark]*

Page 22 — Efficiency and Sankey Diagrams
Q1 efficiency = useful energy transferred ÷ total energy transferred
= 225 ÷ 300 *[1 mark]* = 0.75 *[1 mark]*
0.75 × 100 = 75% *[1 mark]*

Page 23 — Energy Resources
Q1 Any two from: e.g. biofuels / wind / the Sun / hydroelectricity / the tides.
[2 marks — 1 mark for each correct answer]

Page 24 — Renewable Energy Resources
Q1 E.g. solar power produces no pollution when being used *[1 mark]* but production can't be increased to meet extra demand *[1 mark]*.

Page 25 — Trends in Energy Use
Q1 Any two from: e.g. it is a clean energy resource / it is reliable / it provides lots of jobs
[2 marks — 1 mark for each correct answer].

Page 26 — The National Grid
Q1 In an alternating current (a.c.) supply, the current is constantly changing direction *[1 mark]*. In a direct current (d.c.) supply, the current always travels in the same direction *[1 mark]*.
Q2 Live — 230 V *[1 mark]*, Neutral — 0 V *[1 mark]*, Earth — 0 V *[1 mark]*.

Page 28 — Static Electricity
Q1 E.g. an electric field is the space surrounding an electric charge where its effects can be felt *[1 mark]*.

Page 29 — Circuits — The Basics
Q1 time = charge ÷ current = 28 800 ÷ 8.0 *[1 mark]*
= 3600 s (= 1 hour) *[1 mark]*

Page 30 — Resistance and $V = I \times R$
Q1 resistance = p.d. ÷ current = 230 ÷ 5.0 *[1 mark]*
= 46 Ω *[1 mark]*

Page 31 — Resistance and I-V Characteristics
Q1 a)

[1 mark for a straight line through the origin]

b)

[1 mark for correct shape that passes through the origin]

Page 32 — Circuit Devices
Q1 E.g.

[1 mark for drawing an LDR, an ammeter and a battery in series, 1 mark for drawing a voltmeter in parallel with the LDR]

Page 33 — Energy and Power in Circuits
Q1 11 × 60 = 660 seconds *[1 mark]*
$1.5 \times 10^3 = 1500$ W
energy transferred = power × time
= 1500 × 660 *[1 mark]*
= 990 000 J *[1 mark]*

Page 34 — Series and Parallel Circuits
Q1 $R = 2 + 2 + 2 = 6\,\Omega$ *[1 mark]*

Page 35 — More on Series and Parallel Circuits
Q1   3.5 V *[1 mark]*

Page 36 — Investigating Series and Parallel Circuits
Q1   E.g.

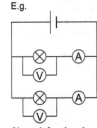

[1 mark for drawing a closed circuit containing at least two bulbs in parallel with a cell, 1 mark for drawing a voltmeter in parallel with each bulb and an ammeter in series with each bulb]

Page 37 — Permanent and Induced Magnets
Q1   At the poles *[1 mark]*

Q2   E.g. permanent magnets produce their own magnetic fields but induced magnets become magnets when they're in a magnetic field *[1 mark]*. When taken away from a magnetic field, an induced magnet will lose its magnetisation, but a permanent magnet will remain magnetised *[1 mark]*.

Page 38 — Electromagnetism
Q1   E.g.

[1 mark for concentric circles, 1 mark for arrows on field lines in the correct direction]

Page 39 — The Motor Effect
Q1   Thumb — direction of the force *[1 mark]*. First finger — direction of the magnetic field *[1 mark]*. Second finger — direction of the current *[1 mark]*.

Q2   35 cm = 0.35 m *[1 mark]*
magnetic flux density
= force ÷ (current × length of conductor)
= 9.8 ÷ (5.0 × 0.35) *[1 mark]* = 5.6 T *[1 mark]*

Page 40 — Electric Motors
Q1   E.g. in a fan/blender to make the blades move / in electric toothbrushes to move the bristles / in hair dryers to move the fan blades *[1 mark]*

Q2   Any two from: decrease the current / decrease the number of turns on the coil / decrease the magnetic field strength.
[2 marks — 1 mark for each correct answer]

Page 41 — Electromagnetic Induction
Q1   The induction of a potential difference *[1 mark]* (and a current if there is a complete circuit) across a conductor which is experiencing a change in magnetic field *[1 mark]*.

Page 42 — Generators
Q1   A coil is made to rotate in a magnetic field *[1 mark]*. This induces a potential difference across the coil, which causes a current to flow through it *[1 mark]*. A split-ring commutator is used to swap the connection each half turn to keep the current flowing in the same direction *[1 mark]*.

Page 43 — Loudspeakers, Microphones & Transformers
Q1   A coil of wire carrying an alternating current surrounds one pole of a permanent magnet and is surrounded by the other pole. This coil is wrapped around a paper cone *[1 mark]*. When a current flows through the wire, the interacting magnetic fields of the permanent magnet and the wire cause a force which moves the cone in one direction *[1 mark]*. When the current reverses, the force is reversed and the cone moves in the opposite direction *[1 mark]*. This repeats as the current alternates, which makes the cone vibrate, which vibrates the air around it

to create a sound wave *[1 mark]*.

Q2   Step-down transformer *[1 mark]*.

Page 44 — More on Transformers
Q1 a)   p.d. across primary coil =
p.d. across secondary coil × (number of turns in primary coil ÷ number of turns in secondary coil)
= 20 × (16 ÷ 4) *[1 mark]* = 80 V *[1 mark]*

b)   power of primary coil = power of secondary coil, and power = p.d. × current, so
power of secondary coil = p.d. across primary coil × current in primary coil
320 = 80 × current in primary coil *[1 mark]*
current in primary coil = 320 ÷ 80 = 4 A *[1 mark]*

Page 46 — Forces and Newton's Third Law
Q1   When the ball hits the wall, it exerts a force on the wall. There is an equal and opposite force on the ball from the wall (Newton's third law) *[1 mark]*. This means that the ball is pushed in the opposite direction, away from the wall, and so bounces back *[1 mark]*.

Page 47 — Mass and Weight
Q1   weight = mass × gravitational field strength
mass = weight ÷ gravitational field strength
[1 mark]
= 820 ÷ 10 *[1 mark]* = 82 kg *[1 mark]*

Page 48 — Scalars and Vectors
Q1   Scalar quantities only have a size whereas vector quantities also have a direction *[1 mark]*. E.g. distance is a scalar quantity, whereas displacement is a vector quantity *[1 mark]*.

Page 49 — Calculating Speed
Q1   First convert minutes into seconds:
2.0 × 60 = 120 s *[1 mark]*
average speed = distance ÷ time
= 660 ÷ 120 *[1 mark]*
= 5.5 m/s *[1 mark]*

Q2   54 km/hr ÷ (60 × 60) = 0.015 km/s
0.015 km/s × 1000 = 15 m/s *[1 mark]*
distance = average speed × time
= 15 × 24 *[1 mark]* = 360 m *[1 mark]*

Page 50 — Acceleration
Q1   initial speed = 0 m/s, final speed = 5.00 m/s, acceleration = g = 10 m/s^2,
distance = (final speed^2 − initial speed^2) ÷ (2 × acceleration) *[1 mark]*
= (25 − 0) ÷ (2 × 10) *[1 mark]*
= 1.25 m *[1 mark]*

Page 51 — Investigating Motion
Q1   Use the light gates to time how long it takes the object to pass between the two light gates *[1 mark]*. Measure the distance between the two light gates *[1 mark]*. Divide the distance by the time taken for the object to travel between the two light gates *[1 mark]*.

Q2   Using a stopwatch introduces human errors like reaction times, which aren't present with light gates *[1 mark]*. This matters more for short intervals, as the reaction time is a larger proportion of the interval being timed *[1 mark]*.

Page 52 — Distance-Time Graphs
Q1   E.g.

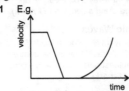

[1 mark for a continuous line that initially curves upwards, 1 mark for the line to finish straight with a positive gradient]

Page 53 — Velocity-Time Graphs
Q1   E.g.

[1 mark for line which is initially horizontal, then becomes a straight line with a negative gradient, continuing until it meets the time axis, 1 mark for showing the line then continuing horizontally along the time axis, and 1 mark for then showing the line curving upwards.]

Page 54 — Free Body Diagrams and Forces
Q1

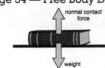

[1 mark for arrows pointing in the right direction and labelled correctly, 1 mark for arrows being the same length]

Page 55 — Forces and Scale Drawings
Q1

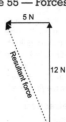

Resultant force = 13 N
[1 mark for a correct scale drawing, 1 mark for correct resultant force]

Page 56 — Newton's First Law and Circular Motion
Q1   The resultant force is 0 N *[1 mark]*.

Q2   The force acts along the string/along the radius of the stone's circular path towards the centre of the circle *[1 mark]*. It is always at right angles to the line of motion of the stone *[1 mark]*.

Page 57 — Momentum and Newton's Second Law
Q1   momentum = mass × velocity
= 220 000 × 250 *[1 mark]*
= 55 000 000 kg m/s *[1 mark]*

Q2   First, convert quantities to the correct units:
45 g = 0.045 kg
10.8 ms = 0.0108 s *[1 mark]*
Then calculate the change in momentum:
change in momentum
= momentum after − momentum before
= (mass of ball × final velocity of ball)
   − (mass of ball × initial velocity of ball)
= (0.045 × 36) − (0.045 × 0) *[1 mark]*
= 1.62 kg m/s
resultant force = change of momentum ÷ time taken
= 1.62 ÷ 0.0108 *[1 mark]*
= 150 N *[1 mark]*

Page 58 — Conservation of Momentum
Q1   Total momentum before collision
= (2.0 × 1.5) + (3.0 × 0) *[1 mark]*
= 3 kg m/s *[1 mark]*
The total momentum before the collision is equal to the total momentum after the collision.
Total momentum after collision
= total mass of trolleys × final velocity
3 = (2.0 + 3.0) × velocity
velocity = 3 ÷ (2.0 + 3.0) *[1 mark]*
= 0.6 m/s *[1 mark]*

Q2   Take 'to the right' to be positive.
Total momentum before collision
= (20 × 3) + (20 × (−2))
= +20 kg m/s *[1 mark]*
The total momentum before the collision is equal to the total momentum after the collision *[1 mark]*.
Total momentum after the collision
= (20 × −1) + (20 × velocity)
20 = −20 + (20 × velocity)
40 = (20 × velocity)
velocity = 40 ÷ 20 *[1 mark]*
= 2 m/s to the right *[1 mark]*

Page 59 — Newton's Second Law and Inertia
Q1   The empty trolley has a smaller inertial mass *[1 mark]*, so less force is needed to change its velocity/stop it *[1 mark]*.

Page 60 — Moments
Q1   moment of a force = force × distance
so distance = moment ÷ force *[1 mark]*
distance = 2.4 ÷ 15 *[1 mark]* = 0.16 m *[1 mark]*

Page 61 — Levers and Gears
Q1 a) anticlockwise *[1 mark]*
b) quicker *[1 mark]*

Answers

Page 62 — Reaction Times

Q1 E.g. click a mouse button *[1 mark]* when a computer screen changes colour *[1 mark]*.

Q2 (final speed)² − (initial speed)²
= 2 × acceleration × distance
(final speed)² = 2 × 10 × 0.162 + 0 *[1 mark]*
= 3.24
final speed = $\sqrt{3.24}$ = 1.8 m/s *[1 mark]*
time = change in speed ÷ acceleration
= 1.8 ÷ 10 *[1 mark]* = 0.18 s *[1 mark]*

Page 63 — Stopping Distances

Q1 Work done by brakes = energy transferred from the kinetic energy store of the car *[1 mark]*.
Energy in the kinetic store of the car
= 0.5 × mass of car × (speed of car)²
= 0.5 × 1000 × 25² *[1 mark]*
= 312 500 J *[1 mark]*
Work done by brakes
= braking force × braking distance = 312 500 J
Rearrange equation for braking distance:
braking distance = 312 500 ÷ braking force
= 312 500 ÷ 5000 *[1 mark]*
= 62.5 m
So the braking distance ~ 60 m *[1 mark]*

Page 64 — More Stopping Distances

Q1 (final speed)² − (initial speed)²
= 2 × acceleration × distance
so: acceleration = (final speed² − initial speed²)
÷ (2 × distance)
= (0² − 16²) ÷ (2 × 50) *[1 mark]*
= −2.56 m/s² *[1 mark]*
Estimate the mass of the lorry to be 30 000 kg
[1 mark for any value in the range 25 000 kg to 35 000 kg]
force = mass × acceleration
= 30 000 × (−2.56) = −76 800 *[1 mark]*
= (−)80 000 N (to 1 s.f.) *[1 mark]*

Page 65 — Work Done and Energy Transfers

Q1 For the book to stop, it will need to do work against friction. The work done will be equal to the energy initially in its kinetic energy store.
work done = force × distance, so
distance = work done ÷ force *[1 mark]*
= 1.25 ÷ 5.0 *[1 mark]* = 0.25 m
[1 mark]

Page 66 — Kinetic and Potential Energy Stores

Q1 gravitational potential energy
= mass × gravitational field strength × height
= 0.80 × 10 × 1.5 *[1 mark]* = 12 J *[1 mark]*

Q2 kinetic energy = 0.5 × mass × speed²
= 0.5 × 4.9 × (2.0)² *[1 mark]*
= 9.8 J *[1 mark]*

Page 67 — Energy Transfers and Power

Q1 As the ball falls, energy is transferred mechanically from its gravitational potential energy store to its kinetic energy store *[1 mark]*. When the ball hits the ground, some energy is transferred away by sound waves *[1 mark]*. The rest of the energy is carried away by heating to the thermal energy stores of the ball, the ground and the surroundings *[1 mark]*.

Q2 power = energy transferred ÷ time,
so energy transferred = power × time *[1 mark]*
5.0 minutes = 5.0 × 60 = 300 s
energy transferred = 12 × 300 *[1 mark]*
= 3600 J *[1 mark]*

Page 69 — Developing the Model of The Atom

Q1 a) The centre of an atom is a tiny, positively charged nucleus *[1 mark]*. This is made up of protons and neutrons and is the source of most of the atom's mass *[1 mark]*. Most of the atom is empty space *[1 mark]*. Electrons orbit the nucleus at different distances *[1 mark]*.

b) The diameter of an atom is around 1×10^{-10} m *[1 mark]*. The size of a nucleus is 100 000 times smaller than this *[1 mark]*.

Page 70 — Isotopes and Radioactive Decay

Q1 C *[1 mark]*

Page 71 — Penetration Properties and Decay Equations

Q1 $^{238}_{92}\text{U} \longrightarrow {}^{234}_{90}\text{Th} + {}^{4}_{2}\text{He}$

[1 mark for the correct representation of uranium, 1 mark for correct alpha particle symbol (He or α) and mass and atomic numbers and 1 mark for the correct mass and atomic numbers for thorium]

Page 72 — Activity and Half-life

Q1 10 × 24 = 240 hours
The number of half-lives in 240 hours is
240 ÷ 60 = 4 half-lives *[1 mark]*
Initially, activity = N

after 1 half-life, activity = $N \div 2 = \dfrac{N}{2}$

after 2 half-lives, activity = $\dfrac{N}{2} \div 2 = \dfrac{N}{4}$

after 3 half-lives, activity = $\dfrac{N}{4} \div 2 = \dfrac{N}{8}$

after 4 half-lives, activity = $\dfrac{N}{8} \div 2 = \dfrac{N}{16}$

The fraction of remaining radioactive nuclei after 4 half-lives is $\dfrac{1}{16}$ of the original value *[1 mark]*,
so the fraction that have decayed = $1 - \dfrac{1}{16} = \dfrac{15}{16}$
[1 mark]

Page 73 — Dangers of Radioactivity

Q1 E.g. Radiation can cause minor damage to a cell that causes it to mutate / radiation can cause cells to divide uncontrollably / causes cancer *[1 mark]*. Radiation can also kill a cell completely *[1 mark]*.

Page 74 — Half-life and Uses of Radiation

Q1 Gamma radiation can penetrate through tissue, so it can be detected outside the body with the radiation detector *[1 mark]*. It is also causes less damage inside the body than alpha and beta would *[1 mark]*.

Page 75 — Fission and Fusion

Q1 A nucleus can undergo nuclear fission when it absorbs a neutron. When the nucleus splits, it will release some neutrons *[1 mark]*. These neutrons can then go on to be absorbed by other nuclei causing them to undergo nuclear fission. This continues in a chain reaction *[1 mark]*.

Page 77 — Density

Q1 E.g. use a mass balance to find the mass of the object *[1 mark]*. Fill a eureka can with water to just below the spout, then immerse the object in the can *[1 mark]*. Collect the water displaced by the object in a measuring cylinder as it flows out of the spout and record its volume *[1 mark]*. Then calculate the density of the object using density = mass ÷ volume *[1 mark]*.

Q2 volume in m³ = 75 ÷ (100³)
= 7.5×10^{-5} m³ *[1 mark]*
density = mass ÷ volume
= $(4.5 \times 10^{-2}) \div (7.5 \times 10^{-5})$ *[1 mark]*
= 600 kg/m³ *[1 mark]*

Page 78 — The Particle Model of Matter

Q1 Solids are generally denser than liquids, which are generally denser than gases *[1 mark]*. The forces between the particles are greatest in solids and weakest in gases *[1 mark]*. This means that the particles are closest together in solids and furthest apart in gases *[1 mark]*.

Page 79 — More on the Particle Model of Matter

Q1 There are less frequent collisions between particles and the container walls in a given amount of time, resulting in a lower overall force exerted on the container wall *[1 mark]*. The particles have a lower momentum, so they each exert a smaller force on the container walls during collisions *[1 mark]*. A lower force results in a lower pressure of the gas *[1 mark]*.

Page 80 — Specific Heat Capacity

Q1 change in internal energy = mass × specific heat capacity × change in temperature, so:
change in temperature = change in internal energy ÷ (mass × specific heat capacity)
[1 mark]
= 1680 ÷ (0.20 × 420) *[1 mark]* = 20 °C *[1 mark]*

Page 81 — Specific Latent Heat

Q1

[1 mark for showing the line as flat at 0 °C, 1 mark for showing the line as flat at 100 °C, 1 mark for drawing a straight line with a positive gradient for temperatures below 0 °C, between 0 and 100 °C , and above 100 °C.]

Page 82 — Pressure

Q1 When the volume of a gas is decreased it results in the particles being pushed closer together *[1 mark]*. This means that the particles hit the walls of the container more often so the pressure of the gas increases *[1 mark]*.

Page 83 — Atmospheric Pressure and Liquid Pressure

Q1 pressure due to a column of liquid = height of column × density × g,
= (320 − 120) × 1000 × 10 *[1 mark]*
= 2 000 000 Pa *[1 mark]*

Page 84 — Forces and Elasticity

Q1 extension of the spring
= 0.20 − 0.16 = 0.04 m *[1 mark]*
Rearrange force = extension × spring constant
So spring constant = $\dfrac{\text{force}}{\text{extension}} = \dfrac{3.0}{0.04}$ *[1 mark]*
= 75 N/m *[1 mark]*

Page 85 — Investigating Hooke's Law

Q1 First calculate the extension of the spring:
extension = 1.3 − 1.2 = 0.1 m *[1 mark]*
energy stored in a stretched spring
= 0.5 × spring constant × (extension)²
= 0.5 × 54 × 0.1² *[1 mark]* = 0.27 J *[1 mark]*

Page 86 — The Solar System and Orbits

Q1 E.g. artificial satellites are made by humans, whilst natural satellites are not *[1 mark]*. Planet 2 is closer to the star *[1 mark]*.

Page 87 — The Formation of the Solar System

Q1 A cloud of dust and gas was attracted together by gravity *[1 mark]*. The cloud collapsed towards the centre and became more dense *[1 mark]*. As the dust and gas was compressed, the temperature increased *[1 mark]*. When the temperature was high enough, hydrogen nuclei started to undergo fusion to form helium nuclei *[1 mark]*.

Q2 The force of gravity does work on the gases in the star to compress them *[1 mark]*. This results in the particles having more energy in their kinetic energy stores, which increases the temperature *[1 mark]*.

Page 88 — Red-Shift and Big Bang

Q1 Observed light from galaxies has all been red-shifted *[1 mark]*. This suggests that the light sources (the distant galaxies) are moving away from us *[1 mark]*. Observations have shown that more distant galaxies are more red-shifted *[1 mark]*, and so must be moving away from us faster than closer galaxies, meaning the universe must be expanding *[1 mark]*.

Index